Witch Way Back

ROBERT WRIGHT

DEDICATION

For all the believers.

CONTENTS

ACKNOWLEDGMENTS

Thanks to the friends and family who encouraged
and supported this book. To my chief editor, cover artist, manager,
and favorite fan – thanks for all the hard work you did and for
putting up with the attitude I inflicted on you (again).

CHAPTER 1

Scom trudged through the darkness, away from what had once been Chell's castle and the place of his greatest disappointment and sadness. Looking up into the air where the red dragon, Regni, had flown the little troll failed to notice a pair of eyes peeking out of the small grove of trees that grew beside the path he was following. His whole attention was focused on following Regni and saving the princess who was his best friend in this world.

Scom froze in his tracks as a rough voice issued from the dark. "Well if it isn't the small little morsel of a troll with no princess around to protect him," the echo of the voice dying with a little chuckle.

Scom straightened up to his full height, which with trolls is not all that tall, then answered back in as firm of a voice as he could muster from his small body. "Who's there and what are you after?"

Out of the dark, Nomi walked with a sad smile on his face,

and a look of pity and admiration for the little troll. "You are lucky that it is I and not some other dragons looking at you now troll or you would be a quick meal about now." Looking around the area and after scanning the night skies, the gold dragon once more focused on the little creature standing before him. "And just where, may I ask, are you headed? Are you entertaining the idea of following one red dragon and trying to go save a certain princess, troll?"

Scom stood as tall as his height would allow him to stand and looked up at the dragon with fire in his eyes. "I am following Regni to save my friend and not you nor any other creature will keep me from that, Nomi."

Nomi looked at Scom with new respect in his eyes and chuckled as he settled down lower to the ground to talk to the brave creature before him. "I must say that I am impressed with you troll and your loyalty to the princess. The braveness that you have shown to me will be needed if you are to complete your mission."

Scom looked at Nomi with a touch of skepticism, but figured any help he could get; even help from a not so dumb dragon would be nice. "And what mission is it you think I need to do, and does it involve saving the princess, Nomi?"

Nomi looked around once again for he knew that saving the princess and going against the Queen's will was not something that he wanted just anyone to hear. He wasn't really thrilled to let a troll in on the secret he knew, but to save the princess he would have to trust this little creature before him. "I know, little one, where Regni has flown, where the portal is that will take you to the world in which the princess now resides."

Scom looked the dragon up and down, quickly thinking that this might be a cruel trick of the Queen's, but then remembered that Nomi seemed to be a friend of the princess's and besides Mr. Blue did seem to like the golden dragon and even greeted him as an old friend when they first met. "Okay, so you know where the portal is so why you don't go through and save the princess?"

Nomi leaned down even closer to the troll and whispered, "If I go the Queen will notice and then will take even more drastic action against the princess. But, the Queen will not miss one insignificant little troll; no offense little one."

"No, no offense is taken dragon, for I see your point very well." Squaring his shoulders back the little troll said in a harsh whisper, "but what is it you will be doing to help the princess while I'm in her world trying to save her from her fate."

Nomi gave a little quiet chuckle, "Don't worry troll, I will be helping the princess in this world by gathering all that defy the Queen under her banner, so that when she returns the princess will have an army to back her up."

"Okay, I see your point again dragon, for surely you are not a dumb dragon as the others are. What I don't understand, though," Scom paused with a thoughtful look on his face, "why the Queen did not kill the princess outright when she had her here. Not that I am complaining, you understand right, dragon?"

Nomi looked down at the troll and grinned. "That is easy to answer troll. First, if the Queen had killed the princess she would have had a hard time with the creatures of this world for the princess is well loved by more creatures than even she knows about. Second, the Queen could not be sure of how her magic would react to killing one such as the princess. You know someone that has her and her sisters' magic within her."

"Oh yes, I do see how that would stop the Queen from causing harm to the princess when she was in this world. The Queen may be very mad, but trolls never thought she was as dumb as some dragons and other creatures we knew."

Nomi gave a little growl low in his throat "Yes, well not all dragons are dumb and some trolls should learn to curb their opinions so that they are not eaten."

Scom took a step back and then bowed low. "I see your point, sir dragon," trying to pacify the large creature. "But enough of this talk; let us follow Regni before we lose him."

Nomi held out a large paw that would swallow a couple of trolls and chuckled, "As I said troll, I know where Regni goes. I want him to get ahead of us so that he will not see us following him. So hop up here in my hand and soon we will be on our way."

Scom climbed into Nomi's paw and laughed a low quiet laugh. "Oh don't worry sir dragon for us trolls have a little secret of our own. It keeps us from getting caught when we don't want to be seen. Just take off and I promise that Regni will never know we are behind him."

Nomi looked at the little troll that settled into the middle of his hand and smiled down at the creature. Yes, there definitely was more to these little trolls than meets the eyes, he thought. With a flap of his gold wings, the dragon took to the air and was immediately lost to sight.

The gray morning light shone through my eyelids slowly waking me from my slumber. As I sat up, the murmur of voices and the movement of pans sounding through the walls slowly sank into my consciousness. As I stretched my arms above my head, I looked around at my surroundings and slowly focused on a sight that I never thought I would see again.

For I was once again in my bedroom, in fact as I looked down at my clothes I could see that I was in the same pajamas I had on before I had been taken from this world to the other by my sister.

I couldn't believe that I was back, back from where I had started my adventure in another world. How could this be, I thought. The last I remembered was my mother casting a spell on Mr. Blue and me . . . Mr. Blue!" I shouted as I looked desperately around for my fuzzy friend.

I threw pillows to the floor searching for my friend and then dived under the covers popping back up with the small fuzzy bear held in both my hands. "Oh, there you are, big guy. Glad to see that you came back home with me; I don't know what I would have done if that witch had harmed you."

A loud knock and my foster mom's voice coming through my bedroom door had me diving under the covers once again, but this time, to hide. There was no way I could explain how different I looked after my adventures.

As the bedroom door cracked open, I could hear her chuckling, "Ceri, I know it's Saturday, but its time you get your butt out of bed. Are you planning on sleeping all day, girl?"

I gave her a muffled reply that seemed to satisfy her because she soon closed the bedroom door and I could hear her laughing and muttering about strange teen behavior as she headed back to the kitchen.

As I climbed out from under the covers, I tried to figure out how I was going to hide my new appearance from those here at home. I thought as I walked over to my dresser that I would need more than the little makeup I had to change my red hair and eyes, not to mention the whole having wings thing to make me look my normal boring self again.

I stopped in front of my dresser and looked around on top of it for some miracle, then looked at the mirror that reflected my image back at me and froze in confusion. What the heck, how did this happen, I thought, as I looked at the reflection staring back. No red anything; no red hair, no red eyes, no wings. A normal blue-eyed blonde in her pajamas was looking back at me, my normal everyday reflection.

I hurriedly rolled up the sleeve of my top and looked for the tattoos that signified my powers. They were also all gone, all three of the ones I had gained from my sisters and my own just like they had never been.

Now what the heck was going on here, I wondered? Now that I thought about it some more, my mom should have been pretty freaked out that I had been gone so long on this little adventure I had and here she was acting like it was any other Saturday morning.

ॐ∾ॐ∾ॐ∾

SLAM! The bedroom door bounced off the wall, startling me from my thoughts and in walked hurricane Dede. For a second there, as the small bundle of energy entered the room, I caught a flash of her as a demon, you know red hair, eyes, little wings sprouting from her back, then bang she was back to being my little sister again. Whatever was going on here was really messing with my mind.

As the small interruption to my thoughts stopped in the

middle of my room, she gave me a once over and then scanned the room looking for areas to make trouble in as she made her announcement in a voice that I'm sure every neighbor in our apartment complex heard. "MOM SAID YOU'RE TO COME GET BREAKFAST NOW BEFORE IT TURNS TO LUNCH."

"Yeah, yeah, tell Mom I'll be right there, squirt. I just want to get dressed."

"BUT MOM SAID . . ." Dede started in again in her loud hear-me-and-obey voice.

"Yeah, tell Mom five minutes, I'll be there in five, "I countered as I ushered her out the door and closed it on her protesting backside.

As I quickly dressed I thought about how lucky I was to have a family like this and not like the one with the crazy sisters and mom who had been out to kill me. I mean Jenna and Bill were great foster parents and the only parents I had ever known. Then Dede, their biological daughter, came along eight years ago and even though she can be oh-so-loud, bossy, and get into my stuff at times, I do love the little bundle of destruction.

As I finished dressing, I looked around the room that I thought I would never see again. All my stuff was exactly where I had put it the night I had been transported to that other world. My homework for school was on my desk so-so completed along with the plate and glass I had left from the snack I snagged while doing a little late night gaming. I popped the game out of the system and saw yeah even same game I had been playing, an old fantasy D and D role playing game I was messing with out of boredom that night.

As I slipped the game back into the rack next to my system and walked out to breakfast, I thought, well maybe it all had been some dream; a strange dream from staying up late and playing games and eating junk food kind of dream. Yeah, that must be it, just a dream; I mean what else could it be?

꿈ꕥ꿈ꕥ꿈ꕥ

Regni flew through the early morning sky headed toward the large mountain looming in front of him. The morning sun peeking over the top of the nearby hills reflected off his red scales and his shadow below him glided along the forested valley. Regni enjoyed the wind flowing over his wings as he glided the last little bit to his final destination; the place where he would be able to fulfill the commands of his queen, and finally get rid of the last of the princesses forever. As the dragon circled a large ledge about half way up the mountain he couldn't shake this nagging feeling that someone was following him, but scanning the clear skies about him the dragon could detect no other creatures. As he landed on the ledge, the dragon turned his back on the large dark cave entrance carved into the side of the mountain.

Sniffing the air, searching for the cause of his unease, the dragon whispered to himself in concern, "Dragon and troll, why do I smell dragon and troll?" Then he froze as some small trees at the base of the mountain stirred as if some large creature had moved through them.

He cocked his head looking all around, smelling the air and listening for the tiniest of sounds, but he could not sense what was causing such unease within him. "HELLO! IS THERE ANYONE ABOUT? PLEASE COME OUT FOR I WILL NOT HARM YOU, YOU HAVE MY WORD," Regni shouted now, almost as in a panic. Worried now he thought to himself that if the Queen learned that he had led someone to the portal, well he knew what the punishment for that would be.

Nothing moved in the air or the dark thick trees below, but there was this whisper of something, some sound as if a creature was breathing so as not to be noticed by Regni. "Well whoever you are I have a solution to take care of this problem," the dragon declared as he launched himself into the air and once again circled the base of the mountain.

"LET US SEE IF YOU CAN HIDE FROM THIS," the red dragon yelled, and then spewed fire up and down the valley, igniting the forest below him. "YES BURN, JUST BURN WHATEVER YOU ARE," he yelled again as he once more landed on the ledge.

His wild laughter echoed up and down the valley, roaring over the flames of dragon fire that now consumed the trees and any small creatures that were not quick enough to outrun the inferno. Watching the flames crackle and snap as it ate through the once pristine forest, Regni soon settled down from his mad rage and once more looked around the base of the mountain. "Well if that didn't get you then nothing will," he whispered as he glanced all around him one last time before heading into the cave entrance to fulfill his Queen's wishes.

❧❧❧

After a couple of hours, the heat from the fire around the base of the mountain slowly died down to smoking embers. Small coughs issued from a large pile of ash as it slowly rose and fell to the side as if some great beast was rising from below. With a shimmer, a gold dragon appears one paw wrapped around a coughing bundle.

"You can put me down now Nomi, for I think he is gone; if you know what I mean, dragon."

The gold dragon slowly opened his claws and spied the dusty bundle of troll and slowly lowered him toward a spot that didn't seem to be smoldering too much. "Be careful where you step troll as there are still hot spots around here."

The troll shook himself off showering ash all over the ground and causing Nomi to back up. "It is a good thing that dragons are fireproof; if you know what I mean, dragon," said the troll as he slowly looked at the destruction around him.

Nomi slowly looked around with the troll at all the destruction that Regni had wroth with his fiery breath. "Yes, but it is not so much that I am fireproof as that Regni was in a hurry to finish the mission that the Queen sent him on. If he had used his full power then it would not have mattered, for only a demon can live through real dragon fire little one." The dragon gave the troll a searching look then chuckled. "What made the difference was the power that you have to make us invisible, that is what really saved us troll."

Scom gave his own little chuckle and then looked at the dragon with a frown. "This is a troll's secret and must never be shared; you do understand, right dragon? Only for the Princess Ceri would I share a secret such as this."

Nomi bowed low to the troll. "Your secret is safe with me, troll, for as you said it was used in defense of the Princess, and right now that is what is important."

With a look of relief, Scom bowed back, which of course is polite when talking to a dragon. Then looking at the ledge above him he wondered what new world it would lead him to.

Nomi followed Scom's gaze upward then held out a paw to once again carry the troll. "Up we go troll, we need to get you up to the cave and inside so that you can go through the portal."

"And once I am through Nomi, then what?" the troll asked as he climbed into the offered paw.

"Then my little friend you need to find the princess and bring her back to this world." With that, the troll in hand, Nomi leaped to the ledge and deposited Scom at the cave entrance.

⁓⁓⁓⁓⁓⁓

Walking into the kitchen, I stopped as Jenna, my foster mom, turned from the stove and gave me that once over that parents do so well. There it was again, that flash as if seeing someone you know change into a creature and then change right back. Man, I must really be tired, I need to get some sleep tonight or I was really going to go crazy with this stuff.

Jenna smiled and then turned back to what she was doing on the stove. "Well, it's about time, young lady, that you got out of bed. Some late night gaming I bet," she said in a teasing voice.

"Yeah I guess a little too late night; I seem to be having these weird dreams or hallucinations."

"Oh, well how about an early bedtime tonight instead of staying up all night playing games. That might help you know," Jenna said with some concern now in her voice.

"Yeah I know, I promise no gaming tonight," I said then noticing the dubious look that flashed my way from Jenna. "Okay, how about no staying up late gaming, how's that sound? Okay, Mom?"

Jenna gave an exasperated sigh. "Well, I guess it will have to do. Now sit down and get some breakfast."

I jumped into my chair next to hurricane Dede and started to scoop some breakfast onto my plate when Bill, my foster dad, laid down some bad news. "Remember Ceri, Mom and I have to go to work today and you promised us you would take Dede to the mall for some Christmas shopping."

I stopped in mid scoop of some scrambled eggs with that news. Yeah, I had forgotten that little promise, oh well so much for killing a Saturday lying around the house reading and napping, I guess. "Oh sure, yeah I remember — mall today with little sis, sure no prob," I stammered, but could tell by the look on everyone's face that no one believed me.

"I tell you what," Bill said as he reached for his back pocket. "Here is enough money for lunch and snacks and your allowance from last week. How's that sound?" he asked as he laid some bills down on the table.

I scooped up the money just as two little grubby hands reached for them. "Yeah thanks, that's great, Dad," I said stuffing the money into my front jeans pocket before I finished loading my plate for the energy I would need for a whole day of shopping with the little rugrat sitting next to me.

Mom came over to the table and sat down to grab her own breakfast. As she settled in to eat she laid down the law on my little sister as she always does when she leaves her with me. "Now Dede, I want you to remember that Ceri is in charge and that you will do everything that she says, and remember the 5-foot rule."

Dede sat there with a look of resignation on her face as she listened to the same speech she hears every time she goes out with me. "Yes, I know Ceri is the one in charge and all that. I remember . . ."

The three of us each gave the little troublemaker a stern look as Dad cleared his throat and then continued the lecture from Mom. "Yes, well if you remember so well then we won't have a repeat of that little incident we had last month, will we?"

The mention of that little episode, wandering away and getting lost for two hours, seemed to make the little one shrink into her chair her head hung so low that her chin brushed her chest. With a quiet whisper, she looked back up at the three of us, "I really remember, I promise Dad."

I felt sorry for the little squirt and reached over and brushed one tear that seemed to have escaped from those lively eyes. "Don't worry guys I'm sure we won't have any problems today, will we kiddo?"

Me getting back on Dede's side seemed to instantly cheer her up for the smile that usually graced her face was once more back. "Oh, right I really, really promise no trouble today."

Mom and Dad seemed to be satisfied with that little

performance from the diminutive faker and started to get up and get ready for work. "Okay girls just so you guys are back in time for dinner," Mom announced as she followed Dad down to their room to get ready. "Oh, and can you guys get the dishes before you leave, okay?"

"Sure Mom, no prob," I answered, stuffing the last of my breakfast down and checking that Dede was on the way to finishing her breakfast so that we could head out to our trip to the mall. God, I thought as I picked up dishes off the table to put in the dishwasher, a normal everyday Saturday. That was one crazy dream I had last night, I don't know how I could have thought a normal everyday girl like me could have had an adventure like that.

༺≈ঔৈ≈ঔৈ≈ঔৈ༻

An hour later we were all walking out the door, parents to work and kids to a day at the local mall. What could happen in a normal little town like Bellingham, to a normal girl like me I thought? As I buckled Dede into Dad's truck and threw my backpack with Mr. Blue in it into the back seat a little itch at the back of my head flashed that those are the kinds of questions that you should never ask. For fate is always lurking around the corner waiting to answer, and you may not like how she responds.

I watched as my parents headed out to work and noticed them glancing over at the steps of the apartment across the driveway. At first, I couldn't see anything and climbed into the truck and started it up to head out for a day with the little troublemaker beside me. As we pulled out of our parking space though I noticed a slight movement under the stairs and another figment of my imagination manifested itself into a large black dragon crouching under the steps.

I slammed on the truck's brakes and blinked my eyes then looked back at the stairway in the next apartment, but all I saw was one of our neighbors, Roc, step out of the stair's shadow. He stood there watching us as I put the truck in drive and we headed out to the mall. As I listened to Dede she told me all about the shopping we needed to do for Christmas. I couldn't help but notice that Roc was watching our truck with an unyielding gaze.

"Are you listening to me?" Dede whined in her pay-attention-to-me-now voice.

As we turned the corner and lost sight of our curious neighbor, I focused on my little sister again, for I have learned early on that it is not wise to ignore eight-year-olds that want attention. "Yes, I am listening to you, chatterbox, and will obey, okay?"

Dede giggled which is always better then the tantrum she can throw. "Well maybe we can visit Santa one more time?" she asked with that pleading little look that she knew I could never resist.

"If you're good for me while we are shopping then we will talk about it. Okay?"

This really set her off and she was almost bouncing out of her seat as we headed down the road. Her enthusiasm was catching because I soon forgot all about bad dreams, flashes of sight, and nosy neighbors as we pulled into the mall parking lot. Now I thought all I have to do is find us a parking space in this mess.

CHAPTER 2

Scom slowly walked into the cave entrance with an anxious heart. The light from outside was soon swallowed by the blackness of the cave as he turned a corner. What I wouldn't give for one of the princess's lights right now the troll thought as he groped the wall with his left hand while waving his right hand out in front of his face so that he wouldn't run into anything. "I would hate to run into anything nasty," he mumbled. "You know like a rock, a wall, or a dragon."

With those words, Scom stopped and closed his eyes to gather his strength for what lay ahead. As he opened his eyes again he could see a small dim blue light shining down the tunnel. I must be getting closer to the portal that Nomi told me about the troll thought as he moved slowly toward the light.

As he moved further down the tunnel he could see, by the growing light that the end had another bend in it and that was why the light had not shown further down the dark tube he had traveled. Steeling himself as he reached the end of the tunnel, the terrified troll peeked around the corner of rock that he stood behind expecting at any second to see a red dragon ready to pounce on a small snack like himself, but found that he was staring at a large empty cave.

Well almost empty, he thought as he stepped out into the cave. For in the center of the cave hung a large exquisite blue light shining and pulsing as if the light itself were alive. Each pulse of the light seemed to beat to the rhythm of the little troll's heart.

Looking around the cave once again for Regni, and satisfying himself that he was truly alone Scom relaxed somewhat and moved toward the light, almost as if he were drawn to it like a moth to an open flame. "You are more beautiful than anything I have ever seen," he whispered as he reached out to touch the shining light.

Scom's hand caressed the light for an instant then disappeared within it. This action seemed to shake the troll out of his stupor and he jumped back from the light, counting each finger on his hand to make sure that they were all still there. "Oh, this is not the time to fall under a magic spell if you know what I mean?" Scom whispered to the portal. "I have a princess to save."

The blue light, as if though understanding the troll, dimmed and the pulses slowed as if waiting to see what the little troll would do next. Scom moved around the cave trying to get up his courage to tackle the magic that was contained in the portal. With a last look around, he straightened his back and marched toward the portal. "I need to save my princess so, however, you send me into her world please give me the power to help her if you know what I mean?"

The portal flashed a dark blue then gave some pulsing light blue flashes. "It is almost like you are laughing at me but I must go through," Scom said as he stepped through the magic of the portal and into his princess's world.

❧❧❧❧❧❧

Dede and I had a great morning shopping at the mall. We had gotten the Christmas presents that she wanted for mom and dad along with some more ideas that she wanted to add to her already extensive list for Santa. Even the hallucinations of seeing people turning into strange creatures that I had been having this morning seemed to have gone away.

We had taken a break from our travels through the crush of people that were crowding the mall hallways and stores. We had just sat down at an empty table we had spotted to have a well-deserved break and lunch when a young girl sat down across from us.

"I'm sorry. Is this your table?" I asked trying to be polite while glancing around for another empty spot in the rush of humanity that flowed around us.

"No," she mumbled in a voice that I barely heard over the

noise of the crowd.

"Oh well, okay." Dede and I looked at each other then proceeded to get set to eat the lunch sitting before us while ignoring our new table mate.

"You are going to be in danger, princess," the girl whispered, stopping both us in mid-bite in surprise.

I looked at the young girl closer as she sat staring down at the cup in her hands that she slowly twirled back and forth. She was a very slight girl with a quiet presence about her. Her face was hidden by the light brown hair with pink streaks in it, but I could feel that she was peeking out through the colorful mop to judge my reaction. "What do you mean danger?" I asked as I looked around the crowded food court.

"Yeah, and what do you mean princess? She's my sister; you can't go calling her names," Dede piped up, adding her two cents to the weird conversation our table mate had started.

The girl looked up at us as I gave Dede my 'be quiet, I'm handling this' look. As I glanced back at her face, I was caught by her eyes. They were large and sort of a nondescript color, but they had this long faraway look to them. God, could this day get any stranger, I thought.

"You know who you really are, princess, and that was no dream you had. I saw that the Queen has sent someone here to put a bounty on your head and . . ."

"Whoa, hold on there. First of all, how do you know about my dreams and who the heck are you?" I asked as I looked at Dede whose mouth was hanging open at the girl's rant and then glancing back at the strange girl in disbelief.

"We don't really have time for this, princess," the girl said as she sighed then looked around as if she expected us to be attacked at any second.

"Okay, you know what? We are getting out of here; we will find another table so that you can sit with whoever you are channeling or whatever it is you are doing," I said as I gathered our stuff together, and glanced around for another empty table in the crowd.

The slight girl grabbed my arm with surprising strength then whispered so quietly I had to bend down to hear her words. "Okay, I will tell you everything, though I don't think you will believe me."

"Try me, you never know," I said as I sat back down at the table and arranged Dede's lunch out for her again. "And you, eat or no visit to Santa after lunch," I growled as I pointed at Dede's lunch.

The girl looked around once again then gave another big sigh as if she was being put out by my questions, then launched into her tale in a quiet voice. "My name is Jamie, princess, and . . ."

"And my name is Ceri, so let's drop the princess bit, can we?" I asked interrupting her story.

Jamie looked at me then I could see a small, slight smile flit across her face. "As you wish Ceri, I will try to remember that. As I was saying before I was interrupted," once again that sly little smile, "my name is Jamie and I am a witch."

"Oh, where are your broom and cat?" Dede asked, looking under the table and around the area for those items. We both stared at the little troublemaker, me with a look of exasperation, and Jamie with a look of amusement. "What? I was just asking," Dede answered with her own look of annoyance.

"Anyways there is a portal here in Bellingham that leads to other worlds. The witches' council, of which I am one, protects this world when the Others come through and cause trouble in this world."

"You mean others like dragons, goblins and such, those Others?" I asked shaking my head in disbelief.

"Yes, those are the Others I am speaking about."

"Okay then, so how come we don't hear about dragons or goblins running around town then, huh, answer that?"

"You don't hear about them because when they come through the portal it does something to them and changes them. Most of them change into human form or some animal form depending on the magic in the portal and . . ."

"Okay, then how do you know who an Other is if you are here to protect this world, huh?"

"Yeah, what my big sister said," Dede stated around a mouthful of fries.

We each glanced over at the little bundle munching on her lunch with a look of annoyance. "What? I thought you would be happy I'm sticking up for you."

"Pipe down pipsqueak and finish that happy meal," I said as I turned back to Jamie and our insane conversation.

"This is getting us nowhere," Jamie actually growled out as she started to rise from the table.

I gently grabbed her arm and pulled back into her seat. "Listen I'm sorry, okay? This is a little hard to handle right now after last night's dream and seeing flashes of weird things this morning and all."

Jamie seemed to accept my apology and continued with her narration. "A witch, princess, I mean Ceri, cannot see an Other unless they do something bad or evil. That is when their true form shows through the portal's magic. When that happens, then we can see the Others and take care of them."

"And by take care of them you mean what?" I asked.

"I mean a witch will destroy the evil Others to save those who live in this world. That is our duty and has been ever since time beginning." Then Jamie hesitated and got this thoughtful look on her face. "Wait, what do you mean you see flashes of weird things, weird as in what way exactly?"

I looked around to ensure that no one but the little nosy package eating her happy meal was paying attention to us. "I mean that I sort of see some people, sort of flash into these Others as you call them, you know dragons, demons, and such. That's the weird things that I have been seeing this morning since I woke up."

We both sat there, each lost in our own thoughts about what we had learned when a small shrill voice broke the spell. "Well when you two are done talking fairy tales, I'm done with my lunch and you said we could go see Santa, Ceri. I mean you did promise and I have been pretty good for you all morning and all, right?"

"Yes you have been good for me and a promise is a promise, so let's get this mess cleaned up and go see Santa, troublemaker," I said as I gathered the trails of a devoured happy meal and a sandwich I barely had touched. "You coming with us to see Santa?" I asked Jamie as she sat there staring at me like I had grown two heads.

"Oh yes," she whispered, "there is more that I need to tell you, and we need to figure out why you are seeing the Others without them causing problems when you are only a half witch." Now it was my turn to stop and stare, trying to figure out how this girl knew things that I had dreamed of last night; but the insistent tugging on my leg from the little bundle that wanted to see Santa brought me back to more immediate and pressing matters. At least, it was immediate and pressing for one anxious eight-year-old, for me there was a whole lot of other things on my mind right now.

So with a mind full of concern and dread overseeing Others and one crazy girl, we headed off to take Dede to see the mall's imaginary Santa. Well, I thought, maybe he is real too, who knew in this crazy world.

⚚⚚⚚⚚⚚⚚

Queen Ellie marched back and forth before her throne, her constant pacing and whispered mutterings making the ogre guards stationed around the throne room nervous as time passed. Ogres may be muscle bound cousins of the trolls in this world but lacked the trolls smarts and guiles. However, these guards had been with the Queen before and recognized the dangerous mood she was in.

As Queen Ellie moved past each mountain of muscle, she could see how her guards flinched as if they were a puppy expecting a blow from its master for piddling on the carpet. "Where are you, Regni and why do I not have my daughter's head before me?" The Queen stops in the middle of the throne room and looks up at the ceiling and yells "AND WILL YOU INFERNAL CREATURES STOP TWITCHING?"

Silence fills the large room as each guard freezes in fright, going as still as the statues around the room. As the Queen, staring at the floor slowly gathers her anger back inside her the only sound that can be heard is the doors to the room slowly opening as a silver dragon's head peeks in.

"Yes, what is it?" she whispers quietly, looking up at the doors, as each of the guards around the throne room slowly tuck their heads down further between their thick shoulders, knowing that tone of voice from the Queen means that someone could die a slow, painful death.

"M-m-my Queen, I have s-s-some news f-f-for you-u-u," the silver dragon stutters in fright for he knows that bringing bad news to the Queen does not bode well for a long life in this kingdom.

"No worries, my friend, come in and tell me what news you bring." The Queen's face lights up with a cruel little smile that is unnoticed by the approaching dragon in his fright.

Gulping and then bowing before his Queen, the dragon shakes as he prepares to deliver his news. "The messengers that you have sent to the other creatures of this world have come back, my Queen."

"Yes, and what have they said?" Queen Ellie asks in an even lower whisper.

The dragon slinks even lower to the floor, his tail splayed out behind him, counting the seconds that he has to live in this world. "They have all rejected your rule and have all sided with the Princess Ceri. Even the creatures that have not been in contact with the princess know of her."

"How is this possible? How could such a small slip of a girl do this?"

"I'm sorry, my Queen, but it is said that she is more

powerful than you and . . ." the dragon looked up and stopped at the rage that he saw on his Queen's face.

All in the room could feel the power ratchet up as the Queen slowly breathed in and out, trying to control the killing forces just waiting to unleash themselves into the throne room. "And what of Regni and my daughter, is there any news of either of them?"

"No, my Queen, but Regni has only been through the portal for one day, and may have to wait till dark to contact the Others in that world."

Slowly the power fell down and all the creatures in the room breathed a sigh of relief. "Go and I want you to gather all my forces together and teach these lowly creatures what it means to disobey me. Do you understand?"

"Yes, my Queen. Oh yes, I will obey," the dragon answered as he scrambled out of the room feeling the power once again growing and pulsing out of his ruler.

"Yes, see that you do, and I want a watch put on the portal to see when Regni returns from his mission."

"The dragon moved faster toward the doors, now grateful that he seemed to have escaped his Queen's wrath. "Yes, my Queen, at once. I will obey your orders."

"Oh and one more thing dragon, send me more guards to replace these, won't you?" The dragon heard the Queen whisper before the doors slammed as if from a large gust of wind. The yells, screams, and sounds of something wet being thrown against the walls of the throne room hurried his feet along the long hallway as he rushed to obey his mistress's wishes.

⇜⇝⇜⇝⇜⇝

As we stood in the long line waiting to gratify my little sister's urge to visit Santa for the fifth time since Thanksgiving, I thought over all the strange things that the quiet girl/witch standing beside us had told me. It was still pretty hard to wrap my head around the idea that my dream last night was the real thing.

Then it hit me. Turning to look at Jamie with an 'I got you now' smile on my face, I whispered so that none of the people around us could hear. "Okay, if as you say it wasn't a dream last night then tell me how I got back here without missing any days? I mean I was in this other world for quite awhile, so explain that, huh?"

"Oh that's an easy one," Jamie matched my 'got you' smile with one of her own. "Your mother didn't send you through the portal. She sent you back here by magic, so she poofed you back here to the next morning."

"Poofed? Really that's what you are going with Jamie? Poofed . . .?"

"You know what I mean. That's my word for being magicked somewhere. You know one second you are there, and the next, poof, you're gone," she said in a nasty voice.

"Okay, okay no reason to get mad. Seems to me she could have just as easily killed me as sent me back home, so why send someone here to put a bounty on my head, Jamie?"

"Oh, that's easy. If your mother kills you then there would be a huge revolt by all the creatures in the Others world. Well maybe except for the dragons, but everyone else would hate to see you die."

"Well that's nice to know, I guess."

I felt a small insistent tug on my leg and some mumbling behind us when I noticed that we had let a gap grow in the line as the two of us talked. We closed up the line as I thought some more on what Jamie had said.

"You know, Ceri, you are part witch and I could probably teach you how to use your powers here in this world."

"Yeah I guess, but that won't get you in trouble or anything, will it? I mean teaching an Other as you call it how to use their magic and all."

Jamie didn't answer for a second and stood there chewing on her lip and looking around like she expected to be trounced upon any second. "Well to tell you the truth my teacher wouldn't like it at all, but I guess what he doesn't know won't hurt him. Besides you really aren't a creature from that other world, I mean your mom was a witch here before she got banished you know," she finally answered.

As we moved up in line once again I thought over some more of what Jamie had been telling me. Seems every time this girl opened her mouth she gave me more questions than answers. "Okay since you know about my mom being a witch maybe you can tell me why she was banished then?"

Jamie leaned in even closer to me and whispered, "I don't know why she was banished. My teacher Saba won't tell me, but I do know that he and your mom once had a thing going on until he sent her away."

"So your teacher is the one that started all this garbage, the one who banished my mom, the woman who is trying to have me killed. Is that what you are telling me?"

"Uhm well, yeah I guess I . . ."

About then we had made it to the front of the line and my attention was distracted by Dede pulling me up to see the red-suited man sitting in the middle of a red and green sparkly display that looked like a large Christmas elf had thrown up in the middle of the mall.

Settling down in the chair with the little bundle of anxiety sitting on one side of the large suited man and me on the other, I looked around as the girl taking pictures snapped a few frames for posterity for our parents. I could see that Jamie was now out in the center of the mall arguing with what looked an odd little gnome with a bush of red growing out of his head.

Paying for the pictures while Dede gave the Santa impersonator her list for the fourth or fifth time, I looked at the pictures and thought it was surprising what embarrassing things I wouldn't do for my little sister and my parents. Then again as Dede bounced up to me and I tucked the pictures into my pack next to Mr. Blue, I thought who was I to complain about embarrassing things when I walk around with a ratty old stuffed teddy bear everywhere I go.

We both walked out of the Santa display and found Jamie and the strange little man standing in the middle of the mall. Looking at them I couldn't help notice how the movement of the crowd on this busy Saturday morning flowed around the two as a stream moving around a rock. Almost as if there was an invisible barrier that kept people from bumping into the two of them.

"Ceri and Dede, this is my teacher Saba," Jamie whispered with almost a touch of what sounded like fright in her voice.

"Hello," I said as I took in the small round man, noticing the pair of crutches he was using to hold himself up with. I glanced down at the spindly little legs that held that round body, and then quickly glanced back up to his eyes, hoping that I wasn't too rude in my observations.

"Yes, well, hello to the both of you," he said, his voice small and squeaky with a tiny smile on his lips that never reached his eyes. I couldn't for the life of me figure out where I had seen eyes like those, they were dark black with an emptiness to them, almost soulless.

Dede bumped into my leg as she sort of hid behind me and peeked at the person standing before us. This sort of woke me up from my musings and brought me back to my surroundings. "So you are Jamie's teacher? So what was that you teach her again?"

"Yes well we have to go now; it was nice, uhm, to meet you two. Come, Jamie, let's remove our self from this place." With that, Saba turned and waddled away from us.

"Yes sir, I'll be right there." Jamie moved closer to me and whispered, "Come to the mall tomorrow and we will talk some more, okay."

I nodded then reached out for her hand. "Jamie, your teacher, are you safe with him? I want to know, I mean it's none of my business, but he does seem a little, well you know creepy."

Jamie smiled a sad little smile then pulled her hand from mine. "Don't worry, I will be fine. Just be here tomorrow at eleven, okay?"

I nodded once again as she turned and disappeared into the crowd as Saba bellowed her name. Then it hit me where I had seen eyes like that, it was the dream I had last night. It was my mother; her eyes looked like Saba's – just before she spelled me.

Oh, this day was so not turning out like I had hoped it would when we headed out to the mall this morning. Grabbing Dede's hand, we headed back to the stores to finish up the shopping we had left to do. That was when I noticed that I wasn't the only one who was quiet. One subdued little girl slowly marched beside me. "You okay kiddo?" I asked in concern.

She looked up at me and I could almost see tears in her eyes. "I don't like that man, and I think things are going to be different after this."

I pulled the two of us out of the crowd and bent down to her level. "Don't you worry, I promise nothing is going to change, okay? And as for that man, we probably will never see him again, ever."

"Okay," she whispered, still not sure.

With that proclamation, I gave her a hug for reassurance then stood up looking around the mall. "Tell you what, how about we grab a frozen yogurt for a cheering up treat?"

That seemed to dry up the tears and chase the worry away for Dede, but as we headed back to the food court for the unexpected treat, I listened to the babble from the little girl beside me with half my attention as I went over the strange events of the day and wondered what else could go wrong.

CHAPTER 3

Regni stood in the alley in the cold, dark rainy night; water dripping off the edge of the building he was leaning against. He pulled the heavy coat around him as the wet cold seeped into his new form. Even as a human he could feel the dragon fire deep down within his body, but even this heat seemed to have trouble combating the dampness.

A small shuffling sound slowly moving toward him catches his attention and makes him forget all about the miserable weather. "Who's there?" he barks out in a harsh whisper.

"It'sss jussst me, Regni," a return whisper hisses from the darkness.

"Where are the other outcasts? The Queen requires that you all hear her proclamation."

"They are comingsss, they jussst sssent me ahead to check it out firssst."

As the huddled creature neared Regni, he could smell a

pungent sickly sweet odor slowly drift off the creature. "Stand back from me creature, before I tear you to pieces. I can see and smell why they sent you out here first to see if this was one of the Queen's tricks."

"Yesss, thisss namelesss one isss expendable, ssso it isss told."

"Yeah, well the others better get here soon or I will take my impatience out on you, vermin."

"No need to need to kill it, even if it is a lowly creature, Regni," a harsh voice sounded behind the dragon.

Regni whirled around and caught a glimpse of a large shadow standing where a second ago there had been dark nothingness. "Roc, I didn't figure that you would be here."

"I'm here to see what all the fuss is about."

"There is no fuss, this is the Queen's orders and you would be well to follow them if you know what is good for you." As the two big men talked, Regni noticed that other creatures had quietly gathered behind the building.

"Well all the others are represented here Regni so why don't you get on with it," Roc said as he leaned against the wall and crossed his muscular arms over his barrel chest.

Regni gave Roc a dark look then stood straighter as he gave the Queen's announcement. "The Queen has decided that she will pardon any Other that will bring me the Princess Ceri's head."

A black mutter erupted at this news and Roc slowly stood straighter and looked at Regni with a flash of heat in his eyes. "And why should we, the ones that the Queen has tossed on this world against our will do her bidding, her killing for her?"

Regni looked at Roc and then around at the creatures gathered around him. "Like I said, the Queen will give you a full pardon and you get to come home with her full support and gratitude."

Roc looked around at the creatures and could see that the ones gathered here were giving the Queen's announcement some serious consideration. "Yeah well I, for one, am not the Queen's lackey. She wants this little slip of a girl dead, she can come and do it herself, and well, as for the Queen's gratitude . . ."

"What's the matter Roc, forgot what is feels like to be a full dragon, to feel the freedom of flight or are you scared of this little slip of a girl?" Regni asked as he laughed along with several of the other creatures in the group.

But the laughter died quickly as Regni was picked up and slammed up against the wall behind him. The water that ran down the wall splashed outward drenching everyone around the two men. "You, Regni, are not my equal; do not make me prove it!" Roc whispered as he stared into the red dragon's eyes, the flame of passion and anger flaring in his dark orbs.

Regni looked away from Roc's eyes and then slowly relaxed

in his grip. With a smile on his face, he said, "Remember Roc, I am the Queen's messenger and no harm can come to me."

"You aren't worth the trouble, Regni," Roc said as he pushed Regni back into the wall and slowly walked away from the group and disappeared into the night.

"Ssso when isss the princesss sssuposed to die, Regni?"

Regni stood up and adjusted his coat and watched where Roc had disappeared a few seconds ago. "What?" Regni looked around at the group watching him. "Oh yes, the Queen wants the princess dead as soon as possible, no excuses and no mercy. Bring me her body when the deed is done."

An older scruffy looking man stepped up and said, "Roc may be right Regni, I don't . . ."

Regni reached down and grabbed the man by the head and gave his head a quick twist. The snap sounded large in the quiet of the night. "NO MORE ARGUING, THE QUEEN'S COMMANDS WILL BE OBEYED!" Regni shouted as he threw the body up against a large garbage can. "Now get out of my sight, vermin, and kill the Princess," Regni ordered as the creatures hurriedly slipped into the night.

❧☙ ❧☙ ❧☙

I woke up Sunday morning to a rare winter day of bright

sunshine peeking through my bedroom window. Laying there, huddled under the blankets with Mr. Blue keeping me company, I went through all that happened yesterday and wondered whether it would be smart to see Jamie again.

I mean she seemed to come up with pretty good explanations for all that had happened to me since I woke up from my "dreams" yesterday morning, but it was still hard to swallow that it had all been real.

I couldn't wrap my head around the thought that I really was a princess and a half demon/ witch to boot. Those things don't happen to normal girls like me, do they? Well actually I guess those kinds of things don't happen to anyone except in some fairy tale, so who was I to complain?

I hung around the apartment most of the morning zoning out gaming and doing normal family stuff, my mind on a million different things. About ten-thirty, I decided that I would, at the very least, meet with Jamie one more time and got ready to go out.

As I was getting ready, it hit me what was different this morning; it was how quiet the apartment seemed. Usually, there is the noise of Dede running around being a little holy terror, my dad watching Sunday football, and mom working on her computer for the day. I guess I wasn't the only one in the house with a bunch of troubling thoughts.

"Hey, I'm going to the mall to meet a friend, be back in a

while," I flung at my parents as I headed toward the front door.

Dad jumped up from the couch like he had been stung by a hornet and Mom's chair crashed back into the coffee table as she leaped to her feet. I stopped in the middle of the room, stunned by their reaction; I mean it isn't like I wasn't allowed to be out by myself.

"Uhm, you guys okay?"

Both of my parents looked at each other with what I could swear was a look of worry and concern.

Mom walked over to me and gave me a hug as Dad sat back down on the couch again. "Listen Ceri, how about we stay home today. Okay? Just have a family day, what do you think?"

I sort of glanced at the two of them, trying to figure out what was going on between them. "Well, I did sort of let a friend know that I would meet her at the mall."

"Can't you call her and cancel? It's been so long since we had a family day together," Mom said as she slid back into her chair and then pulled it up to her computer once again.

"Well no, not really. I don't have her home number to tell you the truth." I noticed that look again that passed between them. "What's going on here anyways? Why is everyone so touchy about me going to the mall, I mean we were there yesterday with no problems?" I asked as I hoped that Dede hadn't blabbed about the strange goings on we

41

had encountered yesterday.

"Nothing is going on Ceri, we want to spend some time with you and your sister," Dad said. "But if you really want to go, be back before dark, okay?"

"Yeah, uhm, sure Dad, no problem," I said as I grabbed up my backpack and stuffed Mr. Blue inside as I headed out the front door. Could this weekend get any stranger, I thought as I headed out the door and down the front steps of the apartment with my head down in deep concentration.

"Going somewhere, Ceri?" a deep voice sounded in front of me just before I reached the bottom of the stairs.

"What the fu . . ." I said, startled as I looked up to see our neighbor from the apartment across the drive standing there looking like he had been starting up the same steps I had come down. "Yeah I'm going out, uhm, Mr . . ."

"Roc, the name is Roc. No Mr.," he said with a slight smile on his face.

Well that name fit, I thought, as I got a close look at him. Actually, mountain would have probably been a better name for this guy with as large and well defined as his muscles were on him. "Yeah well, Roc, I'm running a little late so how about I slide by you and go on my merry way."

He didn't move, just looked up at our apartment door. "Do your parents know that you are going out?"

"I'm sorry, but I don't know who you think you are, but it's really none of your business what my parents know or don't know. Now excuse me!" I said as I pushed by the huge man, knowing that he only moved because he had wanted to, and not by my will.

"Sorry Princess didn't mean to inconvenience you. Be careful out there."

I stopped at my dad's truck and looked back at the mountain of a man that was slowly climbing our stairs and had that flash of hallucination, momentarily seeing a dragon before the image disappeared; I queried his back, "What was that you called me, Roc?"

He just stopped and looked around at me and once again that sly small smile lit his face. "Have a good day, Ceri."

"Yeah, that's what I thought you said," I mumbled as I climbed into the truck and headed out to my date with Jamie.

☙❧☙❧☙❧

Scom lay shivering under the large green garbage can, not even smelling the stench that was emitting from the large metal box. He slowly sank down further into a dark corner closest to the wall of the building that the can butted up against, trying to stay out of the puddles that formed on the pavement from the nauseating drippings leaking from above.

He thought back to the events of yesterday and last night and wondered how a self-respecting troll like himself had gotten into a mess like this. First, there was the problem of the type of creature that the portal had turned him into when he had entered this world.

When he stepped through the portal, he had felt like his whole body had been stretched and twisted like a rubber band and then snapped back when he hit the pavement on the other side. He knew there was a problem when he opened his eyes and looked up and saw how large everything looked in this world.

Looking around he could see a large piece of mirror leaning up against the wall of a building. Stepping up to get a closer look at his new body, he stopped as he caught sight of what the magic of the portal had done to him.

Yeah, he thought, that portal had been laughing at him as he stared at the sight of the tiny little figure that stood on four feet looking back at him with two big runny eyes. As a cold wind whipped down the alley, his new shape shivered as the cool air touched each part of his almost hairless body. Oh, this is not good at all, he thought. What else can go wrong now? With that thought, the sky opened up with a deluge of cold winter rain as Scom scrambled under the garbage can for shelter.

As he sheltered under the garbage can waiting out the sudden downpour, Scom scolded himself for tempting fate as he had and reminded himself, before he dozed off from exhaustion, that the magic in this world was tainted by technology.

❧❦❧❦❧❦

The four coyotes slinked through the bushes that lined either side of the alley entrance. They had moved down from the snowy hills to the town where there were better pickings for the small pack. It made it easy for them to move around unseen as Bellingham had large wooded acreage from parks to private land around the area.

The biggest animal of the pack stopped and sniffed the air. He couldn't quite decide what this new smell was, but the underlying smell said food to his nose. Slowly the others gathered around their leader while moving down the narrow passageway and headed toward a large garbage can that dominated the alley.

❧❦❧❦❧❦

The second problem Scom had occurred as he woke from his slumber sometime in the stormy night. As he lay there trying to get his bearings, he could hear voices in the dark, quietly slithering to the edge of the can. He could see large shadows of different creatures shifting about in the night. He watched as two of the biggest creatures struggled and then one walked away from the crowd that was gathered around.

Shaking off his sleepiness, he caught the tail end of the

conversation that followed the struggle he had observed; and finally figured out that he had fallen, unwittingly, into the middle of Regni's efforts to have the princess killed for the queen.

Slowly backing up under the can so that he would not be noticed, he was startled as a large object hit the garbage can and moved it back a few feet. Listening to Regni scream and the other creatures leave the area, Scom looked out and stared at the unseeing eyes of the creature that had tried to question Regni.

The storm seemed to slow down as the fury of Regni diminished. In the quiet Scom could hear the mumbling of Regni as he reached down and grabbed the dead Other laying on the wet ground. He opened the lid and stuffed the body down into the can. Slamming the lid closed, the dragon walked out of the alley grumbling about Other trash and queens who wanted impossible missions done. An hour later, still tired from his adventures, Scom fell back to sleep.

☙❧☙❧☙❧

Now fully awake with early morning light just touching the darkened alley, Scom shook himself out of his thoughts and slowly crawled out from under his hiding place. Taking a step out toward the building and away from the putrid smell behind him, he caught the slightest whiff of the princess coming from under some doors. Oblivious to all around him, he quickly scurried over to the door where he caught the slight scent of Princess Ceri flowing from under the door.

As he sniffed some more, Scom could tell that this was an older scent; maybe a day or so old at least. Well, he thought, if she was here before maybe all I have to do is wait until she returns. Satisfied with his decision he started to look around the area he had been hiding in when he noticed for the first time the four hungry looking creatures that were now stalking him for breakfast. Oh, this is not good at all he thought as he backed into the corner of the building trying to make himself as small as possible.

He watched as the four animals encircled his position, knowing that his mission to save the princess seemed doomed before it had even begun. With low growls issuing from the creatures, Scom felt scared then slowly mad at the injustice of the situation. As the biggest of the four made ready to leap on the small prey, Scom felt a fire and rage start deep down inside his belly and quickly spread outward. A sudden itch all across his body made him shake and shiver and he could feel fur and moisture fly off his tiny body, obscuring him in a cloud of vapor.

කිළ්ක කිළ්ක කිළ්ක

The four coyotes stopped their attack on the small morning morsel that would have barely given each of them a mouthful as it disappeared within a strange smelling fog. As the mist cleared, two of the smaller animals in the pack slinked down to the ground in fright relieving their bladders before they turned and took flight back to the woods that they had come from.

The other two coyotes slowly backed up from the heat now radiating off the large monster that stood before them. As the leader and his mate looked at the beast, the heat and smoke only increased and seemed to blur the outline of the creature before them. The low growl of warning and the red shining flames burning behind the eyes of their supposed meal decided the pack leader that it was better to go look for breakfast somewhere else.

❧❧❧❧❧❧

Scom watched as the last of the two animals turned and ran from the alley. Slowly he walked over to the small broken mirror and looked down at the image that was shown. The red orbs of his eyes took in the large black body that seemed to be emitting heat and smoke from the tips of its fur. Well, this is more like it, he thought, as he lay down suddenly exhausted from changing to this new form. Now I need to find the princess, he thought, as he fell asleep again.

❧❧❧❧❧❧

I arrived at the mall during the Sunday lunch hour and had a frustrating time finding a parking space. By the time I found a place to park and walked to the mall doors, I was feeling pretty put out by the whole experience. "This is a really bad idea," I mumbled under my breath as I spotted an anxious looking Jamie standing in the crowd outside the doors.

As Jamie gave me a hearty hug she moaned, "Oh, there you are princ… I mean Ceri; I was so worried about you."

"No reason to worry, I came as I said I would," I managed, trying to disengage myself from Jamie's suffocating hug.

"It's not that I was afraid you wouldn't come," Jamie said as she looked around at the crowd. "It's that the Queen, as I feared, put a bounty on your head last night."

"Yeah listen, about that – I still think it was nothing but a dream I had the other night, and this whole thing is getting blown all out of proportion."

As I said this, I watched as Jamie's eyes got huge and she shook her head as though to chase all my negative thoughts away. "You're wrong, Ceri. It was not a dream and your life is in extreme danger," she whispered as she continued to scan the crowd and pulled me to the side of the mall entrance.

"Okay, so say I believe you. What can I do about it since it seems that my magic didn't come back with me to this world?"

Jamie took a deep sigh of air and gave me a quick hug before she spoke. "I may not be as good as my teacher, but I can show you how to draw magic. I mean you are half-witch so that side of you should be able to use the magic in this world."

I took a deep breath and then puffed it out into the clear cold winter air. "Okay, but I need to get something to eat, so let's head inside to the food court and grab some eats, okay?"

"Well I don't know about that, maybe we should just start into getting your powers before . . ."

I grabbed Jamie by the hand and started toward the entrance of the mall. "Believe me, girl, you do not want to be around me when I am hungry."

"Yeah, but what about the Others and the price on your head, Ceri?" Jamie asked as she fearfully glanced at each passing face.

I stopped and grinned at my worried companion. "Listen! If any Other bugs me while I am starving, they are going to have more to worry about than me using magic against them. Okay, so let's just go eat and then you can teach me all you know afterward."

Jamie resigned herself to my needy stomach, especially since it sounded with a low rumble at that second. "Okay Ceri, but right after we eat we head to a place where I can teach you."

"Yeah okay," I answered, but was suddenly distracted but a small voice that I heard from the crowd. I stopped as I cocked my head to hear better, for it almost sounded like a little troll voice from my dreams.

Scom woke up and stretched out his body from the cramped position he had been sleeping in. Slowly he stood and noticed that he was back to the tiny form that he had first entered this world in. Oh, this is so not fair, he thought, as he looked around the back of the building and saw some large sleeping beasts sitting against the building walls.

Then a door in the building opened and a man walked out and up to a red beast. As he did something to the side of the beast, it opened and the man slid inside it and it started to rumble to life emitting noxious smoke out its tail.

Watching the red creature move away it dawned on Scom that this wasn't a beast at all, but a vehicle of some sort that the people in this world used to get around. Well, he thought, as he carefully sniffed the closest contraption to him, at least, I don't have to worry about something else in this world eating me as he lifted his leg and anointed the vehicle.

Moving out toward the entrance of the alleyway, Scom stopped and sniffed the air with excitement. It was almost as if he could catch the fresh scent of the Princess wafting off the late morning breeze. With gathering excitement, he headed toward the side of the building following the smell that drove his tiny legs as fast as they could move.

Jamie stopped and looked at the mass of people around us with fright. "What is it Ceri? Do you see flashes of some of the Others?"

I flap my hand at her to quiet her talk so that I could hear better over the din of the crowd. "Sssh," I hissed, "just hold on. I thought I heard Scom."

"Scom? Who is Scom, Ceri?"

I looked at the young witch and then back around at the crowd before us, for I swear I could hear his tiny voice calling my name.

"Oh right, sorry," a whisper sounded at my side.

"Princess, wait for me. Don't leave me here, wait!" There was that tiny voice again, closer than before, but as I scanned the crowd I couldn't see any troll. This is nuts, I thought, I must be crazy as I turned toward Jamie and asked, "Don't you hear him; I mean that little voice calling to me?"

"I'm sorry, Ceri, all I hear is some little dog yipping. Are you sure you are feeling alright?"

"I feel fine Jamie and I swear I hear . . ." My words were cut off as I looked down at my feet where suddenly I realized that that was where the small voice was coming from.

"It's me, Princess; Scom, really. I'm here to rescue you."

I looked at the small dog then glanced back to Jamie then stared down at the tiny bundle at my feet. "Scom? Is that you?"

"Oh yes, Princess it is me and you are in terrible danger."

As I bent down to pick up the shivering body at my feet, Jamie gave me a strange look. "Uhm Ceri, you do know that you are talking to a dog, or rat, or some kind of animal, I think, right?"

I gave Jamie a scornful look. "This is not an animal, this is my best friend in the world."

"Okayyy, well if you say so, but all I see is a tiny mouse trying to pretend it's a dog."

"Yeah, but you heard him, right? I mean you heard him call out my name."

"Sorry Ceri, all I heard was his, uhm, let's loosely call it a bark if you want."

Scom let out an indignant humph. "HEY!! You can't talk to me like that. Let's dump this girl Princess so I can rescue you." Scom then reached over and sniffed in Jamie's general direction. "Plus she smells funny, Princess if you know what I mean?"

I turned to Jamie, the little troll's, I mean dog's, gumption bringing a smile to my face. "You really couldn't hear him talk just now?"

With a look of frustration, Jamie glared at Scom. "No Ceri, all I hear is the noise that little pipsqueak calls a bark. Why? What did he say? Was it about me? Here let me have him I really will turn him into a rat, and then, at least, he will be bigger than he is now."

"Okay, the both of you chill out! We are going into the mall and get some food before I really get cranky, alright?" I said as I headed toward the doors of the mall.

"Uhm Ceri, I don't think they will let the little rat in there." I stopped and looked back at Jamie who had the good graces to give a small apologetic smile. "Okay, *dog* is that better?"

"Not a problem," I said as I slid my backpack around and unzipped it. "Scom can hide in here next to Mr. Blue. Right, Scom? You and he are old buddies."

"Uhm yes Princess, but it will be hard for me to breathe in there if you know what I mean Princess?"

"Don't you worry little guy, I will set you in like so, and then I will leave the zipper open on the side of the pack. That way you get air and you can see out too. There. How's that?" I asked as I adjusted Mr. Blue and Scom into my pack.

"Oh yes, Princess, that is much better now and warmer too," the now miniature and changed troll said with a sigh of relief.

"Yeah and Scom you need to keep your voice . . ." I could

hear Jamie snicker beside me as we walked into the mall. "I mean bark quiet while we are in here, okay?" I heard a small whimper from inside my pack that I chose to accept as a yes from my newfound buddy.

As we maneuvered and grabbed a table in the back of a quiet section of the food court, Jamie once again gave me a snicker as she looked at the pack I gently set down. "Great. Your life is in danger, we're at the mall grabbing lunch and now we have a mini rat thinking he can save your life. What's next? We all go get a makeover before you learn enough magic to save yourself?"

Through the noise of the people moving around us, I thought I could hear a small growl erupt from the opening of the pack. "Listen, if you don't like it, Jamie, you can always leave me and my uhm dog . . . I mean friend to fend for ourselves."

"No, I'll stay Ceri. If nothing else someone needs to protect you from the Others that are in this world."

"Fine then go grab something to eat first while I save our spot and then I will go get my stuff, okay?"

As I watched Jamie walk off in a huff to get her meal, I unzipped my pack a little wider and peeked inside at Scom huddling next to Mr. Blue, "And you! Watch yourself, you little mischief maker. I feel like I need this witch's help to get myself out of this mess, so play nice, understand?"

Scom looked up quaking, with those small runny eyes

staring back at me. "Oh fine, play nice with the witch for my sake," I said as I zipped the pitiful sight back up into my pack and decided what I was going to have for lunch, not that I seemed to have much appetite anymore.

CHAPTER 4

The Others, with the coming of daylight, fanned throughout the town of Bellingham looking for the Princess and the rewards that would be delivered to the one that killed her. For creatures that lived on the outskirts of the town or in the hills surrounding it, this was an unpleasant task. The technological wonders of this world severely messed with what little mojo, or magic, each creature had brought over from their world.

Part of the problem seemed to be that no creature knew exactly where the Princess lived in this town thus making their job a lot harder. As each group separated, loosely controlled territories were divided up throughout the town by the creatures, and through their wild nature some lines were ignored and fights broke out.

❧❧❧❧❧

Roc gazed out his bedroom window that overlooked the apartment complex parking lot, lost in thought about the slight confrontation that he had had with Ceri earlier and the argument afterward with her parents.

Her parents were probably right, of course. Being in human form, Ceri wouldn't be scented out by the Others looking for her. After all, she had lived this long in this world without being discovered, but Roc had this bad feeling deep down in his aching bones that the Princess's good luck was about to run out.

A large, mangy female cat hopped into his lap and meowed loudly at the dragon. "Yes, I know we need to watch out for the Princess, what do you think I'm doing?" Roc answered the cat.

The cat nudged her rather large head on his arm to get his attention and then meowed loudly again. "What creature, where are you looking?" Roc asked, staring all around the parking area.

Then a flicker of movement alongside the garage below him caught his attention. A large strange mountain of a man was looking around and sniffing the air and peeking around the corner of the garage at Ceri's apartment.

The cat meowed loudly again. "Yeah, yeah I see him now. Thanks," Roc mumbled as he tossed the cat to the floor. The cat loudly protested this treatment, with some indignation, but Roc ignored her as usual.

Roc sighed and flexed his arms as he headed toward the door of his apartment. "Yeah," he said to himself, "looks like the Princess's luck has run out." As he closed and locked the outside door to his apartment, the thought flitted through his mind that it had been getting pretty boring in this world anyways.

Coming up and around the creature from behind, Roc moved up until he was almost on top of him; in fact, so intent was the creature on the apartment he was watching that Roc stood and looked at the mountain of flesh for a few seconds before making himself known.

"Uhm, can I help you?" Roc asked, chuckling to himself as the creature seemed to jump in the air despite his massive bulk and spun around with a surprised look on his face.

The man relaxed as he saw who stood before him, then gave a low growl deep in his chest. "Go away, this is no your area."

Oh great, Roc thought, a fricking ogre what I need today. He looked up and smiled at the menace before him. "Well, since my apartment is right over there, big guy, then I think that yeah, this is my area."

The man seemed to try to process this info as he looked at the apartment that Roc pointed at then around to the place that his senses told him the girl everyone was looking for lived. "You know girl lives here, why not you tell?"

Roc studied the big guy some more, trying to decide how smart (or not) he was. "Listen, I think you got this all wrong, my big friend. The Princess lives somewhere else, not here. Okay?"

"NO, I was tracker for Queen. I know smell of girl. She lives here. You lie."

Well so much for that idea, Roc thought. "Listen this is my area, my house. You need to leave. If the princess is here then it's my right to take her to the Queen, so how about you pack it up and go home my friend, okay?"

"I, no your friend. I know you not Queens's friend."

Roc shrugged his shoulders at the ogre and sighed. "So I guess since you are not leaving we are going to have to do this the hard way then. Is that what you're saying?"

"I no say anything, but I will take girl to Queen."

"Well, okay then if that's the way it has gotta be," Roc said as he turned his body halfway away from the ogre then spinning back, putting all the power he had behind it, he launched his fist into the massive face before him.

As his fist connected with the ogre's face, Roc thought it was like hitting a solid brick wall. Stepping back, expecting the large man to fall he was a little surprised when he saw that the ogre stood there and slightly shook his head, glaring back at him with a puzzled look.

"Why you hit me for like that?" the ogre asked, rubbing his jaw where Roc had landed a solid punch and then stepped toward the wary dragon. "That not nice to hit me." With that short statement, the ogre swung a large fist the size of

Roc's head at his body.

Roc leaped back as the wind from the swinging fist swept past him, then ducked down and under as the opposite hammer of a fist barely missed his head. "Whoa, my big friend, maybe we got off on the wrong foot here," Roc said as he moved further away from the now windmilling blocks of meat being thrown at his head and body.

"I NO FRIEND WITH SOMEONE WHO HIT ME!" the big man said as he tried with all his might to connect with the smaller creature in front of him. The more the ogre swung at the elusive being in front of him and missed the more his temper rose so that soon he was in a killing rage. Now if only he could get his hands on this creature, he would break him in half and make a snack of him.

❧❧❧❧❧

The three of us had a quiet lunch. We didn't have much to say to each other while we ate, all lost in our own thoughts. I could see that Jamie wasn't very happy because I was sneaking Scom my fries and nuggets since I had totally lost all my appetite thinking of all the strange things that had happened over the last two days.

I guess that I had to face up to the truth that it wasn't a dream I had had the other night and that there really was another world out there somewhere full of creatures called Others. Oh heck what was I thinking; I was one of those creatures, those Others from that world.

"Ceri, what are you thinking about?" Jamie asked as she gathered up the wrappers from her lunch.

I looked at her feeling a little lost. "I was thinking that with Scom here, all you were telling me was true. You know the dream, the Others world, and all the creatures in it that I met before, it's all real."

Jamie gave me a look of exasperation. "Well duh, yeah, that's what I have been saying all along."

"Okay, I get it. I never really believed before, but now with Scom here I guess I have no choice."

"So you're telling me you didn't believe the things I told you, but the rat shows up and all of sudden you believe me, is that what you're saying?"

I heard a low growl from my backpack. "Quiet Scom," I said as I tapped the pack lightly and then turned to Jamie, "and you stop teasing Scom. He can't help how he was sent through that portal, okay?"

"Alright Ceri, I'll try. Here let me get rid of this garbage and then we can go over any ideas for keeping you safe."

I touched Jamie's arm lightly and gave her an apologetic look. "And I'm sorry okay? Deep down I really did believe you, it's that seeing Scom made it more real."

Jamie gave me a small smile back. "It's alright, Ceri. I guess I'm not used to dealing with the Others and all this without my teacher around." With that small confession, Jamie grabbed up the wrappers on the table and headed for the nearest trash can.

As I sat and watched the young witch dispose of what was left of our lunch, the thought flickered through my mind that it seemed curious that Jamie wanted to keep her teacher out of this whole mess. Or maybe, I thought, he might be part of the problem and I hadn't realized it before.

Once Jamie disposed of our trash, I saw her head to a small coffee stand at the side of the food court. Guess she thought it would be better to have something in front us while we talked so that people wouldn't come and try to commandeer our table.

As I watched her walk back to the table, I looked at the large Christmas shopping crowd that flowed around us and through the only mall in this little town. That's when I noticed this flash again, a flash of this one guy that looked like, well like a great big ugly, for lack of a better word.

He stared at me with this strange look and then he was lost in the crowd and gone. By this time Jamie had returned to the table and looked at my searching face with some concern.

"Are you okay, Ceri? What are you looking for?" she asked as she now searched the massive crowd herself.

"It's nothing, I guess," I answered as I sat back down in my chair trying to give her a reassuring smile. "Now how do

we do this? I mean with the magic thingy and all."
Jamie gave one last look around the area and then focused on me. "Uhm, it's not some thingy or whatever you want to call it. It is real magic produced by ley lines in the Earth."

"Okay sorry," I said with an apologetic look.

Jamie sighed and then her face softened as she went on with her lecture. "I'm sorry too; it's that I have had this drilled into me by my parents and teacher on how serious and important this is since I was young. I'm not sure that I can teach you any of this stuff on such short notice."

"Don't worry kiddo. I have confidence that you can get it through my thick skull one way or another."

"Well, okay then. The magic is in the ley lines as I said before. The thing is that only a witch can use and manipulate these lines."

"So sort like a magic helper, like Hamburger Helper right, but for magic?"

"OKAY! That's it! I'm outta here if you aren't going to take this seriously!" The people at the tables around us gawked as Jamie let out this sudden outburst and her chair slid across the floor as she got up to leave.

I grabbed Jamie's arm and chair and then pulled her back into her seat, whispering in her ear. "Alright no more being flippant, I'm sorry." Then I turned to the couple that had made a beeline for our table as Jamie stood to go and hissed at them. "We aren't done here yet so go find somewhere else to sit."

The couple looked at us for a second and then headed out into the ocean of humanity flowing around us, looking for a new spot to sit and eat.

"That wasn't very nice, you know?" Jamie said looking after the couple, then looking back at me and giving a little giggle. "There are times when you can be so outgoing and direct, you know?"

"Yeah I know, I have had a few conversations with my parents about that. It's sort of the reason that I do online public school since I used to get in so many hassles with some of my teachers."

"Yes, I could see that about you, Ceri."

"Uhm thanks, I think? Now tell me how will these ley lines help me since I'm only half a witch?"

"Alright, Ceri, but remember one more smart aleck remark and then I am out of here, okay?"

"I said I would be good, Jamie. I'm sorry, tell me about this magic."

With another big sigh and a quick look around, Jamie then got down to the fundamentals of magic. "A witch takes the power of the nearest ley line and draws it inside. Then they use that power to shape whatever magic they want to do."

"Okayyy, seems simple enough, Jamie. So show me an example of this magic."

"What, here? Right now?"

"Yeah. What? Isn't there any line power around here for you to use?"

Jamie huffed at me with an indignant look. "Of course, there is a ley line near here, and I will have you know that I can store power within me also."

"Okay well, and then it should be no problem to show me a small trick . . ." Jamie gave me a stern look. "Of course, I mean a small bit of magic then, right?"

Jamie looked around at the crowd again, then back at me. "Okay, watch my face."

I watched for a few seconds, not knowing what to expect or really seeing anything happening. I could almost feel a small tingle, but ignored the feeling as I started to notice little changes in her face until all of a sudden I was staring at my own face staring back at me. Then as fast as it came the image and the tingle were gone.

"Uhm okay, how did you do that? That was freaky."

Before Jamie could answer I heard a small voice from inside my bag whine. "Princess, what is the tingle that I felt coming from out there?"

Both Jamie and I both looked at my pack and the small

brown face that now peeked out of the opening in the side.

"You felt my magic, rat?" Jamie asked then quickly looked at me and smiled. "Sorry, Ceri, a force of habit."

"Don't say sorry to me. Tell Scom you're sorry."

"Fine Scom, I'm sorry I called you a rat."

"That is alright, I guess, but yes I felt something. Is that what you call magic in this world of yours?"

Jamie looked at me then down to my backpack. "Yes that is magic, but if I can ask what did you feel ra . . . I mean Scom?"

"It felt like a tingling sensation all over my body, and then it was gone."

"And you Ceri, did you feel this sensation also?"

I looked at Jamie and then Scom as they watched me with anticipation. "Well yeah, I guess I did feel a little tingle, almost like a small jolt or spark of electricity running through my body."

With that, I looked down at my arms and saw a faint outline of the tattoos that denoted the powers that I once possessed in another world. "I wonder . . ." I whispered as I opened my hand below the table and thought of a small glowing fire.

"Oh no, you aren't supposed to be able to do that," Jamie said in a loud voice as she brought her hand to her mouth to cover the slip she had done.

"Oh cool, Princess!" Scom said as he leaned further out of the bag to see the small globe of light that was formed in the outstretched palm of my hand.

As we all watched, the fire gradually died as the tingle of power slowly leached out of me. I peeked at my arm and could see that those tattoos were now gone, almost as if I had imagined them.

I looked around to see if anyone had noticed this little display. I know a little late for that but saw that everyone around us seemed to be wrapped up in their own holiday world. "Uhm Jamie, how did that work, and where can I get some more of that?"

Jamie sat there and stared at me for a second and then slowly slid around the table, away from me. "You aren't supposed to be able to do that, Ceri," she said with large frightened eyes.

"Do what? I thought the whole idea was to teach me how to use this magic power of the ley lines."

Jamie whispered so low that I could barely hear her from across the table. "Yes but you took that power from me. Witches can only gather this power from the ley lines, not from other witches. Oh, this is so not good."

I looked at the young witch with surprise written on my face. "No, you're wrong. It must be that there is a line nearby and that's where I got this power from."

Jamie was shaking her head in denial as she looked around like she expected the magic cops to show up any second and take me away. "Listen to me Ceri. The nearest line is in a park about a mile or so from this mall. The line doesn't function around technology; for some reason, it messes with the power."

"Okayyy, well maybe I have the ability to draw that power from here, you think?"

Jamie looked at me for a second then looked down at her hands. "No. What I think happened was that as I used my magic somehow you drew it from me into yourself. That's the tingle or spark that you and Scom felt."

"Listen, Jamie, I know that in the Others world I could take the magic from my sisters and all, but I have been touching your arm quite a few times this weekend and nothing like what happened to my sisters happened to you. So it must be that I drew the power from some line around here."

Right about then a small voice popped out of the backpack that Scom had been hiding in. "No Princess, as much as it pains me to agree with this witch, I think that she is right."

Jamie looked at the pack with the same surprise written on her face as I probably had on mine. "Okay now, this does not bode well when the rat agrees with me."

I let that reference go as we had more important things to worry about right now. "What do you mean, Scom?"

"It's that I felt a flow of magic between the two of you, Princess. That was what the tingly feeling was. I think that this world has different rules for magic and that you can only steal a witch's magic as they go to use it themselves."

"Yeah, but Scom, Jamie is still here, and whole. I mean with my sisters they were gone when I took their magic away from them." I turned to Jamie and gave her a once over. "I mean you do feel alright kiddo, don't you?"

Jamie sat for a second or two and assessed how she felt and then smiled for the first time. "Yeah I feel fine, empty of magic as if I had used all that I had stored up inside me."

"Then that is the thing that is happening, Princess," the little voice from the pack said, "In this world you only take the magic as the witch performs a spell, but leave their living essence still in them."

"Alright Scom, I guess I see what you are saying," I sat and thought of the possibilities of this little power of mine for a minute then straightened up and looked back at Jamie. "Well, it's nice to know that I won't hurt my only friend in this world like I did my sisters in the Others world."

"HEY!" the little voice sounded out from my pack.

"Sorry Scom, I meant my only witch friend, better?"

"Yeah, a little better," grumbled the small voice from the pack. I looked at the bag and then up at Jamie as I heard her trying to stifle a laugh from across the table.

"Okay so here's an idea. How about you stop stuffing your face with food, Jamie, and we head over to this park and load us up with magic from the line that is there."

Jamie gave me a look of indignation and huffed at me. "It was not my idea to stop here, Ceri, and stuff our bellies with food, remember?"

I smiled back at the witch. "Yeah I know, but you are so easy to get a rise out of."

A little laugh sounded out of the bag in front of me which caused Jamie to throw a dirty look at it before getting up from our table and pulling all her trash together to leave. "But you are right, Ceri, we need to head over to the park for I do feel a little exposed with no magic to protect us."

This thought sobered me up and I stood also to clean up my trash too. Throwing my pack over my left shoulder, I began to follow Jamie to the trash can and out to my car. "Yeah you're right. We need to get you some magic mojo and see if I can't load some of this up myself." Looking back at our table, I saw that it was snapped up by a pair of couples looking for all in this world as if they had nothing to do but worry about their Christmas shopping.

☙❧ ☙❧ ☙❧

Urg watched the witch and her friend leave their table and head for a trash can. He may have been an ogre, but he wasn't quite as slow as some of his brethren as he realized that the two females were probably on their way out of the mall.

Urg tried to fathom in his shallow mind why the witch wasn't with her teacher, Saba. He finally figured out that he should follow them and find out what the witch was up to; for Urg may have been an Other, but he was also a spy for Saba ever since he had been caught taking tasty bites out of that hiker last year.

Urg knew that he really shouldn't be helping the main witch that protected this area, but in his small brain, he figured it was better that Saba kills Others rather than himself. Of course, he never gave an ogre over to Saba, I mean even ogres should have some standards, but that didn't matter much seeing that there were so many different types of Others living in this world.

With these thoughts muddling through his mind, Urg stood at the door of the mall watching the two girls approach. As they came closer, Urg's nose suddenly caught the scent of something, almost like a troll, as they passed him.

Then as he moved behind the girls, he caught a whiff from the breeze flowing through the outside doors; not a strange smell, an almost remembered smell of something like home. It almost smelled like a long ago aroma that lingered from when he was once one of the Queen's guards. Almost as if the Queen herself was now in this world, but different somehow. This idea went through his mind as he once again strained all his thought processes trying to puzzle out the new smell.

Urg stopped in his tracks as the connection was made in his brain. It wasn't the Queen he smelled, but the Princess, the one that Regni had told them about. Returning her, the Queen would forgive all crimes and let you come back home, out of this world of technology and back to a world of magic.

Urg's grin turned nasty as he closed the distance between the witch and who he now knew was the princess. Though he was really puzzled on why the two of them were together and acting as best friends. Yes, Saba, he thought, will be very interested in what his little student was doing on her free time at the mall.

❧❧❧❧❧❧

As Jamie and I walked out of the mall, I had this strange feeling that I was being watched, as a small voice from my pack piped up. "I smell ogre, princess, and that is so not good, if you know what I mean, right princess?"

Jamie was ahead of me and didn't hear Scom's warning. As unobtrusively as I could I slowly looked around, but the crowd was so thick coming and going out the doors that I couldn't see anything but the nearest people around us. "I don't see anything, Scom," I whispered moving up beside Jamie as we headed toward my car. "I'm parked over here, Jamie," I said as we moved into the parking lot itself.

"Is something wrong, Ceri?" Jamie asked as she followed my gaze around the parking lot.

"No, nothing. I think that Scom and I are smelling things," I said as we found my truck and we settled into the vehicle for the drive to the park.

CHAPTER 5

Roc ducked once more under the swinging arms of the creature in front of him and swung around behind the ogre. Before the creature could react, Roc took one step forward and landed a solid kick between the legs of his nemesis.

As the ogre stopped and then slowly turned around to face the dragon, the thought flashed through Roc's head that he was now in deep trouble. "Okay now listen big gu . . ." Roc started to reason once more with the ogre as he took one step toward Roc. The dragon stopped talking when he noticed something peculiar about the expression on the ogre's face.

The ogre stopped in mid-stride as Roc heard a low moan and hiss of air slowly escape the ogre's mouth as bit by bit the large mountain of muscle bent over, his knees hitting the ground in front of him. Roc relaxed as he watched the eyes of the big guy roll back up into his head and then as the rest of his body hit the ground, he gave a sigh of relief that the creature had gone down easier than he thought he would.

Roc stared at the ogre for a few seconds "You know you're lucky we aren't back home and I wasn't in my dragon form, ogre, or you would be one crispy critter," Roc said to the now prone and unconscious figure before him. The only answer was an involuntary groan that escaped from the prone body.

Roc looked around the area to see if this little dance had been noticed by his neighbors. Seeing no one out and about, he walked over to the head of the ogre and lifted him up by the shoulders to move him to a more secluded spot. "Damn, I've forgotten how heavy you guys are. You would think being in this world you would have lost some weight there, big guy."

A quiet snort was all the answer that Roc got back from his comment as he laid the ogre's head back onto the ground behind the garage. Roc leaned up against the wall of the garage and relaxed now that the ogre was down and out for the count, feeling every bump and scrape his body had endured in the fight.

A quiet meow sounded at his feet as he felt the large furry body rub along his legs. "Yeah, I'm fine, don't worry about it," he said as he looked down at his cat.

Reaching down and picking the fur ball up, Roc slowly slid down the garage wall to sit and rest after all the excitement of the last while. "And just how did you get out of the apartment?"

The cat yowled back at the dragon as he roughly petted the cat in his lap.

"Yeah magic, right, so how come in this world you can do magic and I can't. Why don't you explain that to me?"

The cat silently looked up at Roc then rubbed her head into the big man's chest and purred.

"Okay, okay, I know you have no control over what happens in this world any more than the rest of us, but still it would be nice to have some power here in this world, or . . ." Roc looked around the area he was sitting in and sighed. "Maybe even get out of here and go home."

The cat sat up swiftly and bit Roc on the arm and then jumped down from his lap as the dragon let out a yelp and stood up. "Hey! What was that for? I said it would be nice to go back home, not that I was going to turn the Princess into Regni. Damn! Give me a break here."

That cat stopped and looked over her shoulder at Roc and meowed once, flipped her tail at the man and strutted away, disappearing around a corner of the building.

"Now that was not a nice thing to call me. You remember that when you come looking for dinner tonight. HEY! Did you hear me? Damn! Now, what's gotten into her lately?" Roc inquired, scratching his head as he looked at the spot where his companion had disappeared.

The only answer was a snort and snore from the prone ogre by his side. "Yeah and I don't need your two cents in this either," he mumbled as he looked down at the body lying on the ground.

⟡⟡⟡⟡⟡⟡

I hadn't realized how much time we had spent in the mall until I looked at the clock in the truck. "Is it really almost four?" I asked not believing my eyes.

"Well yeah, I told you Ceri that we were going to waste a lot of time at the mall. Who knows? By now we could have taught you all kinds of magic if we had started right away."

I looked over at Jamie and smirked. "Yeah but then think, we wouldn't have found Scom, my best buddy then either."

"Oh yes, what I large loss that would have been," Jamie answered dryly. "How would we ever have survived that?"

I laughed as I heard a small growl come from the back of the truck. "Oh hush, Scom, you know Jamie is only kidding around, right?"

With another low growl from the back and a roll of Jamie's eyes, I figured the answer to that question was a big NO."

"Alright, so changing the subject, I take it this is the park you are talking about?" I asked as I moved into the left turn lane and pointed to one of my favorite spots to go when I wanted to get away from it all.

Jamie smiled and nodded. "Yes, that's the one."

"Uhm Jamie, I thought you said that technology ruins or messes with magic and these ley line thingies?"

Jamie looked puzzled and a little annoyed at me as she answered. "Yes, I said that except for that whole *thingie* stuff."

"Oh sorry, well then how are we going to do magic here in the middle of town?"

"Oh that," Jamie said with a look of relief on her face, "you do know how big this park is right?"

"Yeah, of course; like I said before, I come here a lot. Okay?"

"Well, it is big enough to have a small ley line within it. You have to walk away from the entrance of the park to get to it, but it should be enough to load us up with power. Don't worry, I will show you when we get to the right spot."

With that reassurance from Jamie, we pulled into the empty parking lot. Getting out of the truck, I pulled my pack out of the back and reached in and got Scom out and set him on the ground.

While Jamie looked around the park, Scom ran over to a small tree and proceeded to fertilize the surrounding ground with an intense look of relief.

"OH my God, what is that stench?" Jamie exclaimed with small shallow breaths.

I looked and laughed as Jamie put both hands to her face to cover her nose. "I think that was Scom's Mickey Ds lunch coming out the south end of my little buddy," I said, looking at Scom as he proudly walked back toward me.

"Yeah well if there were any of the Others around here, I'm sure that that smell would drive them away. Seriously, Ceri, how can something that small produce something that smells that bad?"

Picking up Scom and grabbing Jamie's arm, I pulled her toward the middle of the park. Laughing, all I could think was that my life may have gotten a wee bit complicated lately, but you sure can't say it was ever boring.

❧❧❧❧❧❧

Urg slowed down as he turned the corner and saw the Princess's truck turn into the park. It's a good thing that an ogre's eyesight was so good. Of course, that and their excellent sense of smell was why the Queen used the creatures such as himself for her own guards and trackers. What ogres lacked in brains and common sense, they more than made up for it in their relentlessness in following their prey.

As Urg crossed under a freeway overpass, he paused a little bit as he caught a slight whiff of an Other's scent. The further he moved under the overpass, the more the smell felt like he was running into a wall of stench made up of a long unwashed body mixed in with a slight reptilian odor.

"Whosss isss moving underss my home?" A hiss, barely heard above the cars moving overhead, was whispered from within a dim, dirty corner.

Urg stopped and peered into the corner and then laughed. "Oh, only you. For a second you scare me."

A small figure, dressed in bundles of rags and a cloak, stepped out of his dim hidey hole facing the large ogre. "Ssso I onlyss sscaress you a little my fine friendss? Perhapss a little bites would changess your mind?" the wrapped figured hissed back at the ogre as he slithered closer.

Urg stepped back from the figure and thought as carefully as his small brain allowed. I have no fight with you. I follow someone, so now out of my way," the ogre said as he puffed out his chest and looked down at the small figure.

"Nos need to be rudess my largess friend. I'm curiousss wheress you are going in sssuch a rush," the voiced hissed now with a slight sound of mocking laughter.

Urg looked at the bundle of rags that was standing before him and some small alert signal was going off in his head that maybe this creature wasn't so helpless as it seemed, but after all, he was an ogre, one of the meanest creatures in his world next to dragons, of course. "I follow witch and girl that is all you need to know."

"Girlss, what girls? Isss Princesss who we follow with the

witchy?" the bundle hissed louder as the creature stepped closer to the ogre.

Urg brushed past the small creature pushing him aside, knocking him to the ground and laughed. "I no tell you anymore creature. I have to go now."

The bundled creature slowly picked itself off the ground where he had landed and looked at the back of the ogre moving out from under the overpass. "Thatsss will be fine ogre, butsss I wonder what the other creaturesss would thinksss of Saba'sss ssspy catching the Princesss," he hissed quietly, laughing as the ogre before him stopped, shoulders hunched as if he had been punched in the back.

Urg stood where he had stopped as if he had suddenly been rooted into the sidewalk under his feet, thoughts slowly processing through his mind. After a few, slow agonizing minutes he saw only one solution to his problem. "Follow me filth, but the witch is mine to give to the teacher. The Princess we will split. Deal?"

"Oh, yesss we have a deals, yesss we do," the bundle laughed as he slithered down the sidewalk behind the ogre. Well, at least, we have a deal until I think it's time to break it, the creature thought with silent glee.

❧❧❧❧❧❧

We followed the path leading from the parking lot to the inner core of the park. Passing the playground, I looked around and thought of all the warm summer days that my sister and I had spent here playing. Slowing, even more, I looked at the playground equipment and the sprinkler system the park had that amused all the little children during the hot, lazy days of summer. I remembered how the parents would sit in small groups on the ground or the few benches and picnic tables spread around the play areas. I grew a little melancholy thinking of how all that could change with what was happening in my life.

Jamie slowed down and looked back at me with a puzzled look. "Is everything alright, Ceri?"

I shook myself as if coming out of a dream. "Yeah remembering better days when I was younger. The park looks so forlorn and barren during the winter with no one around."

Jamie looked around at the area and then shook her head. "Oh I guess so, we never really came here much except when my teacher or my parents came to charge from the ley line or to teach me something. Then it was at night or when there wasn't anyone around, like now. Guess they didn't want a bunch of people to see them do what they needed to do."

"What, you mean your parents never took you to the swings or to play in the water during the summer?"

"No, Ceri, my parents were more concerned with keeping track of Others and saving the town than they were with me playing; and Saba, well let's say that he is only interested in a witch that is perfect in her assigned duties."

"Is that why you haven't told him about helping me or teaching me magic?"

Jamie looked at me slyly as we walked toward a small wooden bridge. "I haven't told Saba what I am doing with you because he wouldn't understand. In fact to tell you the truth I think he might even give you over to the Others, figuring one less of you would be good for this town," Jamie said as our feet clomped on the wood boards of the bridge.

We both stopped in the middle of the bridge as I put Scom down to stretch his legs. Jamie leaned against the bridge railing with her back to the flowing stream under us as I looked over the same railing down into the rushing water. "So then tell me something that I've been wondering about since we met," I said as I peeked over to the witch as she stared out over the area we had left.

"Yeah, sure. What is it, Ceri?"

"Uhm, well you said you saw me in this Others world, right?"

"Yeah?"

"Well, how did you see me, a crystal ball, read some tea leaves, what?"

Jamie smiled and gave a little chuckle. "No, nothing like that. I have a small gift of sight. Sometimes it lets me see things that happen." Then the smile and laughter left her face and was replaced by a frown of concern. "Actually, the sight is why Saba took me on as a student. He thought that I would be able to see Others before they did something. He wanted to use that power or sight to get rid of Others in this world before they caused problems."

"Uhm, not a very nice guy, is he?" I asked.

"Well, he is protecting this town from dangers," Jamie answered, a little defensively.

"Yeah, okay I guess that is one way to look at it, but back to the dream or whatever it was. Did you see the whole thing like a movie or what?"

Jamie smiled and then turned and leaned over the railing like me and stared down into the flowing water below, the stars shining off the rushing current. "No, it was more like a highlight reel as they call it." Then looking down at our feet, her smile grew bigger as she watched Scom poke his nose over the side of the bridge and sniff he air. "You fall in, rat, and I won't fish you out."

I heard a small grumbling issue from near my feet but noticed that the little guy backed up from the edge of the bridge. Picking up Scom, we headed to the other side of the bridge, my laughter bubbling over at the interaction between my two friends; one new, one old. "Come on Jamie; show me where this power in the park is."

As we walked down the path deeper into the park, I was

hesitant about going further as I noticed that the sky was starting to darken over with sinister looking clouds. "Hey Jamie, how long does it take to do this power up thing of yours anyway?"

"Not long, why?"

"Oh, just wondering. My parents didn't want me out of the house today and I told them that I would be home before dark."

"Don't sweat it, you'll make it. We're almost there."

I figured we were close by even before Jamie told me as I could feel that small spark or tingle again as we moved deeper into the park. Scom gave a small whimper in my arms, so I figured that I wasn't the only one of us the line was having an effect on.

Jamie looked over at the small bundle in my arms and frowned once again. "That's strange."

"What's strange? I asked, thinking over the last couple of days with all that happened to me, a small dog whimper seemed pretty normal.

With a look of puzzlement, Jamie glanced at me and then down at Scom shivering in my arms. "Well, my teacher said that Others shouldn't be able to feel ley lines. The only reason I thought that you had a chance to draw power from them was because you are half-witch. Yet the little one here seems to be affected by the magic in them too."

I looked down at Scom with worry. "Are you alright, little guy? Do you want to wait here for us?"

Scom looked around the area of growing darkness and then shivered some more. "Oh no, Princess, if it is all the same with you I will go with you. It would be much safer if you know what I mean Princess, right?"

"Well, okay Scom," I answered, "but how about you ride in the pack with Mr. Blue where you will be a little warmer than out in the open, okay?"

A small chill ran through us all as a breeze whistled through the trees, making Scom shiver even harder than before. "Yes your Princess, maybe riding in the pack with Mr. Blue would be for the better."

We stopped for a minute as Jamie held my pack and I opened it to deposit one small package inside it. Scom snuggled deeper into the pack with Mr. Blue and I noticed that the shivering hadn't stopped completely, but did seem to slow down some.

Moving back down the path with the witch by my side I could hear a small sigh of contentment come from my pack. Well, I thought, at least, he will stay out of trouble in there if nothing else. Then I gave a small snort of laughter as I heard a loud snore two steps later coming from deep within my pack.

Jamie looked at me then gave my pack a quick glance. "Is that . . ."

"Yeah that's Scom," I laughed shaking the pack a little and hearing a loud snort now from inside. "That troll can sleep anywhere, no matter what form he's in."

"I guess so," Jamie said with some amusement in her voice, nice to know that my friend could laugh even if we were in a semi-serious situation like now.

Moving down the path, it was quiet as each of us was lost in our thoughts. Well, I should say, a quiet that was broken every now and then by dog snores filling the air. The crisp wind was picking up now and the clouds that were rolling in on the tail of this wind looked fat with rain, ready to deluge all who happen to wander under them.

Jamie stopped near a baseball backstop off the path we were on and pointed out toward a line of woods near the outfield. "Can you feel it, how powerful it is?" she said with a bright feverish look in her eyes.

I looked around and saw that we were still alone in the park then glanced over where she was pointing. "Oh, yeah I can feel it alright. Believe me, that's all I can feel the closer we have gotten to this line. So now what do we do?"

"Simple. We go down to the line, and open our self up to its power. Nothing to it, Ceri," Jamie said as she headed down the slight hill toward where the ley line was.

I followed Jamie down the hill, mumbling behind her back. "Great just plug me into the recharger like a battery, why don't you?"

"What was that, Ceri?" Jamie asked as she got to the bottom of the hill and then turned her head toward me with a quizzical look on her face.

"Ohhh, nothing, just talking to myself," I said as I thought to myself that I really need to learn to keep these thoughts inside, no sense in peeving off a witch that was looking to load up on magic.

The closer we got to the woods, the more of this spark or tingle I felt flowing through my body. From the back of my pack, I could hear Scom shifting around and knew that he was in the same boat as me.

I stopped about midway through the ball field and looked down at my arms and could see the outlines of my sister's and my power tattoos that I had inherited in the other world glowing on my arms. "Uhm Jamie, what do you mean by opening yourself up when we get to the line?"

Jamie stopped in mid stride and looked back at me with some puzzlement. "Well, you don't think that power flows into a person like a sponge, do you? Because if it did work that way then anyone could get the magic. You have to release yourself and take in the power."

"Oh, yeah, that's what I was afraid you were going to say."

"Why, Ceri? Is there a problem?" Jamie asked as she moved closer to me, her eyes finally catching the glow on my arms.

"Well I don't know if I would call it a problem per se as

much as I don't seem to need to open myself to suck up any of this magic," I said as I kneeled and laid my pack on the ground. I looked inside and found Scom looking at me with small, red glowing eyes. Well, I thought, maybe there is a slight problem after all.

"Uhm Scom, are you okay?"

"Yes, Princess," the small pack traveler answered in a deeper growl that his tiny size should never be able to voice. "I think though that you should not take me any closer if you know what I mean Princess?"

Jamie looked at me and then down into the pack that was now opened and resting between my knees. "Oh, crap! I mean, sorry Ceri, I, I mean he shouldn't be like this."

Scom looked up from his hiding place, his eyes still glowing red and growled at the witch. "We trolls may be the smallest in our world, little witch, but we are the most magical too. We have tricks that the others in our world have no knowledge of.

Jamie looked down at Scom then over to where the line was and said. "Yeah Ceri, I think he is right; he shouldn't get any closer to the ley line."

Looking down where her gaze was directed, I tended to agree with my new friend. "Alright, but I'm going to take it slow in approaching this line too, Jamie," I said as I stood up and wiped my sweaty hands on my pants.

Another growl sounded from my pack as I took a step back

toward the spot we were headed to before. "Princess, I think that it would be a good idea if you stayed with me if you know what I mean?"

"I do know what you mean, Scom," I said as I moved off, "but you know me, I never was good at following good ideas or plans."

I heard a faint mumble come from the pack as we moved off into the growing dark. "Yes, I do know that Princess, and that is why I worry so."

Yeah so do I, Scom, I thought, so do I.

❦❧❦❧❦❧

Urg and his new partner reached the park with no other further troubles to slow them down. The ogre sniffed the air like a relentless bloodhound now locked onto the scent of the vehicle that the two girls were riding in.

"There. That is where they are," Urg said as he turned into the park's parking lot.

"Aress you sssuress that this iss where they aress?" the wrapped bundle asked as he followed the bigger creature into the park.

Urg stopped upwind of his tag-along and frowned down at him. "You no question me, I will find the two girls. They are where I say they are."

A small, scaly looking hand was held up in front of the

bundle and a little mocking laugh came from the top of it. "Oh, by all meansss, my friend; I will not questionsss you at all."

Urg's minuscule brain worked hard to see if the creature before him was truly mocking him, but the effort was too much and for the ogre not worth the trouble right that second. With a huff, he turned and walked down to the only vehicle parked in the lot. "See? I told you the witch and her friend stop here."

The bundle looked around the area and then shrugged his shoulders. "Well thatss iss fine my big friend, but wheress are they now; thisss isss a big park, you knowsss?"

Urg looked around, sniffed the air and then pointed in the general direction of the middle of the park. "They this way," Urg said as he set off in the direction the two girls had taken.

The bundle stood and watched the ogre for a second then followed him to the cover of the trees. Looking up at the night sky and approaching clouds he thought that yes being under cover would be a relief from all the openness of the park's parking lot. His kind were, after all, creatures of the dark and closed spaces; striking from cover with no warning to the unwary. Yes, this was going along so nicely, so nicely indeed.

CHAPTER 6

The once beautiful valley was covered in smoke and ash and the stink of dead and burnt bodies floated on the slight breeze that danced across it. A lone figure watches from a hidden cave as yet another round of dragons flew down through the pass above them and swept the valley floor with more flame of destruction.

Ro lowered his head at the sight before him and the cry from the children behind him in the cave assaults his senses. Slowly he turns as the murmur of quiet footsteps sounds behind him.

"Are the children settled, Da?" Ro asks his larger shifter brother.

"Yes Ro, all are settled in this cave and the others in the mountains," Da answers as he comes up to Ro's side and looks out over the valley that was once their home.

"Good, Da."

Da looks over to his brother and then back out over the valley. "You know brother that the people are calling for revenge for these atrocities, don't you?"

"Yeah Da, I know." Ro sighs and then straightens up. "But both you and I know that we can't take on the Queen and her army by ourselves."

"I know Ro, but if the Queen is treating all her subjects like she is treating us I don't think we will be alone for long."

"Yeah, I guess you're right Da," Ro said as he looked over the burning valley. "I figured that we would have more time to prepare for whatever the Queen threw at us."

Da looked at his brother and asked in a laughing voice, "You didn't really think that witch would give us a month to plan for war after we told her dragon to go bug off yesterday, did you?"

Ro looked at his brother with a grim smile. "No, I thought we would have had a little more time to get everyone to safety."

"Don't worry Ro; those lives that were lost will be paid back in full, including the Princess and Scom's."

"What? You don't believe that golden lizard, Nomi that the Princess and Scom are in another world and that Scom will bring her back here to lead the overthrow of her mother?" Ro questioned his brother.

"Listen, Ro, I liked the Princess and all, but she did just

want to go home, not that I can blame her, of course. I don't see that little troll making it in her world and convincing her that we are important enough to give up what she has there to come back here."

Ro smiles and shakes his head. "I don't know Da, I think that if anyone can do that that little sneak thief troll can do it."

Then another dragon flies low over the valley floor spewing flames over already burnt ruins. "Yeah, maybe you're right there, but for right now how about you and I get together with what people we have left and see if we can't find a way to ruin the Queen's day by thinning out a few of these dragons around here.

Both Ro and Da turn to go back into one of the caves that houses what is left of their people. "Oh yes, my Queen, you shall dearly pay for what all you have done to this world, whether the Princess returns or not, you shall pay a heavy price."

☙❧☙❧☙❧

Roc stands over the ogre as his eyes slowly open. He steps back as the mountain of a man rises from his position and eyes Roc from head to toe. "That was not fair way to fight, dragon."

Roc smiles at the ogre. "Well it may not be fair, but it was damn effective if I say so myself."

The ogre smiles looks around and then scratches his head as a large mangy cat crawls from under the nearest car and moves to stand beside Roc. "Yes that it was; now what we do?"

The cat at Roc's feet meows in a quiet voice then sits and looks up at Roc who has a surprised look on his face. "My friend here thinks that you would make good allies in keeping the Princess safe in this world."

The ogre looks puzzled for a second then looks down at the cat. "But why you want to keep girl safe and from Queen?"

"Because," Roc says as he walks closer to the big man and claps him on the shoulder, "with the Princess safe maybe we can all go back home and then get rid of the Queen and live in peace in our world; the world that we truly belong in and not this world of technology."

"That is big thoughts for one such as me," the ogre says with a largely surprised look on his face. "I had not thought of us all being able to go back home before."

"Yeah well I tell you what, how about you leave this place and think about it for awhile and then come back and let me know what you think."

The cat is now purring and rubbing between the tree trunk legs of the ogre, the sounds of the purring soothing the thoughts of the disquieted creature. "Yes I will go for now and think, but I will be back one way or another."

Roc smiles at the ogre and then looks down at his cat. "Thank you, my friend, that is all I ask for now is for you to think of the possibility of freedom and life back in our own world."

With a shrug, the ogre turns and walks away from the dragon. "I will think."

The ogre stops at Roc's next words, though. "Good, I'm glad you will think it over, but remember it might not be a good idea to tell anyone where the Princess is."

The ogre glances over his shoulder, back at the dragon, smiles and then walks away mumbling, "I will think quietly then."

As the ogre passes out of sight in the gathering darkness, the cat looks up at Roc as he looks down. "What do you think; will he go for it and help us?"

The cat meows and then turns in the general direction of where the Princess left this morning and meows again in a louder voice.

Roc looks back at where the ogre went and then at the direction that his cat is looking. "Yeah I guess you are right. The important question is where the Princess is right now. Maybe it's time we go talk to her parents again and go find her. Come on, cat."

The cat meows once more and then hurries after Roc as he heads towards the princess's apartment.

❧❧❧❧❧❧

The closer we came to where Jamie said the line was, the more power I felt seep into my body. I stopped about fifteen feet away from where I could see a brilliant bright line shining in the grass running along the edge of the tree line. "Wow, it's beautiful," I whispered to myself.

Jamie kept on walking and then stopped as she straddled the line, before turning and giving me a puzzled look. "Come on, Ceri, the line is right here."

"Yeah I know Jamie, I can see it from here, and if you don't mind, I think I will stay right where I am."

Jamie looked down between her feet and then back up at me. "Uhm what do you mean you can see the line, Ceri?"

I looked at the glow that shone in the grass now that night had pretty much fallen, wondering if maybe this girl had taken a little too much power and her brains were rattled. "I mean the line that is glowing beneath your feet like a beacon. That's the line I'm talking about, Jamie."

We both looked at each other as if we each thought that the other had lost our minds. With a smile crossing my face I asked Jamie. "You can't see the line can you, just feel it right?"

Jamie shook her head and frowned as she searched the ground around her for some sign of what I could obviously see, but she couldn't. "No, all I can do is feel the draw of the power. That's how a witch can find a ley line in nature. Jamie looked up at me and smiled. "It has to be your demon half that allows you the ability to see a ley line."

"Yeah okay, I'm good with that, but why don't you show me how you draw in this power or magic before I venture any closer to the line, okay?"

"Well, sure that'll work, I guess." With that Jamie straddled the line once again and with her hands at her side she closed her eyes and took several deep breaths in and out. As the last breath seemed to leave her body, I swear I could see all her tension seep into the air around her, leaving her limp and totally relaxed.

I watched as a small yellow glow started at her feet and then entwined up her body until soon she was covered from head to toe in the golden light. She stood there for several minutes as I watched the glow become so intense that it almost hurt my eyes to look at her. The line in the ground dimmed slightly as it gave up its power to the young witch. Then slowly the color sank down into the ground once again restoring its power to the ley line.

As Jamie stood rooted to the spot, I looked around as I thought that I had heard some noise back by the path that we had followed to get out here. "Uhm Jamie, are you okay?" I asked not really wanting to disturb the young witch.

"Oh yes," she answered in a faraway voice slowly turning and looking at me with a satisfied smile on her face. "That is such a rush, Ceri."

Okay then, I thought, that's nice to know as I looked at the dreamy expression on Jamie's face. "So is that all there is to it then?" I asked.

Jamie looked at me and then had a small body shudder as the dreamy, goofy smile seemed to disappear off her face and her usual expression returned. "Sorry about that Ceri, it's just that it feels so good loading up with magic and all. When you don't have any in your system it feels like your body is empty, or that you're always thirsty, and once you hit a line it feels like you quench that thirst," Jamie said as she moved over to where I stood.

I could almost feel a tiny current of her power leeching to me and took a few steps away from her. No sense in taking out the power that she just loaded up with, I thought. I looked at the line and then back again at Jamie. "Well I guess if it didn't kill you I should give it a try," I said with a shaky voice.

Jamie repeated my gestures, looking at the line and then back at me with a small slight frown. "Remember, take some deep breaths and center yourself. Then let the magic flow in. Whatever you do don't fight it, though, okay Ceri?"

"Uhm, yeah, right don't fight the magic. Anything else I should know?"

Jamie looks at me with this *just get on with it* expression that I have gotten from my mother so many times before.

"Yeah, yeah I'm going," I whisper as I slowly turn and walk toward the bright glow.

As I step onto the line, I can feel the power of the magic beating against my body; pulsing with my own heart beat. Straddling the line and looking down at the glow beneath my feet, all I can think of is the moths that are drawn to the bright light of the bug zapper. Gods I hope I'm not about to be zapped into a puff of smoke like a bug, that would so ruin my weekend.

As I look up at the clouds above, I can feel the release as my body opens to the magic waiting for me, but this is different from what I saw with Jamie. This is not a slow seeping of magic slowly crawling up her body to fill her with its power. This feels like I am engulfed within a thick wall, drowning in the power as the magic slams into my body with a sudden force.

I can't move, can't breathe, can't see anything around me. I can only feel the power in this ley line then as it dims, I feel it pull more power from the earth around me. I can feel the grass, the trees, each individual leaf, the pulse of the lives around me.

The magic flows, I feel like I am going to burst from all this power yet still it flows and fills me seeking, going deeper so that every cell in my body feels like it is powered by this new energy.

Outside my body I can hear faintly a cry, maybe of my name, maybe something else, but all I care about is this thing that is giving me all this life energy, a renewal of strength, of power, of magic.

And then it stops, and just like that, I am back in the park looking up at the cloudy sky as I feel the cold December rain fall on my face. Slowly I lower arms I never felt raised, and look over at the spot that Jamie is standing. I can see her there with Scom now standing at her side, both looking at me with wide-eyed stares of disbelief on their faces.

"What, what's wrong?" I ask as neither says a word.

Jamie points at the ground with a shaking finger and asks, "What have you done to the ley line, Ceri?"

"What are you talking about, I . . .", but I stop my chatter as I look down where the glow of the line had lain is now only a blackened, scarred area of grass.

"Oh damn, did I really do that?" I whisper, looking up and down the line to see if any of the glow is still there, but all I see is its charred remains blackened with a few wisps of smoke rising in the drizzle now falling on it.

I look up again at Jamie and Scom and the thought crosses my mind that maybe straddling the ley line hadn't been such a good idea after all, and that maybe I opened up to the power of the line a tad too much.

"Wow princess, I didn't know that an Other could use their true form in this world," Scom says with a small laugh.

"What are you talking about Scom?" Then I felt the flutter

against my hair, the flutter of wings. "Oh no, this so not happening right now," I say as I try to look over my shoulders at the pair of wings that flick with each movement of my back muscles.

"Oh yes it is happening Princess, and to you, if you know what I mean?" Scom says looking at me then up at Jamie as she slowly backs up a step. "Don't worry, witch, she is still the same person, now in the right form."

Jamie looks down at Scom then up at me and frowns. "But you are a demon, I mean I knew, I mean I heard that you were half-demon, half-witch, but you look like a demon. Is that really you, Ceri?"

I sigh and step from the line. Great, I think I lost a friend because of who I am. "Yes, it's really me. Why? Do I look that different, I mean besides the whole wings things and all?"

Jamie stands her ground after a little growl from Scom and then looks me over from head to toe. "Well, uhm no, not really, I guess. I mean besides the red hair, red glowing eyes, and the swords hanging at your side, no, not that different at all."

We all stand there for a few seconds then I hear a small cough of laughter from Scom followed by the giggles then full outbursts of laughter from Jamie and me. After a little bit of this silliness, we all fall silent and look at each other trying to decide what to do next. The thought crosses my mind that I definitely cannot go home like this and freak out my parents and sister. That would be bad, very bad indeed.

Jamie must have had the same thought because she looks at me and smiles. "Well now that you have this magic let's see if you can use it."

"Uhm, use it how?" I wondered out loud.

Jamie walks closer to me and smiles. "Well, one of the things that you will need to do right now is learn how to disguise yourself, or change your appearance and hold it."

"Okay, I do that how pray tell?"

The smile Jamie gives me is brighter than before. "Oh doing the magic part is easy as long as you have the power, and judging by what you did to the ley line you should have plenty of power to spare, don't you think?"

Glancing back at the line feeling a little guilty then back at Jamie, I smiled at her. "Yeah I guess I do have plenty of power stored up, so now what do I do?"

"Alright, all magic is is taking the power you have in you and bending it to a use. So now we want you to change back into what you looked like before, right?"

"Yes!"

"Okay then, remember what you looked like before you went into the line, and mold that power around you to hold that shape."

"Right so that's all there is to it . . ." I said, feeling the power bend around my body.

"Yeah like that!" Jamie squealed with delight.

"There you go, Princess. Nice job, if you know what I mean?" Scom said.

"What are you two talking about?" I asked then looked down and saw that I was back to my regular form. "Uhm how did I do that?"

"With the magic, silly. When taking shapes or different forms your subconscious takes over and holds that magic for you, Ceri. Different magics like producing fire or water or something like that you have to consciously control."

"So as long as I want to hold this shape I will, even when I sleep?"

"Yes, no matter what you will hold it as long as the magic's power lasts in you or you change your form to something else."

"It can't be that simple, can it?" I asked with disbelief straining my voice.

"And why should magic be hard? It just is, just as we all are here in this world, us, the sun, the moon, the stars it all exists and functions. You don't question all that, do you?"

"Well, no."

"Okay then, don't sweat what is not explainable; know that

it works and it functions according to its own rules, okay?"

'Well okay, I guess that is cool."

"Well your Princess, I would say that it is getting very cold, not just cool, if you know what I mean, Princess?" Scom said as he stood shivering in the rain coming down. Jamie was right, even though I would never say so to his face, but he did look a little like a drowned rat right now.

Reaching over to pick up the small guy, I tucked him as close to me as I could and started to walk back to where we had left my backpack. "Yes, I do you what you mean, Scom. So how about we get you into my pack where you can snuggle up to Mr. Blue and get warm."

"Oh yes, Princess that would be such a good idea."

"Are you coming, Jamie?" I asked the witch that was standing and staring at where the ley line once glowed so brightly. She nodded and turned away sadly and followed us up the hill.

I smiled at her and once more glanced down where the ley line rested, not worried about it as I could see very faintly in the dark where the line had started a faint glow again and where the grass and plants were being revitalized in the dark by the returning power of the line.

Urg and the bundle traveling with him moved through the

bushes and observed Jamie and Ceri's little adventures with the ley line. The large ogre knew that a fully charged witch was not something to take on on his own, but her friend, he now knew deep in his tiny overtaxed mind, was also the Princess that Regni was looking for. Yeah, it was definitely time to go get reinforcements. Urg looked down at his companion and grunted, "We need to get help for this; we go now and come back later."

The bundle of rags shook with silent laughter and then looked out at the two little girls now standing at the edge of the woods. As he watched, the young girl that looked like a demon suddenly changed back to her human form. "Whatsss? Are you afraid of two little sslipss of a girlsss?"

Urg thought once more of tearing the bundle apart into little pieces but knew that there were more important things to do right now. "Fine you stay and watch, I go find brothers to capture the Princess."

"Oh yesss, by all means go for help," the voiced hissed out of the bundled that wrapped him from head to toe.

Not trusting this sudden compliance from his traveling companion Urg glanced down at the two girls as they now climbed toward a lone bag that stood at the edge of the field then back at the figure before him. "You no do anything till I get back, you watch girls," growled the ogre.

"Yesss, yesss just watch isss all I do, now go before theysss ssssee you."

Urg gave a quick glance once more at the girls then slunk back into the dark and went in search of his brothers, thinking how he would enjoy being home again once the princess was captured.

The small bundle of rags moves forward and chuckles to itself. "Yesss you jussst goesss get your friendsss, I will watch the little girlsss, oh yesss I will," he whispers in a hiss.

❧❦❧❦❧❦

We got back to my bag and I stuffed Scom in so that the sopping wet dog could snuggle down deep inside next to Mr. Blue. I knew that the ratty old teddy would give my friend as much comfort as he did me growing up. Of course, the temptation to take Mr. Blue out and see if this magic of mine would bring him back to his demon form was very hard to resist, but right now I knew Scom needed him more. Also, I think that that might be the last straw the one that may freak out Jamie and send her running for the hills, no matter what the witch as seen before; I mean Mr. Blue in demon form was enough to scare anyone.

I stood up with the pack in my arms when Scom peeked his head out of the bag, sniffed the air then growled. "Princess, I smell a naga, and that is not a good smell, Princess, if you know what I mean?"

I looked down at Scom and then at Jamie who had a small puzzled look on her face. "Okay, Scom, what in this world or the Others world for that matter, is a naga?"

Scom sniffed the air some more and looked at some bushes across the path we were standing by. "That is a naga, Princess," he said as he let out a low growl once again.

I looked over and saw a small bundle of rags step out of the bushes. I saw that whatever was there was so bundled in the small pile of rags that I couldn't tell if it was a boy or a girl. I turned to Jamie to see if she had an idea of what we were facing when all of a sudden the smell hit me like a wall.

I could see that Jamie had also been hit by the stench of the person across the path by the look on her face and the wrinkle of her nose. The smell was of an unwashed body that had ripened in the hot summer sun (which was pretty bad since this was the middle of winter), mixed with an undercoating of some oily substance.

"Hello Tiss, what are you doing here?" Jamie asked the small bundle across from us that slowly swayed back and forth in a slow motion.

I looked at whatever was hidden from my sight in that pile of clothes and then back at Jamie. "Uhm you know who or what that is?"

Jamie grimaced at me and then cupped her hand over her nose. "Yeah I know him; he is a homeless person that hangs around here at the park or sometimes at the mall."

I looked back at the small man once again and saw that he

was still standing in the same spot he had before, and was swaying back and forth as though listening to a tune only he could hear. "Uhm listen, Tiss is it? Now is not a good time, so uhm how about you head home or wherever you go to now?"

Tiss swayed back and forth while Jamie and I glanced at each other and then back at the offending, smelly bundle before us. I waited for a few seconds then decided that this was wasting our time and I really needed to get back home, so turning to Jamie I reached out to grab her arm when I noticed that she had this strange faraway look in her eyes, and I could now hear what sounded like a low humming hiss coming from this Tiss.

"Jamie? Are you okay?" I asked as I shook her shoulders.

Jamie stood there as the humming hiss got louder from the bundle that was moving back and forth faster than before. Looking over at Tiss, I demanded, "Okay what are you doing to Jamie? Whatever it is, knock it off right this second before I really get peeved."

Tiss stopped moving and then slowly reached up with one hand and pulled the cloth down from around his eyes. I was looking into two small sickly yellow orbs that shone in the darkness that had now completely fallen since we had entered the park. "Oh Princesss, I cannot helpsss that your friend hasss fallen under my ssspell," he hissed in a voice so low that I had to strain to hear him from across the path.

"Well stop it now and let her go," I said as I took a step across the path ready to wring the little guy's neck if he didn't let my new friend out of the trance he had her in, but I never made it fully across before the small creature made a sudden change and not for the better for either Jamie or I.

The small smelly bundle sprang open and out of it curled a large black snake with red and yellow stripping around its hooded head. Before I could move out of its way, a blur flashed in front of me and I was suddenly airborne and flying backward toward the backstop of the baseball field behind us.

The backstop halted me in mid flight and as I slowly slid down the wire and metal, I saw the snake streak out and strike Jamie where she still stood locked in the creature's trance. As the blackness slowly closed around me, I thought I heard a small, nasty growl issue from my backpack and hoped that Scom wouldn't do anything stupid and would go get some help for us. Then the darkness closed in on me.

CHAPTER 7

Roc and Bill, Ceri's dad, slowly looked at the mall doors and at all the people that were still flowing in and out of the stores on this December night trying to finish their Christmas shopping. "How are we going to find two girls in this entire crowd, Roc?"

"Yeah, well my worry is that someone else is going to find them before us."

"Okay, I get it – you were right. Jenna and I should have never let Ceri go to the mall by herself. We couldn't come up with a story fast enough to stop her from coming out here without arousing her suspicion."

"Really? I thought that demons were good at lying, Bill," Roc replied with a certain animosity in his voice.

"Are we really going to go over this again, dragon, because I think we would be better served to find Ceri before any of the Other creatures find her, don't you think?" Bill said with a tinge of anger in his own voice.

A soft meow sounded from the old mangy cat that was wrapped around Roc's neck and shoulders. "No, you are right. No arguments, we are here to find Ceri, not to reopen old wounds," Roc grumbled as both men got out of the car and headed toward the mall entrance.

"Remember Roc that Ceri's father was my brother too, and I mourn his loss as you do," Bill said as the anger that was there before turned to sadness. "If ever I get a hold of that witch that murdered him, I will kill her myself."

Roc looked over at Bill and then smiled at the thought. "Yeah, but remember she is still Ceri's mother and blood may count in the long run."

Bill relaxed the hands that were curled as though wrapped around an imaginary throat and laughed. "Yeah you're right, Roc. What I still don't understand though is why the Queen decided to drag the poor girl into this mess after all this time?"

There are another couple of soft meows from the cat, then a grunt from Roc as they near the mall.

"What did the mangy furball say, Roc?" Bill said with a hearty laugh as the cat threw him a dirty look.

"She said that it was the only way for the Queen to get rid of Ceri's sisters and bring herself back to the Other's world."

"Yeah, well it's a good thing that your cat has the magic to catch that, otherwise, we wouldn't have had a clue what was up and then who knows what would have happened to Ceri."

As they near the mall's front doors the cat's ears perk up and she wails and meows loudly into the dragon's ears. "Whoa, okay, okay not so loud, damn cat you're going to break my ear drums with that chattering."

Both men stop and look around as the cat struggles to get down from her high perch drawing attention from the passing crowd.

"Now what did she say?" Bill asks as the he watches the strange cat's struggles.

Roc lets the cat down on the ground and keeps his body between the passing crowd and the cat that is now sniffing the ground around the doors. "She says that she can smell ogre and witch."

Bill looks around and then back at the cat. "Oh, that's so not a good combination, dragon."

"Yeah, you think, demon?"

Both men stand there then the cat looks around once more and then peed on a spot near the edges of the door. Bill looked at the cat for a second then turned to Roc. "You know your cat's nasty, you know that right?"

Roc looked at Bill then at the cat that now wanted up. "Yeah I know, but what's a dragon gonna do? It's not like I have control over this thing."

The cat quietly purred into Roc's ear and then settled down onto his shoulder as Bill started toward the doors of the mall. Roc stood rooted to the same place with a thoughtful look on his face.

Bill stopped and then glanced back at Roc and then stepped back toward the dragon. "Now what Roc, what's the hold up?"

Roc looked at the cat and then at the spot that she had recently anointed with her bodily fluids. "Nothing is wrong, I don't like that an ogre was watching something from this area. I tell you what Bill. How about you cruise the inside of the mall looking for Ceri and me and the cat will stroll along the outside for a little bit?"

Bill looked around at the crowd moving past the two men and shrugs his shoulders because he couldn't think of a single argument against the big guy's thoughts. "Well, okay, I guess. Let's say we meet at Target at the other end of the mall and then go from there if we don't find her."

"Yeah, that will be fine, you head inside. We will meet you at the other end," Roc said with an air of distraction in his voice as he moved off down the sidewalk.

"Yeah, well okay then, I guess. I'll head in then," Bill said to Roc's back as the dragon moved down the sidewalk now totally ignoring Bill. "Damn dragons always changing plans and moving in the opposite direction of where you want to go," Bill mumbled as he followed the mass of people into the mall.

ॐॐॐॐॐ

Roc moved forward a few steps completely focused on the area around him when the cat let out a loud screech in his ear again and then leaped down to the ground from her lofty perch.

"What do you mean 'he is here', cat? Who's here?"

The cat sniffed around on the ground then looked up at Roc and meowed loudly once again.

"Well let me get Bill then if she took off this way," Roc said as he took a step toward the doors that Ceri's foster dad had recently disappeared through.

The cat's next loud meow stopped him though and he turned back toward the cat. "The witch is with Ceri? Are you sure?" The cat cocks her head to the side and looks at the dragon with annoyance. "Okay, okay no reason to take offense," Roc said.

"So now where would a witch and Ceri go at this time of night?" Roc whispered, more to himself than as if expecting any real answer from the people moving around him.

The cat meowed once, twice, and then started off toward the parking lot with purpose. Roc ran after her and grabbed her up before the cat leaped off of the sidewalk and into the path of the moving cars.

"What do you think you're doing, cat? You want to get yourself killed?"

The cat struggled in Roc's arms then settled down and looked the dragon in the eyes and replied with several pitiful sounds.

"The park? How do you know that the witch will head to the park?"

The cat gave a low meow and then settled down further in Roc's arms and looked out toward where Roc knew the nearest park lay. "Magic is there? What in the gods name are you talking about, cat? What magic?"

The cat neither answered Roc nor deemed to look at him, but the dragon could feel the tensing in the cat's body and knew that if he released his hold on the cat, even a little bit, she would be off in a blur and heading toward the park and this so called magic that was there.

"Fine cat, we'll go to the park. But you had better be right about where Ceri is or we may lose her to some of these creatures wandering around looking for her."

Roc started toward his car and could feel the cat relax as he looked around once more for Bill, hoping that maybe Ceri's foster father had decided that the mall was a waste of time and would come to find Roc. Who knows? Maybe the cat was wrong and Bill had already found Ceri and they were now on their way to the meeting point.

No, Roc thought, this cat may be moody, strange and

mangy, but so far she had never steered him wrong in any advice she had dispensed. Hell, that's why he kept the mangy cat around his place; 'cause it certainly wasn't for her looks, that was for sure.

As if the cat knew his thoughts, she turned her head and gave the dragon a dirty look as he felt a small stream of wetness run down the front of his shirt. Roc held the cat out from his body for a second then looked down at her. "Oh, there are times, cat, when you come close to using up one of those nine lives I hear you have."

The cat turned and looked at Roc and gave a little rasp and then a hushed meow.

"Yeah laugh it up, but you had better hope Ceri is where you say she is. Now let's quit goofing off and get to the park," Roc said as he reached his car, opened the door and threw the cat inside like an old coat.

❧❦❧❦❧❦

Tiss looked at the two girls that lay on the night shrouded ground with some satisfaction. That stupid ogre thought that he needed help with two tiny little girls, what dumb clods they are. Ogres, he thought with a nasty grim smile widening on his face.

"Well I taught themsss that I wasss no one to trifle with nowsss," he hissed to the air. He thought back to how he had to hide the pitiful creature that the portal had turned him into; the grief and misery that he had to endure from the Others who were more inferior than himself. Yes, he certainly showed them all by capturing the Princess and by killing one of these cursed witches to boot.

Turning toward the Princess, Tiss heard another small growl coming from a pack that the Princess had dropped on the ground as she flew through the air. "Ahh, sssoundss like we will have a sssmall bitesss to eat before I move the Princesss," Tiss hissed to the pack as he moved toward it to inspect what little creature was making such noise.

Tiss moved down to look in the opening of the pack, expecting to see his small dinner quivering in fright, then he suddenly leaped up and back as his hood fully opened in surprise – the pack bursting open and scattering a raggedy old teddy and its other contents all over.

In the spot where the pack had once stood a black shadow rose. Two flaming eyes blinked back at the snake as he moved slowly backward to escape the intense heat coming off the creature. "Whatsss isss thisss, isss not fair. The Princesss isss mine and mine only," Tiss jeered as he slithered around the creature, thinking that he could get around it to get the Princess.

The creature, a huge dog, moved with the snake, always putting himself between the Princess and the slithering creature in front of him. As the creature moved, Tiss could see that wherever the creature's feet touched smoke curled up from the wet grass.

"You leave doggy. The Princesss isss mine," Tiss mocked

the massive creature and then struck out at the moving shadow, but the creature moved faster than its huge bulk suggested it could and Tiss's strike missed.

Unfortunately for Tiss, the shadow creature did not miss with his strike. With a leap in the air, Scom passed over the body of the snake and clamped down just behind the snake's head. Scom tried to sink his teeth even further into the creature in his grasp, but biting down was like worrying on a metal chew toy. Scom shook his head side to side hoping to break the snake's neck but soon found himself being wrapped up within the snake's deadly steel coils.

Scom could feel his body heat up with some internal flame deep down inside himself, but even as the smell of burnt meat wafted to his nose, the snake never let go of him. Slowly the rings of Tiss's body closed around Scom and the he had to let go of the snake's neck to get any breath at all.

"Thatsss wasss a nice try doggy, but now you ssshall die ssslowly for hurting me," Tiss howled gleefully with an evil laugh as he looked down on the creature that he would soon kill and have as a quick meal.

❦✦❦✦❦✦

Roc slowly pulled into the parking lot of the park and the first thing he saw was a lone truck sitting in the dark. "Damn doesn't that looks like Ceri's dad's truck?" Roc said as he pulled up next to the vehicle.

The cat stared out the window with wide eyes and gave a

brief meow as though in answer to Roc's question. "Okay, okay so you were right. Ceri is here, happy now?"

The cat didn't say anything as Roc opened the door, but took one swift sniff in the air, let out a loud screech and jumped out of the car and disappeared in the dark.

"Damn cat where are you going now?" Roc said as he stepped out of the car and then stopped as his ears picked up the sound of some battle going on in the middle of the park. "Oh that's where you're going," Roc said as he slammed the car's door and headed off after the cat.

Slowly the blackness receded as I heard a fight in the field in front of me. As my eyes cleared, I saw that the naga or snake creature was fighting what looked like a huge furry dog. I tried to stand, but a sudden wave of wooziness swept over me as I slid back down the backstop. Oh, this was not so good I thought as I watched the dog slowly being squeezed by the snake.

Watching the snake roll the dog over and over on the ground, I could hear what sounded like a pop of muscle or bone and heard a sharp yelp from the now unmoving body wrapped in the snake's curled snare.

I tried to pull myself up again, hoping to help the black dog in the snake's grip, figuring that any enemy of the snake was probably a friend of mine. Suddenly, out of the darkness, I saw another large shadow creature lunge toward the snake, raking its claws across the reptilian's face.

Landing about ten feet away, I could see that this new creature looked like a large sabertooth tiger. The long fangs hung down on each side of its mouth dripped drops of blood down onto the pathway where it stood, making me think that its claws weren't the only thing that scored a hit on the snake.

❧❦❧❦❧❦

Tiss released the nearly dead doggy to face his new adversary. He stared at this new creature that looked like a big kitty and thought that it wasn't fair that all these creatures were trying to take his prize away from him after all the misery he had suffered in this world. He deserved so much more; after all, he was the superior creature.

"Goesss away kitty, I already killed one of you creaturesss, I will kill you too. THE PRINCESSS ISSS MINE!" Tiss shouted this last, getting frustrated at all these creatures trying to stop him from going home.

With a quick fake to the right and then a strike to the left, Tiss almost caught the creature standing in front of him. Unfortunately for Tiss, he forgot to check on the dog that lay behind him, for as he launched himself at this new enemy, he felt a sharp pain in his tail as Scom gripped it within his iron jaws, ruining Tiss's strike.

As Tiss turned to take care of this old nuisance, the cat launched herself catching Tiss once again across the face.

122

This enraged the huge snake even more and his anger seemed to make him grow even larger than he was before.

❧❧❧❧❧❧❧❧

As I watched the two shadow creatures before me battle the large snake, I saw that though they were fierce fighters that they were still no match for the naga in front of them. Each creature was now bleeding from several bites from the snake and seemed to be slowing down in their movements.

I tried to create a large ball of fire to shoot at the snake, but was too woozy still to get anything, but a small ball of light. Looking around the area, I saw that Mr. Blue was lying among the tatters of my pack, and hoping that at least this magic would work, I snapped my fingers to see if I could bring the big guy around to his demon size.

With a flash of flame and smoke, Mr. Blue was back to his old big demon monster self. He smiled at me and took a step toward me with that wagging tail and big goofy grin of his all over his face when I pointed behind him and shouted, "MR. BLUE GET THAT SNAKE!"

Mr. Blue looked at me and wagged his tail even more and walked over to where the snake was now facing the two creatures before him. Both of the creatures were now panting and dripping blood from the many wounds all over each of their bodies.

I could hear the snake hiss something at them and then

strike toward the dog creature when Mr. Blue came up behind him, grabbed his head with one large paw and the tail with the other, stopping the strike in mid-flight. As the demon turned toward me, I saw the naga struggle in his grip and then watched the light go out of his eyes as Mr. Blue first folded the snake in onto itself then rapidly snap the snake's body outward. There was a loud series of snaps and pops, and then a large ripping sound as Mr. Blue was now standing with two half's of a snake in each of his paws.

With another wag of his tail and a huge grin once more plastered on his face and his tail wagging like a little puppy that had accomplished an exceptionally neat trick, Mr. Blue ignored the two bleeding creatures behind him and walked over to me casually tossing the two halves of what was once a large naga in two separate directions. Dang it was nice to see the big guy again, especially when my butt needed saving as it seemed to quite often the last couple days.

Bending over, Mr. Blue gently picked me up off the ground as I caught, out of the corner of my eye, the two huge creatures that had fought the naga change back into their original forms. The dog creature changed over to Scom, which for some reason didn't seem to surprise me at all. The other creature looked like the mangy old cat that always hung around with Roc, but I knew that couldn't be right for there was no reason why she would be around here at this time at night.

"Ceri, are you alright?" Roc's deep voice sounded from the path that Jamie and I had followed earlier this evening.

Okay, so maybe Roc would be out at this park at this time of night I thought as I looked at him bending down and examining the cat at his feet. Then the thought flashed through my head, JAMIE!

I slapped Mr. Blue on the shoulder and pointed at the prone witch who was still lying on the ground not moving at all. "Over there, Mr. Blue, by my friend. Hurry!"

Mr. Blue ambled over to the still witch and then steadied me as I bent over to check on her. I could see, with the small flame I lit, that she was pale and barely breathing. About then Roc came over and stood and looked at the young girl and saw what I had just noticed. "She was bitten by that creature Ceri; I don't think she will make it," Roc said in a casual, almost bored voice.

"Don't say that, Roc," I whispered as I looked down at my friend.

Now both Scom and Roc's cat were standing with us and looking down at Jamie with a sad faraway stare. "I'm sorry Princess, but Roc is right after all. She is only a witch," Roc's cat whispered. I looked at her, astonished and angered by this thought even though Scom had put forth the same idea a little while ago.

"You can talk?" I asked the cat.

"You can understand her?" Roc asked me at the same time

with a complete look of surprise on his face.

"Of course, I can talk, Princess I am a troll like this male creature next to me," the cat said as she sniffed in Scom's direction.

"Correction, she is a female troll, they are not as powerful as us males, if you know what I mean Princess?" Scom said as he huffed back at the cat.

The eyes of the cat narrowed and she hissed back at Scom. "Watch it male or you will find out how powerful this female is."

"Wait, hold it. You can hear the cat talk?" Roc said once again as he looked at the cat and then back at me, then he stopped and looked at Scom with suspicion. "And the dog can talk too? What the hell is going on here?"

I looked at all three of them then back down at Jamie. "I really don't give a rip who can talk to who, I want to fix my friend," I whimpered into the quiet of the night.

"As I said, Princess, she is . . ." the cat started to say then stopped what she was about to voice as she looked into my eyes. Slowly she slunk down to the ground and took a slow step back from the anger radiating off my body.

"If you finish that statement, cat, I will fry your mangy butt right here and right now," I said as the little blue light I held in my hand turned a bright red and grew larger. "And that goes for either one of you too," I said as I stared down both Roc and Scom, daring them to defy me.

"Uhm Princess, that would not be a good idea to fry her. This female may be able to help your friend if you know what I mean?" Scom said as he stepped between me and the cat.

"And how, Scom, can it help me?" I huffed as I stared down at the mangy worthless looking cat that crouched at my feet.

"I won't help a witch, Scom, and besides, you know that our magic is not to be shown to other creatures," the cat hissed and whispered at Scom.

Scom turned swiftly, baring his teeth at the cat and a low growl escaped from his tiny body. "Female this is the one, the one that we have waited for to save us from the Queen and allow all of us to return to our home. We will do whatever it takes to help her, even if it means saving a witch. Do you understand me?"

With that proclamation, the cat suddenly sat up and gazed at Scom with a strange look in her eyes. "Are you sure, male that this is the one? She does not look like a demon."

"This is the one, female; I was there at her birth. She has already taken out her sisters and she will return and take care of her mother, the Queen, and free us all," Scom said as he puffed out his chest and moved closer to the cat. "Now do your magic and save her friend, female."

The cat stood up and sniffed the air and then walked over to Jamie with a twitch of her tail in Scom's face as she walked by him. "Well fine, no reason to get all huffy about it."

The cat slowly started to sniff all over my friend who was now breathing even slower than before, stopping at her right arm where there were two small puncture marks. "Princess, see these marks, clamp your hand over them and lightly, and I do mean lightly, send a small power of flame through them, then ice."

"And this will help how?" I asked as I looked the cat with little hope in her powers such they were.

"Fine, if you don't want the witch to live then don't listen to me, what do I care about one witch more or less," The cat said as she turned to walk away from Jamie.

"Alright, alright I'll do it, hold on," I cried. Still not trusting the cat, I laid my hand slowly over the marks left by the snake and sent a small pulse of fire then ice through the wounds.

Jamie sort of jerked with each bit of power flowing through her and then moaned as though in pain. "Now what happens?" I asked as the witch seemed to turn even paler than before.

"Now what happens is this, Princess," the cat said as she walked up the prone witch's body and leaned down toward her mouth and inhaled on each of Jamie's exhales. I could almost see a small black cloud of something pass between the two with each breath that they took.

"Don't worry, Princess, the female's magic will make your friend better," Scom said as I felt the warmth of his small body as he leaned into me, watching the cat work her magic.

Soon the cat stood up and then walked away from Jamie and into the dark where I could hear what sounded like her coughing up a hairball. "Now that is so cool, why didn't she tell me she could do that?" Roc whispered as he moved off toward where his cat was.

I looked down at Jamie with some concern and saw that she was not as pale as before and her breathing was now better too. I looked up at Mr. Blue and then at Scom and smiled down at my friend for I could see that her eyes were now fluttering open, but still dazed.

"What happened, Ceri?" she asked with a raspy whisper.

I smiled down at Jamie as Roc came back from the dark, carrying his mangy cat, thinking that it was nice that my friend looked like she would survive her ordeal with the snake. "Don't worry about it, Jamie. We'll get you home and then explain everything there, okay?"

"Okay, but I don't think I'll get very far without some help," Jamie whispered again as she tried to rise up from her prone position.

I laughed and helped her to sit up and then pointed to Mr. Blue. "Don't worry, I have that covered with my own king size transportation."

Jamie looked up at the black demon towering over the two of us and I watched as her eyes grew big. "Oh crap, that's one big doggy. He's on our side right?"

I laughed some more at Jamie's reaction and then looked up at my big buddy from childhood. "Yeah, he is on our side and a good thing he is too."

Jamie nodded then sagged down into my arms. "If you say so, Ceri, then I guess I believe you," she whispered so low that I could barely hear her.

"Come on Mr. Blue, gently lift her and let's get her home." Mr. Blue smiled at the witch with a toothy grin and then very gently lifted her from the ground and headed back toward the parking lot where this particular adventure had begun.

As I took a step after the two of them, I felt a large hand grip my arm. "Uhm Ceri I don't think that taking a witch home with you would be a wise idea," Roc said.

I turned and looked him in the eye, the now large ball of flame bouncing in my hand (seems like I wasn't so woozy anymore). Roc looked at the flames in my hand, then at my face and released my arm and took a step back from me as his cat leaped down from her perch and headed off in the direction of the others. "Uhm never mind, what I said wasn't important after all," Roc stammered as he turned and hurried after the others.

As I followed the rest of the group down the darkened

path before us, I thought yeah I didn't think what he said was that important either.

CHAPTER 8

Bill stood at the entrance of the store watching all the customers pass by. He had been through as much of the mall as he could and had seen no sign of Ceri. Of course, in this late night crowd, he figured he could walk right by her and miss seeing his daughter.

Now if only Roc would arrive at the meeting place, then maybe they could split up and get a better look around the mall. The dragon may be a pain in the butt, but he knew how to take care of business.

About then a group of four large men bumped by Bill and he caught a familiar smell coming from them. Ogre, no mistaking that smell Bill thought as he slowly followed the creatures in front of him. Wherever ogres are there is some trouble brewing, and his sixth sense was telling him that this trouble had to do with his foster daughter. So Bill followed the four men easily as three of them seemed so engrossed in what the fourth was saying none of them was paying any attention to those around them.

We made a motley crew walking through the park and I was glad for the darkness that hid us from everyone's view. I think two girls, a man, a dog, a cat, and one huge demon might raise some eyebrows if we had been traversing this same path during the day. The clouds that had earlier spilled the cold winter rain on us had now broken up somewhat and in the dark, I could see patches of moonlight reflecting off the path we were following and casting shadows from my fellow travelers.

Then it hit me just how dark it was and oh how much trouble I was going to be in when I finally got home. Roc who was walking next to me by now saw the look on my face and correctly guessed what was crossing my mind.

"Uhm just to let you know, we need to stop at the mall and pick up your dad," Roc announced.

Oh great, my dad out looking for me, just what I needed right now I thought. I think I would rather face more of the Others then go home and face Mom and Dad's wrath. "Oh, I am so grounded," I whispered to the cold night air.

"Well actually, Princess that is the least of your problems right now, don't you think?" the cat said as she fell back in step with Roc and me.

Scom stopped and turned to face the cat and growled at her. "Hush female, the Princess knows the trouble that is around her."

We had all stopped at the small wooden bridge Jamie and I had crossed before, watching the two animals in front of us. Roc had a small grin on his face and I was a little worried since the cat in front of Scom looked to outweigh him by a good ten or so pounds.

The cat looked Scom straight in the eyes as she closed the distance between them. "If you call me that one more time, I will leave you in little chunks for the birds to pick up for their breakfast," the cat hissed at Scom.

I had to give it to the small troll or dog as he now was, he didn't back up one step and stood up to that large fur ball eye to eye, not a lot of smarts but definitely some courage. "And what pray tell name is that you are talking about, female?"

The cat bristled even more and then Roc leaned over, the grin on his face now a smile going from ear to ear. "My money is on the cat," he whispered.

"Scom be nice, she did help you in the fight and she made Jamie better," I scolded looking at Scom then at Roc with a look of aggravation.

Roc looked at me, shrugged his shoulders then chuckled. "What? Just saying."

"Yeah well, don't egg them on," I scolded the big guy now.

I heard a loud hiss at our feet and then turned my attention once more to the cat and dog that were still going at it.

"Female, female, female . . ." Scom kept repeating over and over like some two-year-old hyped up on a sugar rush.

I reached down and grabbed Scom and clamped a hand over his mouth to keep this from escalating any further than it already had. Looking down at the cat, I felt sorry for the mangy looking beast that was now glaring daggers at the small dog in my arms.

"Look, I'm sorry Scom is being such a pain, okay?"

The cat glared at Scom one more time and then looked at me. "That is fine, Princess. It is not for you to apologize for we all know that male trolls are of low intelligence, breeding, and of course, they smell bad."

I could hear Roc laugh loudly and hear the growls that came from the still clamped muzzle of the dog, but the cat did have a small point thinking back to the first time I had met Scom and the odor that permeated the air around the little guy.

I looked at the cat trying not to laugh since I knew that that would hurt Scom's feelings and asked, "Well if you don't want to be called female all the time then what is your name?"

"Cat," Roc answered.

"Tessa," the cat answered at the same time.

I looked at Roc and then down at the cat and asked, "Well which is it 'cat' or 'Tessa'?" Knowing the answer, but figuring I could put Roc on the spot now.

Roc stood there with a perplexed look on his face then smiled down at the cat that stood at his feet. "Well, I guess it's Tessa, Ceri."

"Good," I said as I looked at the two of them. Then I turned Scom's face toward mine and looked him in the eyes, "and now that you know her name, you will use it. Do you hear me Scom, or else," I scolded him as I put him down on the ground next to Tessa.

Scom looked up at me with those runny little eyes of his filled with hurt, but I knew this game by now and I wasn't about to let the little guy off that easy. "I mean it Scom, don't test me on this, got me?"

Scom looked at me with that look for a second more then it disappeared as fast as it came and was replaced by a sly little smile. "Yes Princess, I understand."

The little faker, I thought as we all crossed the bridge to get to the parking lot. Now all we had to do was go get my dad and then face the music at home for being so late. Of course, there was also the little point of telling my family that I was half demon and half witch with a whole bunch of creatures after my hide. Oh yeah and then there was the whole 'I have a friend that was a real witch' but hey, one thing at a time, I guess. Looking at Jamie still being carried in Mr. Blue's arms the thought flashed through my mind that this was turning into such a long night. What else could go wrong?

❧❧❧❧❧❧❧

Urg had found three of his kin hanging around the back side of the mall as ogres were wont to do while waiting for some unsuspecting victim to rob, or kill, or maybe even eat. These weren't the brightest of his cousins, and it took a little while for Urg to get across the importance of what he wanted them to do.

Of course, the mere mention of the possibility of killing one of the hated witches who protected this world caught their attention, and who knew maybe after they killed her, a little snack in the park might be just the thing tonight to satisfy four hungry ogres.

As Urg passed the entrance to a major store in the mall, he caught this slight whiff of some creature but was soon distracted by his kin arguing about the best ways in which to cook a witch. Urg shook his head at the other three wondering how it was that these idiots had lived so long in this world without being caught by Saba for all the mischief they had caused. Well, he thought, maybe after I get the Princess and the witch he would happen to mention to Saba where the ogres that killed his student lived. That should take care of these three, Urg though with some amusement.

Now all the ogre had to do was get these three back to the park, for he didn't really trust the creature that he had left to watch the two girls. There was something about it that Urg didn't like. Oh well, he thought, what could such a small bundle do to two girls anyways. It's not like the tiny creature had any magic powers or something in this world, but as that thought crossed his mind some inner instinct made Urg urge the other ogres faster toward the park.

⤬⤬⤬⤬⤬⤬

Getting to the truck and Roc's car without being seen seemed a miracle to me even if we were in a dark park at night. I mean it is in the middle of town and I figured we would run into some people cutting through the park or some teens out for a little fun, but I figured our luck had held until I heard the gruff voice bark at someone to our right.

"You say, two girls, not a whole group, why you lie."

I slowly turned from unlocking my dad's truck and looked over to where other voices were now adding their displeasure to the first voice. There, standing in the middle of the parking lot were four very large men. Oh, this was so not going to turn out well, I thought.

"It is no problem," the smallest of the group answered. "It is only a couple more people and means more dinner for all of you."

Dinner I thought, oh I was so not going to be anyone's dinner tonight. Who were these guys and what was their problem?

By then Roc had come around his car and stood by my side

as we watched the four men come closer. He looked at my face and probably saw the questioning look on it for he leaned in and whispered, "They are ogres Ceri, and from what I can tell the very nastiest of them around here. Let me take care of this."

"And you're going to do what against four ogres?" I whispered back at him.

He gave me a look of exasperation then smiled at me. "Stay here, okay?"

"Yeah sure," I answered; as I thought you want to get your butt kicked go ahead, no skin off my nose.

As Roc moved toward the men in front of us, Mr. Blue came over to stand by me with Jamie still in his arms. I looked over at them and smiled at how the big guy was cradling the hurt witch in his arms like she was delicate china.

Jamie looked at me and then at the men. "Ceri, tell this overgrown puppy to put me down. If there is going to be a fight we will need him fighting not carrying me around."

I looked at them and then at the size of the four men and thought that Jamie had a point there. "Okay Mr. Blue, put her down by the truck so that she can lean on it."

With a large grin, the demon did what I asked and deposited the witch next to me. Jamie leaned against the truck and then looked over at where Roc was standing, waiting for the ogres to get near him. "What is he doing? Is he nuts?" Jamie questioned.

I looked at the four guys, all huge mountains of muscle bulging out everywhere. Even the smallest of them looked like he could pick up the truck we were leaning against and toss it aside like a toy. "Yeah, he might be a little crazy at that," I told Jamie.

"He is not crazy, Princess," Tessa said as she hopped onto the hood of the truck. "He is a dragon, and dragons can take care of themselves against ogres."

From behind the front wheel of the truck, I heard Scom whimper, "This dragon may not be crazy, but he is a little stupid if you know what I mean princess?"

"Hush, you two," I said to the two trolls as I stepped away from the truck and lit up a small fireball in my cupped hand. Looking at the five men that faced each other about twenty feet away, I figured that I could help Roc by evening up the odds a little if the group decided that they really wanted to make a fight of it.

The smallest of the guys, who seemed to be the leader, took a close look at Roc then peeked over at the rest of us standing by the truck. Looking back at Roc, he growled, "What is you doing here dragon? This is not your business."

Roc looked at the four men before him and then glanced behind them. As he locked his focus on the ogres, I could almost hear a smirk in his voice. "These two girls are my business, and you need to leave now."

All four men laughed. Then the smallest said, "Four ogres, one dragon, not good odds."

I stepped forward some more and caught their attention with my movement. "Wrong! Four ogres against one dragon and one demon with fire to play with, how are those odds?" Then Mr. Blue slid up next to me, his teeth bared in a huge grin with his tail wagging happily. I looked up at the big guy and smiled; then focused my attention back on the ogres. "Oh yeah, that's right, Mr. Blue here hasn't had his dinner either."

The four ogres stopped smiling for a second, and then the spokesman of the group laughed some more as he looked at his three companions. "Enough! Is still one dragon, little girl and some beast. We ogres are better fighters." With that, the ogres took a step toward Roc but stopped at the sound of the voice behind them.

"You're right, one dragon and demon in front are good odds, but how are those odds with a fire demon behind you, ogre?" a familiar voice sounded from out of the dark.

I looked as a figure walked out of the night, but I couldn't see his face until his hands each lit up with bright blue flames. "Dad? Is that you?" I questioned the figure even though I could see by the light he created that that was who was standing behind the ogres.

"Hey Ceri, a little late on that curfew, aren't we?" Dad

asked with a wicked grin. Then the grin disappeared as he looked at the ogres that were now trying to divide their attention between all the people around them. "Now you, uhm, gentlemen can walk away from here or be carried from here, what will it be?"

I could see that the three largest ogres were ready to call it a night, but the smallest of the four seemed to have other ideas. I saw him shift his stance slightly and then scream in frustration as he leaped in my direction.

Poor ogre never knew what hit him. I threw a ball of flame that hit him dead in the chest which he might have lived through since it wasn't a big ball if the two blue balls of flames from my dad hadn't hit him in the back and drove him into the ground. Of course, everyone knows ogres are pretty tough and he might have even walked away from our fire if Roc hadn't launched himself into the air and landed dead center in the middle of his back.

After looking at what was left of the ogre as Roc hopped back off of him, I was pretty sure that that was one ogre that wasn't walking out of the park tonight. Roc looked at my dad and some signal seemed to pass between them, for they both nodded their heads and then my dad lit two more balls of flames and threw it at the body lying in the parking lot, lighting it up briefly, before the flames died down and left a small smoking grease spot where once an ogre lay.

This happened so quick that the three larger ogres never moved a muscle. They stood and stared at the spot where once one of their own had been before one of them whispered, "We go now, want no more problems."

Roc looked over at my dad and then gave a wicked smile at the three ogres at he walked over to them and got into their faces. "If I hear that you hurt anyone or cause any other problems in this world, you will end up like your friend there, understand?" Roc said as he pointed to the black spot burnt into the parking lot.

All three ogres looked at Roc and then over their shoulders at my dad with fright clearly written on their faces, before all three started nodding their heads in agreement. "Now get out of here and don't make me come and find you boys because you won't survive the next meeting," Dad said as he moved closer to the ogres and Roc to emphasize his point.

All three ogres moved as if demons from hell were after them as they headed out of the park and back to wherever they had been before. As they cleared out, both Roc and my dad came over to where we were standing while glancing over their shoulders to make sure that the ogres wouldn't change their minds and come back looking for more trouble.

Jamie slumped down onto the bumper of the truck with a look of relief as Scom came out from behind the front tire. "Lucky for them that your dad came along or I'd have had to take care of them," Scom growled from between my feet.

I reached down and picked up the small troll as I heard Tessa behind me on the hood of the truck. "Yeah lucky them they didn't get a whiff of you, male, that would've definitely drove them away," she said with a loud chuckle.

I thought the female troll had a point, but figured that I needed to stand up for my little companion. "Okay enough, Tessa, please; there are more important things that need to be taken care of right now," I said as I looked down at Jamie who was still not looking all that great.

Tessa sniffed at me with annoyance and she hopped over to Roc's shoulder as he arrived at the truck. My dad ruffled my hair and gave me that look that said we would talk later and then bent down in front of Jamie and gave her a big smile. "Well, witch, looks like you have had better days," he said as he gave Jamie a once over.

Jamie looked at my dad with a small look of annoyance of her own before she answered. "My name is Jamie, and yeah you are right, I have had better days."

Dad looked at Jamie with a slight frown and then the smile came back along with a laugh that I was so familiar with. "You're right, Jamie that was rude of me, sorry, so can you get into the truck so we can get you somewhere safer so that we can check you out?"

Jamie smiled at my dad's apology and looked up at me. "Yeah, just get me to my feet and I'll be happy to go anywhere else," she said as she tried to push herself up from the truck's bumper.

My dad helped Jamie up as I moved over to open the passenger door of the truck. Once Jamie was in and comfortable, my dad closed the door and put both his hands on my shoulders and looked deep into my questioning eyes. "I know, Ceri, that you have a thousand questions, but now is not the time. Let's get your friend home where your mom can look at her and then we will talk, okay?"

I nodded at this, I mean what else could I say when Roc walked over to me and my dad with a look of worry on his face. "You know, Bill, taking a witch to your house will not help matters, right?"

I looked over at Roc, ready to blast the big man when my dad growled at him. "Dragon, I thank you for saving my daughter and her friend, but it is still my house we are going to and I will not let a little one out by herself with all the Others stirred up as they seem to be, do you understand?"

Roc looked at my dad with a frown and then over at Jamie sitting in the truck. "Yeah, yeah you're right, thought I would remind you of the trouble she could cause us."

My dad stood back from me and clapped Roc on the shoulder. "Don't worry, dragon, I have taken into consideration the problems she could bring." Then he turned to me and said, "And you, young lady, take this motley crew and get right home, and have your mom look at your friend, understand me?"

I looked down at my feet, gave a small nod and whispered, "Yes sir."

"Good, now get home while Roc and I clean up this mess," my dad said as he looked over at the black spot in the middle of the parking lot.

"Come on, Scom, let's go home," I said as I snapped my fingers and watched Mr. Blue turn back into the ratty old teddy bear friend of mine. Snatching up the teddy bear from the ground and walking over to the driver's door, I opened it and tossed both dog and teddy bear into the middle of the seat.

As I climbed into the truck and started it up, I could see Roc point over to the area where we had had our little tiff with the naga and the two of them started off toward that part of the park while talking and throwing glances over their shoulders at the truck. Guess they wanted to make sure that we were headed home like my dad told me to. Geez, don't know what they were so worried about, I mean I always do what I'm told . . . well most of the time, okay some of the time anyways I thought as the two men disappeared into the dark.

We hit a red light at the entrance to the park when a particular odor wafted across my nose. I looked over at Jamie who looked back at me, her nose as wrinkled in disgust as mine. "It's not me!" we both echoed.

We looked down at Scom and Mr. Blue as the little troll looked at the two of us with small runny eyes. "What?" he whispered.

"Oh you are so getting a bath when we get home, troll," I said as I quickly rolled down the windows of the truck to let some fresh cold night air waft through them.

"Yeah and if she doesn't give you one, I will, rat!" Jamie said as she turned her face toward the now rolled down window, her once white complexion down to a slight sickly green.

Scom sniffed the air around him and in a hurt whisper said, "It's not that bad."

With that, the light flicked to green and I gunned the truck off toward my apartment. The cold breeze blowing most of the stink from the small troll out the windows and letting us breathe in peace. Now, I thought, once Dad got home I guess I wasn't the only one that had some explaining to do. Then it hit me if Dad was a demon then what about Mom? Or Dede? Wait yeah I could picture Dede as a demon alright, no other way to explain that little pest of a sister except for her being a demon.

CHAPTER 9

Roc and Bill made their way back across the park where Roc had seen the fight between the snake, trolls, and Mr. Blue. Roc thought back to coming on the scene and watching the two creatures that he now knew were the trolls and thinking that they were some fire creatures from hell.

The heat emanating from the creatures and the way that the large snake whipped around them had kept him from rushing in to help, and then watching that huge demon monster come along and rip the snake apart like it was a child's toy made him hesitate once more.

Yeah, he thought, those two girls didn't do too bad taking care of themselves with the friends that they had with them. They may have been a little beaten up some, but they came out of the whole endeavor pretty much in one piece.

As they reached the area of the fight, Bill reached down and picked up the head part of the snake. Holding the head up and looking at the dead lifeless eyes, he thanked once again whoever gave Mr. Blue to Ceri for their foresight in their choice of protectors.

He looked over at Roc and said, "Hey dragon, see if you can't find the other half of this creature, will you?" as he started to drag the half he had to the asphalt path.

Roc grunted and walked over to a line of bushes that the tail end of the snake was draped across. Grabbing the tail and slinging it over his shoulders, he headed over to where Bill was waiting for him.

Dropping the tail half of the body with the head half, Roc took a step back as Bill lit up a small flame in his hands and then threw it on the body of the creature. A large greasy black puff of smoke issued from the body, the flame lit up even more then slowly died down to nothing as the vile creature was consumed by the fire. "Well that takes care of that problem, even though I would like to know what a naga is doing in this world," Bill said as he wiped his hands off on his pants as though to get rid of the slime of the creature.

Roc looked at the burnt spot and then over at Bill. "And what pray tell is a naga? Cause I know it doesn't come from my world."

"No, you're right. It doesn't come from your world. It comes from mine," Bill said as he looked up at the night sky. "The question we need to ask ourselves is why this creature crossed over into your world and then ended up here in this one?" he said as he looked back at Roc.

"So you're thinking that someone sent this creature after Ceri or are you thinking that your family was its main objective, Bill?"

"No, I don't think that the naga was sent here for Ceri. I think it was looking for Jenna and I and it happened to luck into Ceri with all these Other activities going on," Bill whispered with some concern in his voice.

"Oh great, so not only do we have Ceri's natural mother after her, now are you telling me we have your enemies after you also? Oh, this is shaping up to be such a great night," Roc said, the anger making his voice sound deep and loud in the cold, dark night air.

"Yeah this is not a great development, we can only hope that the people that are after Jenna and I stay in our world and don't cross over to this one like they have in the past," Bill said as he looked around at the stuff spread out all over the ground from when Ceri's pack had burst open. "How can one girl carry so much stuff in one small pack?" he said with a smile now crossing his face.

Roc bent down and started to help the demon pick up the stuff spread all over the ground, then stood up and looked around the area. "Hey, have you seen that cat around?" he asked.

Bill who was bent over scanned the area looking for the familiar sight of Roc's cat. "No, I thought she was with you. Did she go with the girls in the truck, you think?"

Roc shrugged his shoulders and started to pick up more stuff off the ground. "Yeah, that's probably what happened, knowing that cat. From what I saw with that damn snake, she can take care of herself and the girls if need be."

Bill grunted and then both men became quiet as they bent to finish the chore of picking up all the stuff from the ground, each of them thinking once again that there had been more stuff in that pack then one girl could possibly use in a lifetime.

Queen Ellie's castle was a dark forbidding place in the best of times, but the two golden glowing figures that approached the gates emphasized the blackness and hopelessness of the towers and walls surrounding it.

The guards stepped out of the gatehouse, looking at the approaching figures with thoughts of murder and mayhem in their hearts. Soma, the leader of the guards, stepped in front of the two figures as they reached the gate and swung the huge ax that was by his side up and over onto his shoulder.

"What do you want here?" he growled.

The two figures looked up at the large ogre from eyes of deep blue and smiled. Their smile was warming and bright like a sweet summer day and made the ogres behind Soma take a step forward as though they were moths drawn to an open flame.

Soma took a breath then looked around at his men then back at the two figures still standing in front of him and growled once again. "What do you want here?"

The smallest of the figures smiled wider than before and answered the large ogre. "Why we are here to talk to your Queen," she answered in a sweet honey voice, with the melody of her voice sweeping over the guards that stood before the two figures and causing a drowsiness to seep over all of them.

Soma stared for a second then shook his large head as if he was in a stupor. He once more looked at the other guards and saw that they, like him, seemed to be in some kind of trance created by these creatures before him. Kicking and slapping those nearest to himself Soma got his men back into some semblance of order.

Turning back to the two figures, Soma held his ax in a guarded position with both of his hands and took a step toward the two intruders. "You use magic on us?" he growled, ready to swing the ax he handled and swipe these two puny people out of his life.

The larger of the two golden figures held up a hand and Soma stopped in mid stride. "Yes, you are right my big fellow. We have used magic on you, and now you will take us to your Queen."

Soma growled louder in answer as the golden man sighed. "So be it, you lesser creatures must always do it the hard way, mustn't you," then he flicked his hand at Soma.

Soma felt the ax drop out of nerveless fingers then felt himself engulfed in a golden glow. As the light increased, he could sense an intense itchy feeling and then for a split second a burning sensation as all his skin and muscle disappeared from his body.

As the other guards looked on, they saw their leader standing there whole one second and then in the next a large bare skeleton was wearing Soma's armor. As bone and armor hit the ground, the smallest of the glowing figures turned to the ogres that stood before the gate and pronounced in that sweet singsong voice, "Now take us to your queen."

In a flash, all the guards but one disappeared into the gatehouse and all that could be heard was the rumble of the chains as the gate was opened. The smallest figure looked at the ogre before them and smiled. "So it seems like you are our guide to your queen, please lead on."

The ogre looked around in surprise at finding himself alone with the two creatures before him, and then at what was left of their once large leader and stammered. "Yesss, jussst thisss wwway, pleassse."

The larger of the golden couple looked with some annoyance at the ogre and started to wave his hand at the poor unfortunate creature, but the girl grabbed his hand

and admonished him as the ogre ducked down into his armor, expecting at any second to end up in the same shape as Soma had. "No, we need him to lead us to the Queen; he is only a frightened creature," she said

The boy looked down at the girl then over at the ogre and shrugged his shoulders and then looked at the castle with some disinterest. "You are right, but make it not speak or else."

The girl smiled and waved her hand toward the ogre as he felt his mouth clamp shut with such force that he nearly broke his teeth and bit off his tongue. "Remember our mission, brother," the girl said, bringing his attention back toward the job at hand.

"I will remember, sister, now lead on, creature," he said as the two figures followed the guard into the castle, leaving behind his cowling companions in the gatehouse.

※ ※ ※ ※ ※ ※

I drove the truck into the parking lot of the apartment and parked in our assigned space without meeting any further problems. After I turned off the ignition, I looked over at Jamie, who was leaning against the passenger window with closed eyes. "You okay Jamie?" I asked, worried since she now looked a little paler than she had when we had left the park.

Jamie opened her eyes and slowly looked over at me and gave me a small smile. "Yeah I'm fine Ceri; just need to rest."

I looked at the steps leading up to my apartment and then at my friend wondering how hard it was going to be to get her up to the door and inside where Mom could take a look at her. Jamie seemed to read my mind as she looked at the stairs and then back at me. "Don't worry, as long as you help I'll get up the stairs."

"Okay," I said as I got out of the truck and moved around the front to open Jamie's door and get her started up the steps.

As I put my hand on the door handle, a large mangy, furry head popped up from the bed of the truck. "Hey, what you doing, Princess?" a small voice whispered in the dark.

I jumped back in fright, the door handle of the car behind me digging deep into my back. As I bounced back toward the truck again, I lit a ball of flame in my hand before I realized that the head belonged to Tessa and that she must have ridden in the back of the truck from the park.

"Tessa, that is so not funny," I said as I killed the flame in my hand. "You could have given me a heart attack with that kind of behavior."

I heard a low chuckle from the back of the truck where the cat had hidden when I lit the flame in my hand. "Sorry, Princess, I wanted to see what you were doing."

"Yeah well, that's fine Tessa; don't scare me like that, okay?" I said as I opened the door and started to help

Jamie out of the truck.

I started to shut the door of the truck when I heard another small voice shout from inside the interior, "HEY WAIT FOR ME!"

I juggled Jamie in one hand with an arm around her shoulder and opened the door and looked in at Scom. "Well alright then, come on and hop down."

Scom looked at me then down at the ground and then back at me while dancing on the truck seat. "Oh Princess, it is way too far for me to jump if you know what I mean Princess?"

Just then Tessa jumped from the back of the truck with the ease of a cat and looked up at Scom with some scorn. "Oh like a male troll to get stuck on such an easy jump, right Princess?"

I hated to admit to the cat that she might have a point and hurt my friend's feelings, but I really needed to get Jamie back up to my apartment. Reaching in, I grabbed Scom by the scruff of the neck and pulled him out of the truck and by bending both Jamie and I down toward the ground I let go of him and dropped him. "There now, you're down. Think you can get up the stairs by yourself?" I asked as I straightened Jamie and myself up.

"Oh yes Princess," Scom answered with a hint of hurt sounding in his voice.

"Great," I said as once more I tried to shut the truck door.

"Mr. Blue," Jamie whispered. "You can't leave the poor thing out here all by himself, Ceri."

Oh for heaven sakes, I thought, as I reached in for my fuzzy old teddy bear. "Here. You will have to hold him," I said as I thrust him at Jamie and then slammed the door of the truck. "Now can we get up to the apartment and out of the dark, guys?" I asked as I moved Jamie toward the steps.

No one answered, so I took it that everyone was ready to traverse the steps of the apartment. We had gotten up two of the steps with no problems when our apartment door opened and my mom stuck her head out the door.

"Ceri? Is that you? Who is that with you?" Mom asked as she came to the top of the steps. "Where have you been? Do you know that your dad is out looking for you? Oh, you are in so much trouble, young lady."

I let this tirade wash over me, figuring that with the night I had had being grounded or in trouble about being home a little late was no big deal. "Uhm Mom, I have a friend who is hurt," I said, looking up at her as she ended her rant and took a breath.

Got to say one thing, when my mom sees something or someone hurt she will drop everything else to help. She bounced down the apartment stairs in two bounds, scooped Jamie from my side like she was a small feather and was gone inside the apartment before I could blink.

I looked down at the dog and cat at my feet as they looked

back up at me. "Oh, I think everyone in this house has some explaining to do." Both animals sort of nodded and we all followed my mom back up into the apartment.

❧❧❧❧❧❧

I got us all in the apartment and the door locked, when I heard my mom's soothing voice sounding from the living room. I walked around the corner where I saw that my Mom had been looking at the wounds that the snake had inflicted on Jamie.

"Just what bit her, Ceri?"

Before I could speak up Scom piped up in his small voice, "Oh she was bitten by a naga, a very nasty creature if you know what I mean?

Mom looked back at Jamie's wound and started to mumble to herself without showing the slightest surprise that a dog answered her. Of course, the slight squeal that came from the hallway showed that at least someone was surprised that Scom could talk.

"Hey that dog talked Ceri, did you hear him talk?" Dede said as she came out from the hallway.

"Yeah, I heard him and he is a troll not a dog, pipsqueak," I said as I watched Mom grab a box from under the couch and start to rummage through it as though looking for something specific.

"Well, he looks like a dog," Dede said with some doubt in her voice. "Well okay, maybe a rat then, but I don't think he looks like a troll at all."

"Hey!" Scom scolded as he looked at Dede standing there in her winter PJs. "A rat? Indeed!"

Tessa walked up to Dede and rubbed at her legs and laughed. "I like this little one," she said.

Dede hopped back in surprise and looked at the cat and then back up at me. "Uhm Ceri, the cat talked too. So is it a troll too?" she asked a look of concern now on her face.

Before I could answer Mom looked at all of us with that "mom look" that said we had all better do what she said if we all knew what was good for us. "Okay enough Dede, you take the animals into your room. Ceri, I need you to fill a pot with water and put it on the stove. When the water boils, put this stuff in it," she said as she tossed me a cloth bag.

We all moved to do what Mom had said. Even Scom and Tessa seemed to sense that this was no time to stand around and make idle chatter when Mom got this way. As I entered the kitchen, I could hear Jamie ask Mom, "Am I the only one that can't hear the dog and cat talk?"

Mom laughed, "Don't worry dear, it's not you. It's because we're demons so we can hear them."

I lost everything else that was said from the sound of water filling the biggest pot I could find. Putting it on the stove, I turned it on and then noticed that it was very quiet in the next room. I peeked in and saw that it looked like that Jamie had once again fallen asleep or had passed out. "I got the water on, Mom," I said as she looked up at me.

"Good girl. Now when it boils, pour in the whole package then let it simmer for ten minutes."

"Uhm yeah, no prob; but is she going to okay?" I asked starting to get worried all over again.

Mom looked at Jamie and then felt her forehead with one of her hands. "Yeah she'll be alright, someone got most of the poison out of her system or she wouldn't have made it this far. The stuff I gave you will draw the rest out and help heal her so that she won't have any lasting effects."

After a few minutes, I heard the water start to boil and ran back into the kitchen to dump the mixture into the pot. As I opened the bag and tipped the contents into the pot, the smell from the mixture could have given Scom a run for his money on which smelled worse.

As I turned the burner to simmer and turned a timer to ten minutes, the smell of the mixture changed to a honey/clover smell and wisps of green and silver steam now rose from the water.

I thought back to how I had met Jamie and how I thought she was such a strange girl. Now a tear trickled down my cheek as I hoped that Mom was right and my new friend would be okay and back to normal. Well as normal as any of us seemed to be in this household at least.

The timer went off and I was going to take the pan off the stove when Mom came into the kitchen. "Here let me in there, I need to drain the mixture to get it to the right consistency," she said as she grabbed the pan and moved over to the sink.

I peeked in at Jamie and saw that she was quietly lying on the couch so I went to watch whatever it was my mom was doing with that mixture. I watched as she drained the ugly looking water from the pan and then washed it down the disposal. The stench from the water seemed to be fighting the sweet smell that issued from the pan until the water was all washed down the drain.

I looked over at Mom as she plopped the mixture into a bowl and asked, "Uhm when did you learn to do this kind of stuff?"

Mom smiled and got a wistful look on her face. "A long time ago in another world, I was trained as a healer." She gave a small sigh. "Then I met your dad and I left that life behind."

"Oh," was all that came out of my mouth as I followed Mom back into the living room and then watched as she sat next to Jamie on the couch. I guess you never know all you need to know about your parents from when they were younger.

Mom took the arm that Jamie had been bitten on and

turned it so that the wound was facing her. "Ceri, I need you to press down on your friend's shoulders to hold her down," Mom said as she reached down once more and pulled out a wicked little knife out of the box she had been looking through earlier.

I looked at the knife then at Jamie and made a small gulping noise. "Uhm is that really necessary to do, Mom?" I asked as I felt like all the blood was leaving my face and my legs became wobbly.

Mom looked at me in exasperation and pointed the knife in Jamie's direction. "Yes Ceri, it is necessary if you want your friend to get better. Now hold down on her shoulders because she is going to feel this."

I pushed down on Jamie's shoulders and Mom reached down and made two large cuts in the shape of an X on Jamie's arm. It was a good thing that I was pushing down as Jamie's eyes popped open as soon as the first cut happened and she tried to sit up on the second cut.

As Mom rubbed the wound, the blood slowly oozed out of the cuts and gave off a sour smell that filled the living room with its nauseating aroma. Mom took one look at the wound and then smiled as she applied the sweeter smelling mixture to it. "Well, at least, it was better than I thought it would be," she said as the sweet smell of the medicine now permeated the air.

I looked down at Jamie's arm as Mom laid her hand over the mixture and whispered some words that I didn't catch.

The wound under her hand glowed and I caught a whiff of burnt sulfur wafting up from the bites. With this action, Jamie settled back down on the couch with a loud sigh and then fell right back to sleep.

I looked at Mom as she looked at Jamie. "She will be alright now Ceri, she needs some rest for her body to repair itself," Mom said as she looked at me with a reassuring smile.

I sighed with relief and quickly glanced over at the hallway, and then back to my friend on the couch as I heard a meek voice ask quietly, "Can we come out now?"

"Yes, you can," Mom said as she looked over at Dede and started laughing so hard that tears were coming out of her eyes. I looked over and couldn't help laughing right along with her at the sight before my eyes.

There stood Dede with Tessa behind her rolling on the floor in laughter. In Dede's arms, Scom lay dressed in a pink dress with a glittering tiara on his head looking like the small troll wanted the floor to open up and swallow him whole right about then. "This is not a way for a troll to be seen Princess if you know what I mean?"

I couldn't help it as I laughed harder then rushed over to the living room table and picked up the camera that sat on it. "Oh I know what you mean Scom, but this is too good of a picture to pass up. Jamie will love these when she wakes up," I said as I clicked a few snapshots of the disheartened troll.

With each click of the camera, Scom sunk lower and lower into Dede's arms. "Oh this is so not good, so not good at all," moaned the embarrassed troll.

CHAPTER 10

Queen Ellie watched as the two golden figures glided slowly across the floor of her throne room led by the lone ogre gate guard. She had seen the two figures approach the castle and wondered what they would do when her guards tried to stop them from seeing her. Satisfied by the display of their power, the Queen allowed the two people to enter without any further interference by her guards. Who knows, she thought, they may be interesting partners; and well, if not, she had some magic of her own she could show them.

The two golden figures stopped before the throne of the queen and each gave a quick polite bow to the seated figure above them. The queen looked down at the two figures, one male, and one female, but almost identical in looks. She could see that each had long blonde, wavy hair that reached down past their shoulders. Their slight figures were each covered in a white gown that shone with a glare in the golden light that surrounded them, but it was the eyes that drew your attention. They were eyes of the sea, eyes of such a deep blue that the black iris of each looked lighter than the color around it.

"What is it you want here, creatures?" Queen Ellie asked as she rose out of her throne; standing and crossing her arms over her chest.

The male of the two straightened up as though offended by the queen's demand and even the tone of her voice, but the smaller female laid a restraining hand on his arm and whispered something to her companion.

"My good queen, my name is Sara and my brother here next to me is Michael," the small figure sang out in that sweet voice. "And we have come seeking information and to maybe help with a certain problem that you have?"

The queen looked around the throne room and then smiled down at the couple below her. "I have no problems, Sara, is that what you said your name was?"

Sara looked up at the queen, a slight look of annoyance flashing across her face, but then replaced by the sweet smile of sunshine that graced it before just as quickly. "Forgive me then your majesty; for I was talking about your daughter, Ceri, I believe it is. But obviously that problem seems to have been taken cared of then," Sara said with a hint of sarcasm in her voice.

"Uhm yes that is not so much a problem, as it is an annoyance right now, Sara," the queen answered, her smile disappearing from her face to be replaced by a frown as she stared down at the two below her.

"Oh yes, I see that now your majesty; do please forgive my error," Sara said, her smile growing with the annoyance of the queen. "But then since you don't have a problem, then maybe you can help us with a slight annoyance of our own?"

"And this, uhm, annoyance is what, pray tell?"

"Oh, it is a couple of people, of no importance, who have left our world without telling us where they were going and we are so worried for their safety."

"Yes I'm sure you are worried," the queen said, her smile returning and her own bit of sarcasm thrown down at the girl.

The look of annoyance once more returned to both of the figure's faces standing below the queen, and this time painted them in an ugly glow.

As each group stood looking and taking the measure of one another, they knew that each was very dangerous in their own right and were not to be trusted. "So how long have you been looking for these people, Sara?" the queen asked, finally breaking the silence that had descended in the throne room.

Sara lowered her head as though in anger and then looked back up at the queen once again, the sweet smile once more residing on her youthful face before answering. "sixteen years we have been searching, your majesty."

The queen smiled also and then moved down the stairs toward the young couple before her. As she stood in front of them, she looked over the two people before her with a questioning look. "Such a long time for such children as yourself to be searching for two lost souls, isn't it?"

Both of them looked at the queen and smiled. "We are older than we look, your majesty," Sara said after glancing at her brother and getting a slight nod.

"Yes, I see," said the queen as she moved around the young couple and then stopping behind them as she spied a pair of small white wings attached to each of their backs. As she looked, she could see each set of wings move lightly as the couple shifted around to look at the queen over their shoulders.

"And what are these creatures that you are looking for?" the queen asked as she once more moved to stand in front of the couple.

"The people," Sara emphasized, "are demons from our world, actually part of the royalty of their, uhm, species."

"Demons? You mean like the demons that come from dragons? Those demons?" the queen asked with a puzzled look.

"These demons are not from dragons, but actually from our world of Haven," Sara said with a wicked smile.

Queen Ellie stood there, rooted to her spot as though in thought then asked, "That aside, have you thought that maybe the ones you seek are on another world, my children?"

As the queen stood and watched, she saw Michael bristle at the "children" remark and thought to herself that of the two of them, he was the dangerous one. Sara once more laid a hand on her brother's arm and then turned and spoke to the queen. "We have searched other worlds that they could be in and this world and your old home world of Earth are the last to be checked."

"I see," said the queen, "and you think that they are here in this world?"

"Well your consort, Ceri's father, was here and so we thought that these two would be here or passed through and are on your home world," Sara said.

"And my uhm, this consort as you called him and these people were what to each other?" the queen asked with a thoughtful look on her face.

"One of the people we are looking for is your consort's brother."

"Oh yes, I do see now," the queen said.

Both Sara and Michael glanced at each other and then over at the queen. "We also have one of our minions looking for these people on your old world. So we have come here to narrow down the possibilities, in case these two are hiding here," Sara said.

"Well," the queen said as she started back up to her throne, "I can assure you that these two people are not in this world, so that must mean that they are on Earth, wouldn't you say?"

"Yes that does seem likely, after all then," Sara said.

"Good," the queen said as she once more sat down on her throne and smiled down on the two figures below her, "then I expect that you will leave this world now as soon as we have concluded our business here."

Sara looked at the queen for a second and then glanced at her brother and gave a slight shake to her head. "As you say, your majesty, we have no further reason to be in this world and will move on. You are right that our business is done here."

"Very well then you can show yourself out of my castle as I will need to talk to my guard here, if you don't mind?" the queen said as she spied the small ogre that had, through this whole conversation, been trying to make himself go unnoticed by his queen and the two strange creatures before her.

As Michael turned with his sister to leave the throne room, he waved his hand thus releasing the jaws of the ogre. As the doors of the throne room closed behind them, the brother and sister smiled not so sweet smiles at the screams that reverberated off the walls from behind those doors.

After rescuing Scom from my little sister, I figured that now was as good a time as any for a quick bath for the little guy. I left Jamie sleeping on the couch while my mom and Dede were sitting in a rocker as Mom read to her.

Scom was even unhappier with a bath than he was with the dress he had on, but seemed to settle down for his fate, that is until Tessa showed up at the bathroom door. "Oh yes, Princess, give him a good bath for those males do so stink, don't they Princess?" the cat said with a snide little laugh.

I looked down at the poor suffering dog in the tub, which now did resemble a drowned rat more than a canine and then glanced over my shoulder at Tessa. "Yeah well, I know one cat that isn't so sweet smelling herself, and if she is still here when I'm done with Scom she will be next."

I had to smile at the sound of scrambling feet and the look on the cat's face as she exited the doorway. Looking down at Scom, I saw a small smile on the wet troll's face. "Thank you, Princess," he said as he shook some of the water all over the tub and me. "Females can be such a problem if you know what I mean Princess?"

I looked down at the troll with a look of annoyance. "Well as I'm one of those problems Scom, I'd say that I don't know what you mean," I said as I dumped a large cup of water over his head.

"Sorry Princess," I heard through the cascade of water.

Scom sputtered and looked so crestfallen that I took pity on the small fellow and grabbed him out of the tub and started to dry him off with a thick, soft towel. I had broken out the hair dryer and was running it over the still wet troll when I heard my dad and Roc come in the front door of the apartment.

I couldn't hear what was being said at that point so I hurried to finish drying off Scom so that we could head out into the living room and hopefully get some answers to the questions that were floating inside my head.

❧❧❧❧❧❧

It got pretty quiet as I walked into the living room with Scom, all conversation stopped and everyone was standing around looking at each other waiting for the others to start talking. In the awkward silence, I saw that Jamie was now awake and that Dede was sitting over by my friend with a glass of some juice.

I walked over and looked down at the witch. "How are you doing?" I asked, noticing that her color was back to normal and her eyes were clear and focused.

"I'm okay, thanks to your mom. Even though I wish I could remember what happened in the park," she said as she looked over and took in all of us that were there.

"Did I really see you turn your teddy bear into a demon

that carried me to the truck?" Jamie asked with a confused look growing on her face.

"Yeah, you did see that; don't worry the big fuzzy is on our side," I said with a smile, hoping to put my friend at ease.

"Oh okay, but is someone going to explain what happened out there?" Jamie asked as she settled back into the couch.

The three grownups looked around at each other for a few seconds. Then with a sigh, Dad walked into the kitchen, saying, "Yeah, okay we will tell you everything, but first Roc and I need to get something to drink."

Walking back into the living room, Dad handed Roc a can of soda and then went and sat down next to Mom on the smaller living room couch. They both looked at Dede, who by this time was sound asleep in Mom's arms, and then at Roc.

"Yeah, I'll take her and put her in bed for you," Roc said as he walked over and gently lifted the bundle from my Mom's arms and headed toward her room. As he walked down the hall, I turned and faced my foster parents and looked at the people I thought I knew.

We all sat there again in silence for a few seconds until my curiosity got the better of me and I finally spoke up. "Okay what is going on here?"

"Go ahead Bill might as well tell her," Mom said as she settled back into the couch to relax for the long tale to come.

Dad shook his head and then let out a small laugh. "You know, Ceri, we had hoped that this day was a long way off, but now that it is here I feel better in letting you know the truth."

"Okay and the truth is what, Dad?"

"Well, the truth is that your real dad was my brother and . . ."

"And my clutch brother," Roc said as he walked into the room and sat down on the rocker, the last open seat in the living room.

"What?" I asked now totally confused and they hadn't even really started explaining anything yet.

Dad gave Roc a dirty look while the dragon smiled back at my dad. "Enough Roc or you can go home," Mom said anger tingeing her voice.

Roc looked down at Tessa, who took that moment to hop in his lap, and the smile slowly faded from his face.

Dad looked at Roc for a few more seconds before he looked back at me and went on with his explanation. "Let's start with the broader picture here, okay?"

"Yeah sure," I said

"Good then just to let you know that there are many different worlds out there in the universe, and as many different people and creatures as well. Your mom and I come from a world that is called Haven."

"And Roc you come from there too?" I asked looking at the man that was sitting quietly petting Tessa.

Roc snorted a laugh and gave my dad an evil look.

"No, Roc comes from the Others world, which really doesn't have a name . . ."

"Those of us that care call her Mother," Roc said with a low growl.

Dad nodded at Roc and went on. "Okay point taken, but it has no formal name. Anyways in these worlds some have many portals that will take you into other worlds and a few like Earth have only one portal to another world. The portals allow people to travel from one world to the next with its magic, even though in some cases the magic can have some unusual effects on creatures."

"You mean like with Scom and Tessa, where trolls are turned into cats and dogs type of effects?" I asked hugging my little friend who had braved the portal to come and save me.

Dad looked over at the two mentioned creatures and smiled. "Yes like those two and like our friend Roc here, who was a dragon in the Others world," Dad said as he nodded toward the big man.

"Anyways in our world of Haven there are two different types of people; here on Earth you call them demons and angels."

"You mean there really are demons and angels and all that stuff," I asked as I looked at Dad and Mom.

Dad looked at me and smiled. "Yes we are a very old race and some of our people came to this world when it was young to hide out from the war. These people were demons, and when they were hunted down by the angels, they were also vilified in this world so that demons would always be looked down on as evil."

"Oh," both Jaime and I said at the same time.

"So what was this war about?" I asked

"The war was over the rights for demons to live their lives and to be treated as equals. You see the world of Haven is a world of two different lives. In the good part of Haven, the angels live in a land that is fruitful and beautiful. In that part of the world, life is easy and food and water and all things needed to live are plentiful."

"Sounds perfect," Jamie whispered as I nodded at her assessment.

"And the other part of the world?" I asked.

"Yeah the other parts of Haven are wastelands where demons scrape out a living and where the children can die young, that is if the young are born at all. Dad stopped and looked over at Mom and then took her hand in his. For a long time, we struggled under the angels' rule and more of our young died."

"Not good," I said and then turned to Roc. "But how do you both have the same brother then if you are from different worlds?" I asked still confused on what was happening here.

"Well, a long time ago, it was thought that dragons could be used to overturn the angels of our world. So demons secretly hid their eggs amongst the dragons so that hopefully a demon would one day rise and rule the dragons and lead them against the angels in our world, thus freeing us to live our own lives."

"And my dad was one of these demons?"

"Yes and your true dad was the one that rose to rule the dragons and would have led us to freedom if not for your witch mother."

"Guess she ruined not only the Others worlds but yours too huh?" I said taking in the three adults sitting around the living room.

"Well, wait a minute. If Ceri's dad was a demon and Roc is a dragon then how is her dad both your brothers?" Jamie asked with a look of confusion etched on her face.

"Oh that's an easy one to answer," Dad said with a laugh. "You see Ceri's dad came from my mother and father, basically demons, and the dragon's clutch that he ended up in was Roc's parents. So you see, he was born from my demon parents and raised with Roc's as a dragon."

"Well that must have been quite a surprise for your parents when my dad popped out as a demon instead of a dragon," I said looking over at Roc.

Roc smiled in remembrance of some past visions. "Oh, you don't know the half of it, for in our world all other dragons would have killed your father as soon as he was born. But due to some accident, only your dad's egg and mine survived to grow and hatch. My mother, though a dragon, still couldn't bear the thought of killing either of us so that she stole us away and raised the two of us until we were old enough to fend for ourselves."

"Okay well, that sounds a little lonely," I said as I looked at the dragon.

Roc smiled some more at me and shook his head. "No actually, it was quite fun for the two of us. We learned how to live on our own after a time. You see, after awhile, our mother began to regret leaving the other dragons and left us to go back home."

"Okay I guess she wasn't 'Mom of the Year' material, was she?" I asked

A small growl slipped from Roc's lips as he looked at me with a tiny bit of fire in his eyes. "My mother was a dragon and she did the best that she knew how to do for her species."

"Roc," my dad whispered, "she doesn't know any better."

Roc looked at me and then at my dad with a frown. "Yeah,

you're right. Sorry Ceri.

"Yeah I'm sorry too, didn't mean to say anything bad about anyone's mother."

"Anyways," Roc continued, "your dad and I watched out for each other and grew up to be the strongest of the dragons in our world, and that's when your foster dad here, or I guess I should say your uncle, contacted us and we learned what was really going on."

"Yeah but by then your mother had been in the Others world for awhile and she caught your dad's eye with her magic," Mom said with a grimace, the first time she had spoken since Dad had started telling us their history.

"So then I was born?" I whispered.

"Yes and then you were born and your dad would not leave you to help free our people like he should have," Dad said with a bitterness in his voice.

"Oh!" was all that came through my lips as I thought of all the suffering that a people had to endure because I had been born.

Mom looked at me sadly. "It wasn't your fault Ceri, and you must not dwell on what could have been. Right, Bill?" Mom said as she landed a hard elbow into my dad's ribs.

"Oh yeah right," Dad said as he shook himself out of his funk. "No, it was not your fault at all. Your dad chose his path to live and unfortunately it cost him his life."

"Yeah okay, I guess it seems to suck that because I was born that you guys and your people lose out."

"Yes well, after you were born and your dad chose to stay in that world, Jenna and I had to flee to another world and we decided to pick the most backwater world there is and so here we are."

"HEY!" Jamie said, sitting up on the couch and then slowly sliding back down to a resting spot.

Roc looked over at my friend and let out a loud laugh before trying to calm the witch down. "Granted little one, your world is full of technology, but magic is what rules all the other worlds and most look down on technology as being backward and useless, so to most worlds this is a backward place."

Jamie looked at Roc and then a snide little smile crossed her lips. "Yeah well if we are so backward with our technology, then how come it seems to stop you from doing magic, huh? Tell me that, dragon."

Roc's smile from before disappeared from his face and I could see Mom and Dad sitting there trying not to laugh at the dragon's discomfort. "Yes well, it is true that we from my world cannot draw on the magic in this world, but still it is not what I think little one, but what the rest of the worlds that are out there think."

After watching this exchange I turned and gave my dad a questioning look. "But you did magic with no trouble, so I take it then that technology doesn't bother you or Mom?"

"Oh it can bother us, but as demons we can draw upon the ley line magic of this world, in that way we are much luckier than the Others that live here and it has allowed us to hide in this world so far," Dad said

"I guess I can see all that, but still how did I get here and how did I end up living with you guys as my foster parents?" I asked, still full of questions and wanting to make up for all the lost time of not knowing what was the truth about my life.

Dad started to speak and answer my questions but stopped as Mom laid her hands over his while glancing over at Jamie lying on the couch. "Listen Ceri," she said, "I know you have a lot of questions but your friend needs rest and it is a school day tomorrow, so how about we save the rest for tomorrow?"

I started to protest then peeked at Jamie who looked like she could barely keep her eyes open anymore. "Well okay, I guess," I said then it hit me all of a sudden what Mom had said. "Wait you don't mean I still have to go to school, do you? I mean with all that is happening we don't really know if we are even going to be around here right?"

Mom smiled as Dad shook his head at me. "No, young lady you will be on your computer tomorrow for school, and we will act as if nothing has happened until we figure out how to keep you from being returned to the Others world," Dad said as he pointed toward my bedroom.

"Great," I mumbled as I headed back toward my room with Scom in tow. "I got monsters coming out of the woodwork looking to take off my head for my evil mother and I have to do school work tomorrow, just great."

The quiet laughter of the three grownups followed me down to my room where for a second I thought long and hard on slamming my door but remembered that Dede was fast asleep and it would only disturb her. "Come on Scom; let's get to bed so that tomorrow we can go back to our boring old life again."

"Well yes Princess, but as boring as it may be, it was a safe life, if you know what I mean Princess?" Scom said as I tossed the little guy on my pillows.

"Yeah, yeah," I said as I grabbed my pajamas and headed out the door to hit the bathroom to get my nightly bedtime routine done. Out in the hall, I could hear Mom and Dad talking to Jamie asking if there was anyone to call to let know where she was.

As I listened to her explain that neither her parents nor her teacher kept track of where she was it was no problem for her to stay here until she felt better or at least through the night. Yeah, I thought maybe Scom was right, a nice boring life was safe especially when you have people who actually care about you.

CHAPTER 11

Scat sat against the wall next to the trash can with his two brothers listening to the two of them grumble. As they tried to stay warm in the cold winter night a quick flash of light lit up the night. Before their eyes across the small alleyway, two small teens stood looking down at the ogres.

"Well, well what do we have here, Sara?" the young boy said as he looked at the three shocked ogres with a strange disturbing smile on his face.

The young girl stepped forward, stared at the ogres then smiled that same disturbing smile and glanced over her shoulder at her companion. "Oh Michael, I think we have found the ones we were hoping to find when we came to this world."

All three ogres came out of their stupor and surprise and jumped up off the ground. "Who are you?" Scat, the largest of the ogres, asked looking down at the two adolescents before him and then around the area to see if there were any adults around to come to the kid's rescue.

"My but they are big and scary, aren't they," asked Sara as she slowly looked at all three creatures standing before her. "Now what shall we ever do if they try to eat us?" She turned and walked back, giggling, to stand beside her brother.

All three ogres thought that eating the young ones before them was a grand idea, but their lack of fright and almost casual manner set off alarm bells within their tiny brains. Since they had already once run into trouble tonight with magical creatures, all three ogres slowly spread out and looked around for a trap or someone that was going to pop up and save these two meals that had shown up out of thin air.

"I said, 'Who are you and what you do in our area?'" Scat asked once more, now taking a step toward the young ones expecting to see a look of fright cross their faces. Instead, all three ogres were awarded those creepy smiles that the teens wore.

The boy stepped forward and waved his hand and laughed as all three ogres froze in place. "Why, my big friends, we are travelers that have come to check out this world and to look for a lost friend of ours."

All three ogres tried to move, but their bodies were as immobile as if they all had been made of stone. Only their eyes could move and they shifted them to follow the beauty of the young girl as she slowly circled each ogre in the group, stopping before the last one in line.

"Now you will tell us what you know of our friend or we may have to play not so nice with our dinner, boys." Scat heard the girl purr and then a loud unearthly scream sounded from one of his brothers behind him, then a gurgle and then silence.

"Oops and then there were two," the boy said as he walked up and looked Scat in the face.

"Now that was a little taste of what we can do," the girl laughed from behind Scat.

"Make sure that one lasts longer sister, remember we still need answers," the boy said as he looked behind Scat at the girl and Scat's brother behind him.

"Oh yes, brother it will be my pleasure."

The boy smiled at his sister and then looked Scat once more in the face. "So now tell me about a friend of mine that lives around here, a naga, you know a snake creature per se. Goes by the name of Tiss in this world."

Scat looked down at the small boy before him and growled deep in his chest wishing to break the magic holding him so that he could smash the two small figures. "I know no Tiss you . . ."

"Wrong answer, my big friend," The boy said as once more he waved his hand and Scat felt his mouth slam shut.

The screams that issued from his brother seemed to go on for a thousand years, but soon slowed then died. The boy stood and watched whatever unholy action that was being played out behind Scat with a wide grin on his face.

"Okay enough sister," the boy said as he once more waved his hand and Scat could feel his jaws release. "Now my friend, I don't think your pal can take much more of this little playfulness from my sister. So how about you be a good boy and tell me about my friend Tiss."

Scat looked down into the eyes that stared back at him and the thought ran through his small mind that they were the color of the deep ocean and that he and his brothers were going to drown in their depths. "I am telling you truth, I know no naga named Tiss. We no know any snake people."

The boy held up his hand and shook his head as he said, "No, not yet sister."

Scat heard a large sigh behind him in the cold winter night air and the slight panting of pain from his brother, but even with the cold, he could feel the sting of fear sweat starting to run on his body.

"Well if you have not seen our friend Tiss then maybe you have spotted a demon and his mate running around in this world?" the boy said as he looked closely at Scat's face.

Scat hesitated as he thought of the magical creatures that he and his brothers had had a run in within the park earlier. Even though he felt mad at the ones that had sent them on their way with no meals, he couldn't make himself give them up to this creature before him. "I know no demons."

"My, my that is too bad because, my big friend, I think you are lying to me," the boy said as he once more casually waved his hand at Scat's face and the big ogre felt his mouth slam shut once again.

The boy stood there and laughed as he patted Scat's face and then walked back to where the girl and Scat's brother stood. "Oh it is so fun when they resist isn't it Sara, my dear sister?" Slowly he could feel his body rotate with the boy's magic until he was looking at the two teens standing before what was left of his brother.

"Oh yes, it is so fun indeed brother. Would you like a taste of this one?" The sweet voice of the girl echoed off of the walls of the building's alleyway.

That was when the screaming behind locked lips sounded from Scat's brother, and the thought flashed through his brain that he would soon be next since no one could last long with what these creatures were doing to his brother. He only hoped now that it would be quick when it came to his turn with these two monsters. He was wrong on both counts.

❧❧❧❧❧❧

I woke up on Monday morning and looked out the window at the cold cloudy winter morning. It wasn't raining yet, but the low dark pregnant clouds looked like they would open up any second and deluge the town with their wet offspring.

With a snort and snore from Scom, I looked over at the little guy and saw that he was curled up in the blankets at the bottom of my bed looking warm and toasty. Deciding that he had a good idea, I dived back under the blankets and tried to get back to that blessed sleep I had awoken from.

Through the closed door of my room, I could hear voices float down the hall from the kitchen, and then the running of small feet. A timid knock on my door sounded ahead of a quiet voice. "Ceri, are you awake?" Dede asked as she peeked around the now open door.

I looked at my little sister, still couldn't think of her as my cousin, and smiled for Dede was never this quiet nor so seemingly unsure of herself. "Yeah squirt, I'm up. What's on your mind?"

Dede glanced down the hall then came into my room and shut the door. She stood there wringing her hands in front of her and staring at the floor. I patted my bed and she looked up with a sad smile. I lifted the warm covers in invitation, "Come on and hop up here and tell your big sis what is eating you."

With that, she hopped on the bed and we both dived back under the covers to keep the cold morning chill from our bones. "So what's up kiddo?" I asked.

Dede was quiet for a few seconds and I was going to press her a little to see what the problem was when she finally gave a quiet sigh and a few tears flowed down her cheeks. "I heard you guys talking last night," she whispered.

"Oh," I said thinking that this wasn't good news and that maybe Mom or Dad had better talk to the little troublemaker and answer her questions. "Uhm, well, I guess we all thought you were asleep last night there, kiddo."

"I pretended, and when Roc went down to the living room I snuck back down the hall and listened to you guys talk. I mean it's the only way I can learn things around here since everyone treats me like a baby and doesn't tell me things," Dede said looking a little sad and a little angry at the same time.

"I know it's hard," I said giving the little squirt a big hug. "But there are some things that grownups talk about that small kids don't need to know about. It's not that you are a baby, but some things aren't for kids your size and are for parents to solve."

"Okay I guess," she said as the sniffles and the tears dried up. "But is it true?"

"Is what true?" I asked the little bundle next to me.

"That you, Mom, and Dad are demons?

I laid there for a minute and thought what I was going to say, wishing that Mom would come in and see where Dede had gotten to. Yeah, I know big scaredy cat, but I was at a loss for words right then.

"I mean demons are bad, right? So you guys can't be those things, right?"

I looked down at the worried face lying under my covers and gave her a small smile. "Listen do you think deep down that any of us are really bad or evil?"

"Well no!" the small voice whispered.

"Well okay then, besides think about it since Mom and Dad are demons and they have these powers, what does that make you, you little troublemaker?"

Dede laid there, a thoughtful look on her face that slowly turned into that mischievous little smile she gets when she is plotting some Dede trouble. "That means I'm a demon too?" she asked, a look of wonder on her face.

"You got it kiddo, and even though you may not have the powers of a demon yet, most likely you'll grow into them soon."

Dede's smile grew as the thoughts of the trouble she could cause flashed through her mind. Then she looked up at me with a set of those eyes she uses when she is trying to get her way. "Will you help me learn how to use those powers, Ceri? I mean Mom and Dad still think of me as their baby and wouldn't even really tell me what was going on."

"Yeah I'll help you but we don't keep secrets in this family and we don't tell lies. Remember those are the two big sins for Mom and Dad."

Dede nodded with her eyes going wide, probably remembering the one time she had told a lie and its consequence. "I'll tell Mom and Dad right now that I know what is going on," she said as she hopped out of my bed and headed toward the bedroom door. "Oh, and by the way Mom said you got two minutes to get up and get out there for breakfast because it's a school day," she said laughing as she went out the door.

I hopped up out of bed myself looking for a pair of sweats and a sweatshirt to throw on; thinking thanks a lot kid for telling me that now. I grabbed my standard grubby school clothes and threw them on thinking that if there was one nice thing about doing an online school is that a fashion sense is not necessary to attend.

As I walked toward my bedroom door, I heard once again a loud snort coming from the end of my bed. I walked back over and then looked down at the peacefully sleeping troll all curled up in the blanket's warmth and thought you know if I have to be up?

"Scom," I whispered

Nothing no movement or acknowledgment that he had even heard me, yeah well I was getting hungry by now and the little guy was getting up with me, I thought.

"SCOM! LOOK OUT A DRAGON!" I shouted.

Scom jumped up about two feet in the air and came down on the bed, a growl issuing from his throat. As he spun in a circle looking for a dragon, I couldn't help but feel sorry even though I was laughing at the look on the poor creature's face.

Scom stopped and sat breathing hard and threw me a dirty look. "Oh that was so not nice, Princess if you know what I mean?"

"Yeah Scom I'm sorry," I said now feeling really contrite for scaring the little guy, but fighting back the giggles in seeing the look on his face.

"That is fine Princess, now if you don't mind I will go back to sleep where I was having a wonderful dream of home," the troll said as he circled his sleeping spot three times and planted his body back down into the warmth of the blankets.

"Oh sure, no problem Scom. You go right back to sleep while I get some of Mom's great breakfast," I said as I walked out the door of the bedroom.

"Hey, breakfast? Wait for me Princess." I heard a small voice yell and then a thump as Scom hit the floor and then raced by me, headed toward the savory aromas wafting from the kitchen.

Walking out into the kitchen, I saw that Jamie, Tessa, and

Roc were still here and that everyone seemed to be enjoying a great hearty breakfast of Mom's creation.

"Leave anything for me?" I asked looking at the empty plates and bowls that lined the table which everyone else was sitting at.

"Don't worry honey I saved you some food. It's in the oven keeping warm," Mom said as she got up and started to clear off the table. "Here you can sit in my spot since your Dad and I need to get ready for work."

"Yeah it is about that time I guess," Dad said looking up at the kitchen clock.

I stopped pouring the glass of milk I had on the counter and looked at both of my parents with concern. "You're not staying home today?"

"No honey, your Dad and I still need to work," Mom said as she put the dishes she had gathered in the sink.

"And anyways Roc said that he would stick around and keep an eye on you guys," Dad said as he picked up the dishes that Mom hadn't gotten and threw them in the sink with the rest.

"Oh that should be so much fun," I said looking over at the dragon.

"It is not my first choice to babysit either, little one, but we must all do what is necessary to survive," Roc said with a grimace.

"Yeah, so what, you have a job that you don't have to show up for there, dragon?" I asked

"Ceri!" Mom scolded. "That's just rude. Roc is here to help us."

'Yeah sorry, Mom I don't trust dragons," I said giving Roc a dark look.

"It is alright little one for I too do not trust dragons. But to answer your question, I have no reason to work. When I fled to this world I took my dragon hoard with me letting me live here without problems such as this world's money.

Oh well okay then," I said as I thought that I really needed to learn not to insert my foot into my mouth and I really should learn all the facts before I speak. Yeah, one big bad habit I seemed to have had all my life.

I looked over at Mom and Dad and caught their eyes as I nodded at my little sister who was in the process of filling in Jamie on the varieties of games that she had on her gaming console, and which were her favorites.

Mom came over as Dad headed to the back of the apartment to get ready for work and gave me a quick hug while she whispered. "Don't worry Dede already told us that she was up last night and that she knows the score. Just be careful in what you teach or show her, okay, for young demons have been known to sometimes lose control of their magic."

"Oh great," I moaned looking over at my small sister. Not

like she wasn't a little pain in the butt at times, now I had to deal with her learning magic too. Oh, this was so not going to be good, I thought.

"Don't worry you'll survive," Mom said as she patted me on the arm and headed back to follow Dad in getting ready for work.

I grabbed my breakfast and milk and headed to the table to save my friend from the endless chatterbox that was my little sister. "How are you feeling today?" I asked Jamie as Dede took a lone breath in between the wave of words that had washed over us.

"Oh she is fine, right Jamie?" the little chatterbox answered for my friend.

I gave Dede a sour look that did nothing to wipe off the smile on her face as Jamie smiled at my sister and then turned toward me. "Yeah what she said."

"Well glad to hear that you're feeling better. Are you going to stick around here with us too or do you have school to get to?" I asked as I handed down some bacon to the small dog that was begging at my feet.

"I don't go to regular school either, in fact, I'm home schooled by my teacher at his place, so yeah I probably should head over there," she said as she rose up to put her stuff in the sink with the rest of the dishes.

I looked over at the mess in the sink with a heavy heart knowing whose job it would be to clean up the pile stacked up there as Jamie and Dede headed out to do whatever it was they needed to do. Geez shouldn't being a princess have some perks like I don't know maybe any more chores.

Oh well, at least, it seemed like we were all trying to get back to a normal life, I thought as I finished my half of the breakfast on my plate while feeding the other half to Scom who was happy as a clam from the sounds he was making under the table.

❧❧❧❧❧❧❧

I had finished up my meal and was loading the dishwasher like the good little kid I was when Mom and Dad came out from the back of the apartment all ready for work. "Listen Ceri treat this as a normal school day and such," Dad said as he gathered his pocket junk off of the counter where he always stashes it, much to Mom's displeasure.

"Yes, help get your sister set up for classes and help her when you can, okay?" Mom asked

"Sure guys, don't worry I know the drill."

"And listen to Roc if there is any trouble," Dad said with a smile. "I know he can be a pain, but he will watch your back in a fight."

"I heard that!" sounded a large growl from the living room.

"Yeah well you were meant to," Dad threw back to the living room, then turned and gave me a quick hug. As he headed out of the kitchen and toward the front door, I could hear him calling for Jamie to shag it along if she wanted a ride to her teacher's house.

Mom stood there looking at me and then hugged me also as she said, "Try not to make it too rough on Roc, okay kiddo?"

"Who me?" I asked trying to put my innocent face on.

"Yeah you," she said as she laughed and then once more turned serious, "and try to keep out of trouble."

"Yeah no prob, Mom," I said as we headed out to where everyone else was gathered.

The morning ritual of hugs and goodbyes were dispensed with and my parents and Jamie were seen out the door, each to go to their separate destinations finally. Turning to look at my little sister and the mismatch of clothes that she had chosen for this day of school, I let out a sigh and started to march her back toward her room.

"But why? You're a princess so I should get to dress up like one if you're not going to," she whined as I took her in the room and started to grab some warmer clothes for her.

"Yeah well wearing a tutu and a t-shirt is not going to cut it in the middle of winter, kiddo."

"But it's warm in here and I want . . ."

"Oh no, it is not that warm and I will not have you coming

197

down with a cold this close to the holidays. Mom and Dad would ground me until I was thirty if you got sick on my watch, so change," I said as I pointed at the stuff I had laid out for her.

"I can't wait until I'm old like you and can do and wear whatever I want," Dede said as she started to change.

I looked over at the cat that was rolling on the bed laughing and snickering at this exchange and pointed at her. "Keep it up kitty and you're going to find yourself turned into a rug."

Tessa stopped laughing and with a sniff and her nose in the air, hopped off the bed and flipped her tail at me as she walked out the door.

"Can you really turn her into a rug Ceri?" Dede asked her eyes wide and fringed with fright.

I laughed and hugged my sister which seemed to relieve her fright. "No I can't, but that mangy cat doesn't know that. Now come on and finish up dressing so we can get your teeth brushed and get ready for school.

Dede finished dressing and as we headed down to the bathroom the thought crossed my mind that it was time to get back to that normal boring life where nothing happens except doing dishes and helping with my little sis at school. Yeah, such a dull normal life I live.

CHAPTER 12

Saba paced back and forth in his living room wondering where his stupid student had gotten herself to now. Didn't that little girl know that something was very, very wrong in this town, something that needed the two of them together to investigate?

First, there was the early morning patrol he had made. The patrol that he always started in the park so that if needed he could charge his magic from its ley line, but when he arrived at the park he saw that it looked like there had been several fights using magic there.

He could see and smell the magic used and the charred ash of Others that someone had tried to hide. At first, he thought of his student but realized that whoever had fought these creatures wielded a different kind of power than witch magic.

Then there was the ley line itself. Saba had never before in his life seen that line so drained of power. He could see that the power was slowly seeping back into the line from the earth, but it was still so low that the witch went to another ley line to draw his needed magic.

The second problem started when he found the three bodies of the ogres that were left behind the back of the local mall, or he should say what was left of the bodies. However they had died, Saba was certain that it was neither easy nor quick.

Saba burned what was left of the remains with the evil stench of whatever creatures that had killed the ogres filling his nostrils with its rancid smell. Afterward, he tried to trace the creatures, for now, he was sure there were two of them, to their lair, but lost them in a wooded area close by the mall.

As the most powerful witch, Saba was chosen by the witch's council to hunt for the portal that led to the Other's world or failing to find it to at least protect innocent lives from these foul creatures.

Saba stopped pacing as the thought crossed his mind that maybe he was looking at the problem of these new creatures all wrong. By all the evidence that he had found so far it seemed as if these creatures cared no more about the Others than he did; so maybe instead of destroying them Saba could persuade them to join him in getting rid of all the creatures that had crossed over the portal from the Other's world.

A slow evil smile slid over his face as the thought filtered through his mind that these creatures, whatever they were, most likely had also crossed the portal and with their help he could find it and crush this bane of his existence for good.

"I mean, once the portal and all the Others are wiped out then I can get rid of these new creatures and free this world of all these abominations," he whispered with a feverish semi-crazed look in his eyes. Lost in these thoughts, Saba began pacing back and forth plotting out how he would rid the world of the trash within it, and cursing his student for not being here when she was most needed.

❧❧❧❧❧❧

Bill followed Jamie's directions in taking her home but was still worried about the young friend of Ceri's. He knew that even with Jenna's healing powers the girl should still be lying in bed and resting after her ordeal, but he kept his opinion to himself so as not to embarrass her.

Of course, his wife had no such problem and was grilling Jamie on how she felt, where her parents were and how her teacher treated the young witch, which was another reason why he wisely kept his mouth shut.

"Listen, I really appreciate all the worry and the ride and all, but you can drop me off here," Jamie said as she pointed at an empty bus stop.

Both demons looked at each other and then smiled, as the same thoughts crossed their minds. They had been together for so long that most of the time their thoughts were as one. "Yeah, that's not happening Jamie. We would be remiss if we didn't see you to your door," Bill said slowing down the car somewhat.

"Yes, after what happened to you last night you still need rest, and besides there could be Others out there looking to even the score with some lone young witch," Jenna said. "So let us know where your home is, okay?"

Jamie sighed and slumped back into the back car seat and huffed, "Okay it's down the block on the right, the big old gray house, with black trim."

"Thank you, dear," Jenna said with a smile trying to soothe the young teen's feelings.

"I can take care of myself," floated quietly from the back seat of the car as both of Ceri's parents smiled and thought that no matter what, kids always think that they can take on the world. That is until the world bites back.

❧❧❧❧❧❧

Saba stopped pacing and rushed over to the shaded window when he heard the car door slam in his driveway. He watched as his student leaned over and spoke to the two people inside and then as Jamie waved to the departing car.

He slowly walked over to stand in the middle of the living room, picking up his two crutches that leaned against a ratty old couch. Usually, he wouldn't bother with these implements, but all the traipsing around last night, and the pacing this morning seemed to have caused his power to dip down and bring out the pain in his legs.

Jamie stopped inside the doorway and the smile that she had been wearing slipped off her face and hid behind a mask of indifference that she had long ago learned to use around her teacher. "Oh you are up sir," Jamie said as she quietly closed and locked the front door.

Saba stood there, his small round pudgy body leaning on his crutches and stared at his student before speaking. "Yes I'm up and where have you been, and what is that smell all over you?" Saba said as he moved closer to the young girl standing by the door.

"Smell? I'm sorry, sir I don't smell anything," Jamie said shrinking within herself, for she knew that when her teacher was in this kind of mood she was in trouble.

Saba stopped and then sniffed the air. "Come here, girl."

Jamie moved slowly forward then stopped about five feet from her teacher. "I'm sorry I was late sir, I was out hunting Others."

Saba's lips curled up into a cruel smile and he moved closer to Jamie. "Oh, so you were out hunting, girl, is that what you were up to?"

"Yes sir, hunting for any Others that were causing trouble like I am supposed to," Jamie said with a tremor in her voice.

"I see," Saba said as he looked up at the young witch's eyes, "and where pray tell did you do this hunting of yours, girl?"

"Uhm at the mall and the park, sir?"

"LIAR!" Saba screamed as he lashed out at Jamie with a wall of power that sent the young girl into the downstairs landing.

Looking down at her as she lay curled up by the bottom steps of the landing, Saba fought to catch his breath for a minute. "I can smell dragon on you and something else, yes something else that is almost like what I smelled last night around those ogres," he said as he moved toward the downed girl.

"What is that smell? Who were you with last night?" Once again a wall of power hit Jamie as she lay on the steps and slapped her back down into the floor.

Jamie cried out and held up her hands in submission. "I promise, I wasn't with a dragon sir, really. I was at the mall with a friend, that was her parents who dropped me off. Please, sir, I must have gotten the smells from the mall, sir, please?"

Saba stopped and looked down at the young girl, a look of disgust crossing his face. "Quit your whining girl," he said as he turned his back on Jamie and then walked into the living room. "Nothing disgusts me more than hearing you whine."

As Saba settled himself into an old smelly chair that was as disreputable as its owner, Jamie slowly picked herself off the floor and followed after her teacher. With her eyes cast down on the floor, she stood before her teacher in silence.

Saba stared at the girl and frowned, thinking that this girl was such a waste. How could she ever be taught how to be a proper witch if she cried every time she was punished? Thinking back to his teacher and the punishments that had been inflicted upon him, he knew that this girl would never make it as a true witch.

"If it is alright with you teacher I would like to go up to my room?" Jamie whispered hoping that what had happened before would be the last of it today.

"THAT IS NOT YOUR ROOM!" Saba yelled, the spittle flying out of his mouth and hitting Jamie as she stood silently, but cringing inside expecting another magical blow from her teacher.

"I'm sorry teacher, you're right."

"Yes I am," Saba said as he took a deep breath to calm himself. "Remember girl this is my house, my rooms, why I let your parents talk me into taking a stupid girl like you to train as a witch is beyond me."

Jamie stood silently again, head down watching the spittle from her teacher slowly run down her arms, an unfathomable hatred building deep within her.

Saba was lost in thought again for a few seconds and then

startled as he looked up at his student once more. "Go on, get out of here. Go up to your room and ponder why I keep you around here, girl."

Jamie slowly moved out of the room, expecting any second to receive a blow in the back as she headed for the stairs and the sanctuary of her room. As she looked back, she could see and hear her teacher mumbling to himself.

"Yes that friend, that smell was almost like that. We must find that friend," Saba said with a faraway look glazing his eyes.

Jamie ran up the steps and then stood there at the top to see if she could hear any more of what her teacher was mumbling about, but soon gave up and wandered into her room thinking that somehow she needed to let Ceri and her parents know that there may be trouble from a new source, namely her teacher.

❧❦❧❦❧❦

It was a typical quiet morning at the house if you didn't count the sulking dragon that paced all over the living room and the two trolls that seemed to be getting on each other's nerves along with my last one.

By lunch time, I had enough of school for a while and could see that Dede wasn't really into whatever she was supposed to be learning either. "Okay kiddo, how about we take a break while I get some food together for lunch," I said as I reached over and disconnected her from her class on the computer.

A big smile beamed from her small face as she bolted out of her chair, grabbed Scom up in mid-stride and headed toward her bedroom. "Dress up time, little doggie," she said as Tessa followed in her tracks, the cat's laughter bouncing off the hall walls.

I started for the front door when Roc stepped in front of me with a scowl on his face. "And where do you think you are going, Princess?"

"Uhm to get the mail if some big, dumb, self-important dragon would get out of my way," I said as I tried to move around the wall of dragon that was now blocking my way.

"I'm sorry Princess, but I will get your mail, you need to stay in and get your lunch for you and your sister," the big guy said as he puffed out his chest and stepped backward into the hall thereby totally blocking my way to the front door.

I was really getting tired of being treated like a kid and the anger burst out of me as I got up in Roc's face to tell him that when he got this wary look on his face. "Uhm Princess, do you think you could stop waving those swords in front of my face?"

I stopped and looked down at the hands that were held in front of me wondering what this guy's problem was now when through my anger I could see that I was indeed holding my two swords, one red for fire and one blue for ice.

"Ceri, is that you?" I heard a small whisper from the edge of the hallway.

I turned and looked at Dede, my small innocent sister standing there with large frightened eyes staring at me. Both Scom and Tessa were standing by her side, each looking at me as if they were seeing a stranger standing in my living room.

As I moved toward the small waif to comfort her as I had dozens of times before, I could feel the flutter of wings against my shoulders and the thought flashed that losing control of my temper like this really, really did not help my concentration.

"It's alright honey," I whispered as I kneeled down in front of the small frightened child before me. "It is really me; I didn't mean to frighten you, okay?"

Dede came closer and stood inches from me staring into my eyes, "Oh it is you Ceri," she said as she threw herself at me as she slid her tiny chubby arms around my neck and hugged me for all she was worth.

As a single tear slid down my cheek, I could feel all my pent up anger leave me. Dede stood back from our embrace and then looked at me again, but this time with an expression of wonder. "There you are, Ceri, back to being you."

"That's all thanks to you squirt," I said as I stood and

looked over at Roc. "And I'm sorry for the outburst, dragon.

"It is alright, little one, I have been protecting you for so long that it comes to me as second nature," Roc said with a small smile on his face.

"What do you mean protecting me?" I questioned.

"You don't know Princess?" Roc asked with a small smile. "Well you see, Nomi is a cousin of both your dad and mine. When he found out that you were in danger from your sister's he sent me with you to this world. I knew that I was ill equipped to handle raising a child so I found Bill and Jenna and gave them to you to raise, but I have always been nearby to protect my brother's offspring."

Geez, not much a girl can say to a confession like that except, "Thanks, Roc and sorry for thinking bad about you."

"Alright then, Princess, since all that is settled then how about you get a lunch ready for your sister and I will get your mail," Roc said

"Yeah that sounds good, and you, young lady, what do you want for lunch?" I asked Dede as I watched Roc head toward the front door.

"Ice cream?" Dede asked with a small smile forming on her lips.

"Yeah nice try, kiddo, want to try for strike two?" I said as

I ruffled her hair and then headed toward the kitchen.

"Okay how about grilled cheese sandwiches," we both said at the same time since this seemed to be a favorite lunch time meal for all small bodies in this house.

I stopped as we both laughed at the answer and how it was given by the two of us. Yeah, I know stupid thing to laugh at, but it seemed to bring us both back to a normal routine. With that Dede ran off toward her room and both Scom and Tessa followed me into the kitchen.

As I was digging through the cupboards and fridge for today's lunch, both trolls sat on the floor and watched me with a particular interest.

"Go ahead tell her male, before the dragon comes back," I could hear Tessa say in a quiet whisper.

"I will, I will the Princess is busy," Scom said back in an even quieter whisper.

"Well if you don't tell her, I will," Came back a fierce reply from Tessa.

I turned toward the two on the floor that were, by this time, totally ignoring me and snarled. "If one of you doesn't tell me soon what you two are cooking up, we may be having cat/dog stew for lunch, get my drift?"

Both of them gave me a worried look and then Tessa gave a small laugh. Scom stayed somber and said, "Oh I do not think she is kidding, female."

"Oh," was all Tessa squeaked out as the laugh died a quick death.

"So what is so important that Roc can't hear about it?" I asked the silent duo.

"It is Princess the real reason that I came here to bring you back to our world."

"Yeah, fat chance of that happening, Scom. Remember a mother who hates my guts trying to kill me. You do remember that little problem, right little guy?"

"Yes Princess, but you see your mother will take out her madness on all those that were left behind, and that will not go so good for all that live in that world if you know what I mean Princess?" Scom said with a deep frown on his face.

I stopped and remembered all my friends in the Others world and the ones that had fought alongside us in getting rid of my three sisters. "I'm sorry Scom, as much as I would like to help there is no way that I can go back anyways even if I wanted to."

"Well that's not quite true, Princess," Scom said with a small smile crossing his face. "I mean how did you think I got here?"

"Oh yeah that's right, I forgot all about that in all the excitement yesterday," I said thinking back trying to remember if the little troll had told me how he had arrived in this world.

"There is a portal, a magical portal that lets you travel to this world and back," Tessa said.

"Yeah a portal with a wicked sense of humor," Scom said with a little laugh as he glanced at Tessa and himself.

"Okay well, that's all fine and good, but there are still creatures out there hunting for my head according to Jamie and those ogres and that snake we met last night seemed to confirm it," I said as I began to prepare our lunch.

"Princess, you need to go back to your world and save the people in it," Scom said with a pleading look on his face.

"Okay, listen you two, this is my world and that other place will have to do without me. Do you understand that?" I said my temper starting to rise. I couldn't figure out why these two didn't understand how I felt.

Tessa and Scom stared back at me after my little temper tantrum and were quiet for a few seconds until Tessa got up and started to walk out of the kitchen. She stopped at the doorway and then looked back at me and gave a small snarl. "You are wrong Princess, your world is ours, and if you don't go back then a lot of creatures will die all because you want to stay here and be safe." With that little announcement, Tessa flipped her tail in the air and walked out the door.

I looked at the doorway and then glanced down at Scom. "You understand, right little guy? It's not my problem?"

Scom looked at me with a look of pity on his face then

spoke. "I'm sorry Princess, but this time, the female is right. This is not your real world and if you don't go back and fight your mother all those in the Others world will suffer, including me."

"What do you mean Scom? You're here safe with me."

"I'm sorry Princess, but as much as I love you, I need to return to our world and join the fight against the Queen." With that Scom walked out of the kitchen following Tessa, leaving me to my own thoughts.

All I could think was that yes I had been born in the Others world, but this is the world I had been raised in and the one that I knew best. Why couldn't those two see that there was no way I could go back and win against my mother? That I owed no one in that Others world, I mean yes there were people who helped me and all, but they were warriors, fighters that knew how to take care of themselves. What good could one girl do in a battle against an evil magical queen I thought to myself?

I came out of my self-imposed funk when I heard Roc come back into the apartment from getting the mail. I finished with our lunch and threw some hamburger in some small plates for the two trolls and set them on the floor when Dede came bouncing in the room and stopped and looked at me. "Are you okay Ceri?"

"Yeah I'm fine, I have a lot on my mind," I said as I put our lunch down on the table.

"Oh okay," Dede said as she sat down at the table and started digging into her lunch.

As I sat down next to her, Roc walked in and looked at me and frowned. "Are you okay Princess?" he said.

"Yes I'm fine and the next person in this house that asks me that question is going to have a very nasty burn to contend with. Does everyone get that?"

It got really quiet in the room, so quiet that I could hear the footsteps of the little trolls walking back into the kitchen, probably drawn by the smell of the food I had put out for them.

I looked over at the two others sitting at the table and settled down and let my temper die a quick death again. "Alright how about we all have a nice quiet lunch and then maybe after we are done cleaning up, I think you and me, Dede, should head back to school."

Dede gave a small groan then relented as she looked over at my face, and then everything went quiet again as we all dug into our lunch.

CHAPTER 13

Sara and Michael slowly moved through the town looking for a certain house on the block they were walking on. They had spent all day sniffing out the creatures from the Others world and trying to find someone that knew where their missing prey was hiding. It took most of the day as the Others were hard to find since most of them lived outside of the town where the technology would not affect them, but the isolation made it easier for the two to interrogate these creatures without much interference.

Slowly they stopped across from the dark gray house with the black trim and stared at it, waiting to see if there was any life behind the closed dark windows. "I say we go in and find this witch and his student and find out what he knows," Michael said as he looked over at his sister.

Sara slowly shook her head at her brother's impatience and smiled. "No, we will wait and see what this witch does. Who knows, brother, he may lead us to the ones we want without our uhm, help."

"As always, you are right sister, but it is no fun standing around waiting for something to happen."

"I know brother," Sara said as she looked at the houses around them. "Let's wait in here," she said as she walked up the walkway of the house that was across from the witch's.

Sara saw the curtains move and flutter as they reached the porch and the inside door was opened by a small old woman as Sara reached out to knock on the outer door.

"Who are you two?" a gruff loud voice issued from the old lady standing in her doorway, looking at the two young kids through thick bubble-like glasses.

"Why we need to stay here for awhile to watch for some old friends," Sara sang, her voice flowing through the air.

"What? What was that? You can't stay here, go away!" the woman said as she started to slam the door shut on her two intruders.

"Oh I don't think that will work, old one," Michael said as he slammed open the outer door and then pushed open the inner door with such force that the old lady bounced off the wall and landed on the floor of her living room.

As she looked up, the look on the young man's face froze her blood. She slowly tried to back away from him as he entered her home. "You need to leave my home now. This is my house if you don't leave I'll call the police," she pleaded as she reached out for the phone that sat on an end table.

Michael waved his hand and the old lady froze in place. "Oh, I don't think we want this police person to visit right now do we old one?" Michael said with a grin.

Sara watched from the doorway and then looked around the other houses in the gathering dark to see if anyone else had noticed this little interplay between her brother and the old woman of this house. Slowly she entered the house and closed both doors as she watched her brother move toward his next meal. Oh, this place was so fun, she thought. There didn't seem to be anyone who could stop their playtime. Who knows, maybe after they find their missing prey her and her brother may stay in this world for a little while since it was so abundant with playful food.

❧❧❧

Even though Saba had been up all night and had a turbulent morning with his student, he found it hard to sleep. Some little nagging thing was hitting at his subconscious and he couldn't pinpoint the problem.

It was something familiar about his student's friend. Something about the smell of her seemed to bring back memories of a time long ago. Saba fell asleep finally the thought of that smell weighing on his mind.

As he slept he dreamed of the one love that he let go, the love that he betrayed and banished to another world, the world that had spawned all these vile filthy creatures that came and infected his world.

Flashes of his dream took him to his past, the past where Ellie and he were in love and happy, and where they worked together to protect this town and world from the Others. Then his accident chasing that dragon down and saving Ellie's life while he lost the use of his legs.

The jealousy of watching her move around and being whole, fighting the Others, watching as the Witches' Council sent another to fight alongside his love, the one he had saved from certain death.

Stephen, yes that was his name, the one that tried to take his love away, even as Saba worked to become whole again. Oh, how they denied it when he had confronted the two, but no he knew better, for no one could love a man that was not whole, not able to protect his love from harm anymore.

Saba tossed around in his sleep as he remembered the look of horror on Stephen's face as Saba showed him how powerful he was. The look that was wiped out by Stephens's death. Then the panic of what he had done set in, and Saba had to do something, anything to save his hide for wasn't he really the only thing standing between this world and the creatures that were out to destroy it once and for all?

Saba grumbled in his sleep and rolled on the bed tossing the blankets and pillows to the floor as the dreams continued. The images swam through his brain of his love, the look on her face when the Council found her guilty of Stephen's death and banished her to the Others world for what she had done. The last smell he had of her as she faded into nothing disappearing from this world . . .

Saba bolted up in his bed as that idea lingered in his head. That smell that his student's friend had given off, it was almost the same as Ellie's, but somewhat different, but how could that be?

Then it hit him. Her friend, his student was hanging with Ellie's daughter, but where and how did she come to be in this world? But if her daughter was here, was Ellie here as well? Saba sat there thinking on how he could get his questions answered when he heard his student quietly moving around the house, getting ready to leave.

Yes, that was the way, he thought. I'll follow the stupid little thing and she will lead me right to the source of all theses troubles. For he knew, deep down, that all the extra creatures he had been encountering lately must come from Ellie. Yes, they must have been sent to torment and test him, that is what his old love is doing.

Saba quietly got up and changed his clothes and got ready to follow his student. Wherever she went, he knew that she would lead him right to Ellie's daughter. Then with a little magic that would loosen the brat's tongue, he would find Ellie and this time, he would make sure that she paid for her betrayal. This time, there would be no easy little thing like a small banishment, no this time she would share the same fate as that cheat, Stephen.

Jamie tried to move quietly around the darkened house so that she wouldn't wake her teacher. She had learned early on that once Saba was in the mood he was that she would pay the price unless she found some way to stay out of his sight.

It was easier now that she was older and could get out on her own, but there had been times when she had been found by her teacher and he had taken out his frustrations and madness on her.

Looking at her watch, Jamie saw that it was close to six o'clock and the darkness should hide her from any prying eyes. She put on an old winter coat that she knew would keep her warm for the long walk to Ceri's apartment and as quietly as she could, she slipped out the door and headed down the block, congratulating herself on getting out of the house without having Saba causing a scene.

Who knows, she thought, maybe if she was lucky she could talk Ceri's parents into taking her in if she explained how her teacher treated her. If not, then maybe, after all this mess was done, she would take off on her own. No matter what her parents, the council, or her teacher thought she was a witch that could take care of herself.

Saba watched from behind a tree across the street, as his student moved down the block. He felt secure in his vantage point as he had popped up here with a shield around him that he knew the dumb student would never penetrate. Yeah, he thought, after this maybe it was time he found someone more suited to his talents; someone that would obey him as he trained them as he once was trained.

As Jamie turned the corner, Saba noticed her stop and slowly look around, then head to her left and into the main part of town. Just as he stepped from behind the tree to follow his student, a sweet singing voice sounded from behind him. "Why look sister, a witch, now where do you think he is off to?

⌘⌘⌘⌘⌘⌘

Finishing up some last minute school work, I noticed that it was close enough to three o'clock and decided that the school day was over for Dede and me. "Come on kiddo, time to take a break since Mom and Dad will be home in a little bit," I said sliding over to Dede's school area and looking at where she was on her homework.

"Okay," the chipper little voice rang out as Dede started to shut down her class page. "I was pretty much done anyways, and besides this is all so boring."

Yeah, well it may be boring, but you don't want to grow up to be ignorant do you?" I asked as I logged back into her class work. "And besides, you know Mom wants me to check your work each night before we shut down."

Dede grimaced at me and slid out of the way so that I could scroll through her classes, checking to make sure that all her work was done. "Well, did I pass?" she asked with that little smirk of hers brightening her face.

"Yeah, looks good for today," I answered knowing that as much of a pain the little troublemaker was, she never had had trouble getting her work done. It was just that Mom and Dad had me check in case Dede ever got it in her head to slack off.

Getting up and stretching to get the kinks out, I remembered that I had promised my Mom that I would get some dinner going this evening since we would have guests. Who knows maybe even Jamie would stop by and make the merry crowd bigger.

Walking into the kitchen, I noticed that I had a little shadow following me. "You know, you can go play or something kiddo, right?" I said as I looked over my shoulder at Dede.

"Oh yeah, I know," she said as she grabbed one of the kitchen chairs and pulled it up to the end of the counter.

"Okay," I said as I started to pull stuff out of the cupboards and fridge. As I cut up the ingredients and threw them in a big pot, I glanced over at Dede and noticed that she seemed to be lost in her own thoughts.

"Uhm Ceri?

"Yeah what's up kiddo? Something on your mind?"

"Well yeah," she said as she squirmed in her chair. "I was wondering if you could teach me how to do the things you can do?"

"What, you mean what you saw this afternoon kind of stuff kiddo?"

"Yeah, that."

I finished up filling the pot and then added some water and turned the stove on medium as I thought about what Dede was asking. I knew that this was something new to her, but I still wasn't sure that teaching her the tricks I knew would be such a smart idea. I mean she was such a troublemaker as is, that teaching her how to control elements such as fire or water would only increase her trouble factor by a thousand.

"Okay kiddo I'll teach you how to do the elemental magic, but I don't know for sure if you have it in you to do it yet," I said as I walked over to the counter where Dede sat.

"Yeah but Mom and Dad can do magic so I should be able to do it, right?"

"Well, we will see. Remember it could be that you aren't old enough yet for the magic to manifest itself, okay?"

"Yeah okay," Dede said with a slight frown on her face. "But we will try, right?"

"Yeah we'll give it a go right now," I said as I pulled up a chair next to my sister.

"Okay now hold still, I want to check something," I said leaning in closer to Dede.

She backed up a little with a small look of fright on her face. "Uhm what's you doing?"

"Just checking to see if I could feel any magic coming from you," I said with a small laugh at the look on her face. Usually, it was me that was worried what the little troublemaker was up to and not the other way around.

Dede sat up straight again and gave me a sheepish smile. "Oh, right. I knew that."

"Right, sure you did," I said as I laid my arm on hers. "Now quiet and hold still while I concentrate for a second."

I sat there for a few seconds trying to feel the power that I had felt in Jamie and the ley line, that magical spark within, and sure enough there it was. A tiny little spark almost like a heartbeat all its own that lodged deep within the little one that sat before me.

"Well?' a tiny little voice sounded and broke my concentration.

I held out my hand for her to see as a minuscule bright flame formed in the palm of my hand. "See this; this is your first lesson to make a flame like this."

"But how?"

"Hold out your hand flat like I have and think of a small flame in it," I said as I took Dede's diminutive hand and opened it flat on the counter.

"That would not be a good idea, little ones," Roc's voice sounded from the kitchen doorway.

I turned to look at the dragon and was going to tell him what I thought about his advice when I felt a flash of heat and a tiny yell come from beside me. I turned back and saw that Dede seemed to be lost in some trance and there was a large flame emitting from her open palm.

I quickly grabbed her hand within mine and closed it into a fist, hopefully extinguishing the flame while with my other hand I shook Dede to get her out of the trance she seemed to be in.

"DEDE STOP, NOW!" I yelled and shook her hard as I felt our hands heat up.

Dede blinked her eyes and then I could feel the heat in her fist die a quick death. "Did I do it?" she asked as she came back to this world looking confused, but excited at the same time.

"Oh yeah, you did it little one," Roc answered in a sarcastic breath as he walked out to the living room, his quiet laughter following in his wake.

Dede looked at Roc with a puzzled look on her face and

then turned to me. "What's up with him, Ceri?"

"Nothing but the usual, kiddo," I said with a small laugh of my own. "Now let's try that again, but this time not so much concentration and a little less fire, okay?"

"Uhm sure," Dede said with a look of confusion on her face.

I opened her hand again and laid it out on the counter before us. "Think of a small flame, but stay focused on it. Don't concentrate so hard that you lose yourself in the heat and fire."

"OH, like that?" Dede said with a small laugh as a tiny blue flame lay flickering in the palm of her hand.

"Yeah that's a girl," I said as my earlier qualms disappeared with the sound of her laughter ringing in my ears.

❧⚜❧⚜❧⚜

An hour later after all the practice, one exhausted little girl was lying on the couch watching Spongebob while I was setting the table when I heard the front door open and my parents walk into the apartment.

Did I say, exhausted little girl? I guess that must have been me that was tired, because as soon as the front door opened, a streak left the couch and the whole neighborhood heard all about the cool stuff that I had taught her.

I could hear Mom and Dad's laughter as they listened to Dede's chatter and hear Roc's grumble about teaching young ones magic when the teacher was still learning their own limitations. I smiled to myself and walked out into the living room.

"Hey, guys dinner is almost ready," I said.

"Smells good, what did you make?" Dad asked as he took a deep whiff of my cooking slowly wafting in from the kitchen.

"Oh threw in some ingredients and made a big pot of chili," I said with no small amount of pride.

Everyone then separated and headed to their own little before-dinner chores. Ten minutes later, we were all sitting down at the table when I heard a tiny knock at the front door. "I'll get it," I said as I hopped up from the table figuring that it was Jamie at the door.

"Ceri stop!" Dad said, his tone of voice stopping me in midstride.

Dad looked at Roc and the dragon nodded back at him and then headed to the door. I looked at my dad and sighed with frustration. "It's Jamie, Dad."

"Yeah, well we will see, okay. Remember it's better to be safe than sorry."

"Yeah okay," I said then gave him a pointed look as both Roc and Jamie walked into the kitchen.

Dad smiled but ignored my look as his smile slowly disappeared. It was then that I turned and looked at Jamie and saw that she was sporting a black eye and bruises on her face.

Mom was up out of her chair and across the room as soon as she noticed Jamie's face. "What happened to you, dear?" Mom asked cupping her face with both hands looking closely at the bruises.

"It was nothing; my teacher, for some reason, was a little mad at me I guess. Something I did wrong this morning when I got home," Jamie said a single tear slowly coursing its way down her check.

Dad came and stood next to Jamie, the look on his face telling me exactly what he would do this teacher if he had been here right this moment. I looked over at Roc and saw the same look that my dad wore and noticed his fist opening and closing slowly at his side.

"Come on honey, I have something for that, it will take away the pain," Mom said as she steered Jamie out of the room and toward the bathroom.

Jamie stopped in her tracks and turned back to all of us and took a deep breath. "It's okay, it doesn't hurt that much."

"I know, but no sense being in any pain at all; go with my wife and she will help you."

"Alright, but first I need to let you know that my teacher is also mad at you guys and I think he will be coming after you, especially you Ceri," Jamie said.

"Me? Why me?" I asked puzzled wondering why someone else was picking a fight with me. Couldn't these big, bad, and uglies go beat up on someone big like Roc?

"I'm not sure, I know that my teacher seemed real out of it and was losing what little sanity he had in the first place."

"Not to worry little one, if he comes here I think he will find more than he bargained for, right Bill?" Roc said with a wicked smile lighting up his face.

"It will be alright, you go and let Jenna take a look at your face, and I think it would be better if you stayed here with us for awhile too," Dad said as Mom led Jamie out of the room.

The rest of us sat back at the table even though none of us was really all that hungry anymore. Heck, even the trolls ignored the food that I had set out for them and sat quietly until Mom and Jamie's return.

The silence was broken about ten minutes later when Mom entered the kitchen and sat down at the table. I had seen the look she now wore and I knew that it did not bode well for whoever it was aimed at. "Jaime will be out in a second, she needed to get cleaned up," she said through clenched teeth.

Dad looked at Mom and before he could ask, she quietly sighed and looked around at us all. "The marks on her face are not the only ones on her body. That child does not go back to that monster, Bill."

Dad said nothing for a second and then opened his mouth to respond when we all heard a loud pounding at the front door and someone yelling at the top of their voice to let them in.

CHAPTER 14

Saba turned toward the voice behind him, his face a mask of confusion and shock wondering how somebody could see through the magical shield he had thrown up around him. Then his face fell as he noticed the two young people standing before him.

"Seems like the witch here, brother, is not so happy to see us, don't you think?" the young beautiful girl whispered to the equally stunning boy standing next to her.

The boy smiled a smile that lit up his face, but in some small measure seemed never to reach his dead eyes. "Oh yes, Sara, it does look like you are right. He does not look very happy to be seeing us."

Saba glanced back up the street and saw that his student was out of sight of the three of them and dropped his shield as he turned back toward the young couple. He had been caught unaware for a second, but with a sniff of the air, it hit him who these two were. "So you're what I smelled last night – angels," Saba spit out the name as if a bad taste had suddenly manifested in his mouth.

"Yes angels," said Sara as the golden glow around her lit up even brighter, "come to save your world."

Saba looked at her with a look of loathing and disgust. "Save it, spawn, for me and the Witches' Council know what kind of creatures you really are."

Sara frowned as the glow slowly died down around her as she glanced over at her brother. The look on his face was blank and she could not tell what was ticking behind those eyes which could not bode well for those around him.

Turning back, a smile returned to her face as she looked at the witch before her one more time. "We find that we need your help, witch, and for that, we will return the favor."

"And what kind of help would such as you two need from me?"

"Well, we seemed to have lost two of our people and this seems to be the only world that they could be on. So you help us find our, uhm, friends and we might find it in our good graces to let you know where a certain portal to the Others world is."

Saba looked down at his feet and then back up at the couple, an evil smile lighting up his face. "What makes you think that I need your help in finding this portal, creature?"

"Watch your tongue, witch," Michael growled. "For you

are not as powerful as you think, and we are not as weak as you wish us to be."

The smile slowly slipped off of his face as he thought over the boy's words. "Alright, who are these friends of yours? Lost angels, I take it?" Saba said with a small chuckle at his own little joke.

Sara reached out in a flash and grabbed the small, chubby witch by the throat and pulled him close to her body, her face only inches from his. He could feel his bladder release as he looked into those dead eyes, and watched as her face slowly morphed into something hideous. The skin of her face seemed to pull tight against her skull and her teeth lengthened into razor-sharp daggers. The smell that wafted from her breath stank of death and decay as from an old open grave.

"We are looking for demons, witch, and it would be in your best interest to help us with no back talk. Do you understand?" Sara said as she tossed Saba up against the tree behind him.

As he righted himself up against the rough bark of the tree, Saba looked up at the female angel and saw that her face was back to the angelic form it had been before. "Alright I will help you, but you have to show me where this portal is."

Michael looked down at the witch and smiled. "Fine, witch, if you help us find these demons then you will have your portal."

Saba didn't really trust the angels, for he knew that down through the ages others before him had had dealings with these creatures and not always for the betterment of the witches involved.

"Okay, and when you find these demons, then what happens?"

Michael looked down at the witch and then reached down to help him back off of the ground. "Why then we bring them back home where they belong," he said as he brushed the dirt and dead leaves off of the witch's clothes.

"Now do you, or do you not know where these demons are?" Sara said as she slid closer once more toward Saba her anger once more bubbling toward the surface of her being.

"Sister, sister please this witch is now our friend. There is no need to hurt this one," Michael said as he slowly moved his sister away from Saba.

As Sara moved away from the two men standing on the sidewalk, Michael looked back at Saba and gave him an apologetic smile. "You must forgive my sister, usually, it is me that is so, uhm how shall we say temperamental. It must be something about you, witch, that sets her off so, don't you think?"

"Yes, well I not sure," Saba said as he warily eyed Sara.

"That's alright, don't worry about it, witch, I'm sure that you and she will become fast friends soon," Michael said with that peculiar smile of his lighting his face.

"Yeah well, don't hold your breath on that thought," Saba said gaining some of his former bravado.

Michael looked at Saba for a moment, the smile fading before it returned full force a second later. "Yes well, now about these demons?"

Saba stood there and looked at Michael and then back at Sara who was now slowly making her way back to the two of them, the same strange smile as her brother's once again lighting her face.

"Well, yes I think I know where they are or at least I think my student knows where your demons live."

"Oh, and where is this student of yours?" Michael asked in a sugary voice.

Saba once again became alert to a certainty that he was in a danger that he still didn't fully comprehend. "I was following her, she was that girl that went around the corner, just as you snuck up on me."

"Oh, so that is why you were hiding out here, witch? So that she could not catch you spying on her. Why she must be very powerful indeed that you need to follow her in secret, don't you think sister?" Michael said glancing over at Sara with a wide grin.

Saba straightened up as much as he could on his crippled legs, puffing out his chest insulted that these two creatures could think that he was afraid of his student. "I am not afraid of that stupid girl, of someone with no power at all. I will have you know that I am the most powerful of all the council in this area."

Slowly Saba stopped as he realized what he was blurting out to the two angels and watching fearfully the slow predatory smiles that were crossing each young face. "Why thank you for that information, witch, don't you think that was nice of him to tell us this sister?"

"Oh, yes I do Michael," Sara said as she stepped forward and waved her hand in Saba's direction.

Before he could move Saba felt his whole body freeze as if it was made of stone, and no matter how he tried he could not move anything except his mouth. "What have you creatures done to me?" he whispered through frightened lips.

"Why nothing at all, witch, we think that it is time to get rid of the trash," Sara said with a small laugh.

"Wait, please," Saba whispered as Sara moved closer to him, once again her face taking on the look that had so frightened him before.

"And we should wait why witch?" Michael asked as he held his arm up in front of Sara to stop her from killing the lowly creature before him.

"Because there is the girl, the Other that is with my student and you will need my help to get rid of her," Saba said knowing that if he didn't win this argument he would soon be dead.

Both Sara and Michael stood quietly staring at Saba then each glanced over at the other at the same time. "And this Other, you think that she is with our demons witch?"

"Yes, please I can help, you will need my help. It is she that drained the power from the ley line last night, and killed some creatures in the park, I think."

"Creatures, what creatures were these witch?" Michael asked.

Saba thought quickly back to last night to what he had detected at the park and answered the two angels. "One was an ogre at the park's parking lot and at the ley line, I could detect some other creature's essences, something like a snake or some such creature, I'm not sure exactly what it was in that I had never seen or smelled anything like it before."

Sara looked at Michael and sighed, "Guess our little pet Tiss met his match in this little friend of his student." Michael nodded his head in agreement.

Saba looked at the two creatures as sweat slowly ran down his forehead. He wasn't surprised that he was sweating even in the cold winter air in that he now figured that he was fighting for his life, never mind that he was probably giving information that could be dooming his student and most certainly her friend to their own death.

Michael waved his hand and Saba could feel that once again he had full control of his body. "Witch, you are very lucky this night for you will live a while longer. Now how do we find this student of yours?"

Saba flexed his arms and legs and then leaned back against the tree behind him for support. "First, you must promise me that I will live, and then I will give you my student, her friend and the demons you seek."

"Witch, you push your luck with us," Michael said stepping toward Saba, his hands balled into fists. "You know not what tortures we can inflict on you."

But this time, it was Sara that held out her arm and held her brother back from tearing into the witch in front of them. "No, wait brother he is right. It would take us awhile to find his student and then we would not be sure that we would find this friend or the demons. Besides, I think I am kind of starting to like this scum."

"Uhm, yeah, thanks, I think?" Saba said as he looked over at Sara with relief.

Sara glanced over at Saba and smiled. "Oh you are welcome, witch, but don't think for a second that I will not kill you just like that," Sara said snapping her tiny fingers under Saba's nose.

"Yes, yes fine I understand, I need to live because without me then who will protect this world from creatures like the Others," Saba said puffing out his chest once more trying to impress the two angels with his own importance.

Michael smiled and looked Saba up and down and then looked over the street they were on now realizing that they had been standing in the open far too long. Even though the street was dark and quiet, it was still not good to draw attention to themselves even if there really was no one in this town that could really hurt them.

Sara caught her brother's look and then motioned to the witch in front of her. "Alright. witch then how do we follow your student now that you have let her go?"

Saba looked at the angel and sputtered a little bit then mumbled something under his breath that neither of the other two could catch. "What was that witch?" Sara said a sick smile once again crossing her face.

"Nothing, forget it," Saba said taking a deep, calming breath.

"Yeah that's what I thought you would say," Sara said. "Now tell us how we follow your student, witch."

"No problem really, I put a magical trace on the stupid little girl that only I can track. She will lead me right to her friend and probably your demons."

"You mean to lead us to the ones we want?" Michael whispered.

"Yeah, yeah sure that's exactly what I mean."

"Sure it is, witch, sure it is. Now lead on and let's go find our friends," Sara said giving Saba a not so gentle push toward the corner that Jamie had disappeared around. As Saba staggered down the block, both brother and sister looked at each other and smiled at the knowledge they shared that this was going to be the witch's last night on this world.

☙❧☙❧☙❧

Saba lead the two angels across town thinking of ways in which he could escape or kill the two of them, for he had no doubt in his hate filled mind that once his usefulness was done he would die. After all, he thought it would be what he would do to any Other that he had caught in a similar situation, use them and then get rid of them when they were worthless to him.

The magical trace he had planted on his student was working perfectly and soon lead the trio toward a group of apartments. Saba stopped at the entrance of the driveway and walked over to an empty dark bus stop and sat down on the seat, for the long walk was killing his still crippled legs.

As he leaned his two crutches against the wall of the bus stop, he once again thought why he was in this condition and cursed the one woman who he blamed for his problems. Looking up at the two angels he could see that they were rather annoyed at this stoppage in the hunt for his student, but at the moment, he thought I could really give a damn what these two think.

"What's the matter witch, not as powerful as you thought you where?" Sara asked in a mocking tone.

Saba stared at the other two and grumbled, "We're almost there, I can feel her close by. I need a second to rest."

Michael pulled Saba to his feet and shoved his crutches toward the witch. "You can rest when we find her and not before then, witch."

Saba sighed, here was another act or proof that his life was so overburdened, but what was a righteous person to do, but carry on. "Fine, fine let me get settled," Saba said as he slid his arms inside the round metal parts of his crutches.

"Where exactly is your student?" Sara asked looking around at the large, long apartment building that stretched before them.

Saba pointed with a crutch toward one side of the apartment complex. "Over there on that side. As we get closer to her, I'll be able to narrow it down for you."

"Okay well then let's go, we waste time standing here and talking," Michael said as he gave Saba another not so gentle push toward the apartments.

The three moved toward what looked like the main office and a fenced swimming pool as they entered the drive and the two angels watched Saba as he stopped and then slowly turned in a half circle sniffing the air.

"That way," Saba said as he moved down the driveway now passing a gray block of metal mailboxes. Slowly the trio moved down the drive, passing a smaller drive that leads to their left. Passing a group of garages on both sides now they came to another small driveway and parking area to their right.

Saba stopped once more and then looked over his shoulder at the two angels with a wicked smile. "This way, she is in one of these apartments to the right," he said as he headed off at a fast shuffle down the drive.

Michael and Sara followed the witch to the end of the apartments and saw that the entrance way was set up for a group of four apartments. The two to the left both upper and lower looked bigger than their companions on the right. "Well, which one is it, witch?" Sara hissed.

"I'll have to go up to the doors and see which one she went through," Saba hissed right back. "Just stay here and I'll call you when I see which one it is, alright?"

Both angels were not keen on this idea but figured that if Saba's student, her friend and two demons were in one of those apartments sending the witch in first might not be such a bad idea after all. "Alright, witch, but no tricks."

Saba nodded and then walked to the bottom two apartments and stopped before each door. The two angels could see him slowly shake his head at each then walk back to the bottom of the stairs that lead up to the two upper apartments. Sighing and putting both crutches in his right hand he grabbed the railing and hauled himself up the stairs.

At the top, he hauled himself to the door on the left and sniffed at it and then turned and smiled at the two angels and gave them a thumbs up. Both Sara and Michael were puzzled by this action but figured it meant that he had found his student when Saba started pounding on the door. Now both angels slowly pulled back into the dark and watched what would happen next before following the witch into the apartment.

⌒✦⌒✦⌒✦

Dad went and opened the door this time with Roc and Mom following close behind him. Jamie had emerged from the back room and stood at the end of the hallway as I felt Dede's small hand slip into mine.

Seconds later a small dumpy man with red hair flying all around his head followed Dad down the short hall from the front door and into the living room. Dad stopped next to the other two adults thus blocking any further attempt by the man to come further into our house.

There we all stood for a few minutes, all of us looking at our strange new visitor. He was quiet until his eyes finally found Jamie cowering by the hall. "There you are, girl; you need to come home with me now."

Mom shook her head and Dad and Roc stepped forward toward Jamie's teacher. "Are you her parent?" Dad asked as he looked over the disheveled wild-eyed man that stood before us.

"No, I'm not, but it is none of your business who I am," he said as he looked at each of the adults before him. Looking once more at Jamie, he growled, "Come along girl, don't make this any worse for yourself."

Roc let loose his own growl and stepped toward the little man, but stopped as Dad blocked his way with his arm. Saba looked over at the two and smiled. "Careful dragon for I know what to do with the likes of you."

"Yeah, I think Jamie will stay here with us, so you can leave our home," Mom said as she stepped up closer next to Dad.

Jamie's teacher took in the three standing before him and then looked at the three of us kids standing over by the kitchen, then glanced around the living room. "You call this a home, more like a hovel," he sniffed." Give me my student now!" he said in a low menacing voice.

"Yeah well as my wife said, Jamie stays here and you can leave our home."

"Yeah I don't think so," the man said as he pushed a balled fist toward the three adults that soon found themselves lying on the floor unable to move or even to cry out.

Jamie's teacher looked at them and over at us and smiled a crooked, evil little grin and moved into the living room. "Now if you three little children don't want the same, you will come with me."

The three of us stood there for a second in shock that is until all hell broke loose for the chubby little man before us.

I could feel the power rolling off the witch and before I could think about it, I reached quickly with one hand and pulled all his power out of him. With my other hand, I threw the power of earth at the witch and he froze in place with an astonished look on his face.

Unfortunately, for him his bad night didn't end with being turned into a statue, for no sooner did I act then Dede, Jamie, and the two trolls hit him seconds later. I saw a flash of water fly by my head followed closely by what looked like a small ice ball.

As the water and ice hit the now rock solid witch at the same time, I heard what sounded like a large crack of ice and saw him glitter, that is until the two trolls that were now fire demons hit him. As all three of them hit the floor, I heard and saw Jamie's teacher disintegrate into a small pile of rock and dust.

Oops, I guess that was a little overkill I thought as both trolls backed off of what was left of Jamie's teacher and Mom, Dad, and Roc climbed off of the floor.

Everyone was silent for a minute until Roc looked over at us three girls and laughed. "Oh yes, little ones really remind me not to make you mad at me, okay?"

Mom and Dad looked at Roc and then over at us and shook their heads. "Well you did warn him to leave, Daddy, didn't you?" Dede asked in a low voice.

"Yeah honey, your daddy did indeed tell him to leave," Mom said as she slowly walked over to Dede and started her down the hall. "Come on, time to pack some stuff for a move while your daddy and Roc clean up the mess."

"Oh okay, Mommy," Dede said as she happily turned to the two trolls who had now turned back into a regular cat and dog. "Come on Scom and Tessa, let's go get our stuff packed."

Both trolls happily followed the little troublemaker and Mom down the hall to the bedrooms.

"Uhm was that Dede that threw the ice?" Dad asked.

I shook my head looking at the pile on the floor remembering another pile of ice that I once saw like this one and a small tear rolled down my cheek. "Don't cry, Ceri, he isn't worth it, believe me I know, I lived with him long enough," Jamie said as she leaned over and hugged me.

I smiled and hugged her back. "Yeah I know Jamie; thinking of someone else.

Then it hit me what Mom had said and turned to ask my dad what move we were going to take when another knock came at our front door. Both Roc and Dad looked at each other and both shrugged their shoulders as they moved toward the door.

I slid over and listened as they opened the front door and started to answer the questions of our downstairs neighbor.

After about five minutes, Dad and Roc moved back into the living room after getting rid of our nosy neighbor. Dad looked at me and then over at Jamie with a weary look. "Okay, Ceri how about you get some stuff together for you and Jamie for we're going to leave in about a half an hour."

"What? But why are we going anywhere?" I asked.

Dad looked at the pile of dirt that was once Jamie's teacher.

"Oh, yeah, that. Uhm can't you sort of magic it away or something?"

Dad smiled and shook his head. "No sorry honey, it doesn't work that way. We need to move and besides, I think too many people know where we live."

"So where are we going?" Jamie asked

"Well . . ." Dad started to say when Roc cut him off.

"I have a place down on the Southside of town that overlooks Boulevard Park," Roc said.

"You have room for all of us?" Dad asked

"Yeah don't worry, I got all the room we need," Roc said. "As I said, with my dragon hoard I thought ahead and I have a couple of hidey holes spread around the state."

Dad took a deep breath of relief and then turned to Jamie and I. "Okay girls, go get some stuff together, and Ceri only the necessities, okay."

"Yeah okay, Dad," I said as I grabbed Jamie by the arm and hurried her toward my room.

CHAPTER 15

Sara and Michael watched from the dark as the downstairs neighbor went back to his apartment. "Well looks like the witch met his match, doesn't it brother?" Sara said with a small smile.

"Yes, I guess sending him up to check out the situation by himself was prudent, sister."

"Yes it was, now we need to see what comes out of the apartment."

Michael looked at his sister as she stared at the apartment with a feral look on her face. "You think they will move to someplace else, Sara?"

Sara glanced over at her brother and then back at the apartment. "Yes I think that they are smart enough to know to change their position once it has been compromised, I mean they have been on the run for a long time."

Both of the angels settled down in the cold and dark, not moving as the wind whipped around their thinly clad bodies until the door that they had been so focused on finally opened up. Michael started to step forward, but Sara held him back and shook her head, as the multitude that emerged from the apartment crowded into a car and truck and took off into the night.

Michael turned with a seldom manifested anger toward his sister. "We could have had them, sister, why did you stop me?"

Sara looked back at her brother and smiled. "You did see that they had a dragon with them, didn't you?"

"So what is a dragon to us? I also saw that they had three young ones with them too. They would have been distracted by trying to protect them and the dragon would have been an easy kill."

"Brother, oh brother then you did not notice the two hell beasts that were with them or that one of those young ones was their offspring?"

Michael's eyes got wide at this news and then looked back at his sister with renewed respect. "Are you sure that one of them was their offspring, for then we would not need them and it would be so much easier if we could kill them instead of taking the demons alive."

"Oh yes, I am quite sure brother. It was the youngest of the children, the one that the female demon carried, and you are right it will make it much easier to use her than her parents for our mission," Sara said with an evil laugh ringing through her words.

"Well then, I think we should still have attacked them and taken the girl, sister."

Sara reached up and slowly patted Michael on the face lightly, something that always annoyed him even though he loved his sister in his own way. "Don't worry, we will get them. But I want to even the odds a little more so that they are, let's say, in our favor brother."

"And how do you propose to do that, sister?"

"Well, we hear that Queen Ellie has someone in this world that is looking for her daughter, and that that someone has put a price on her head, brother?"

"Well, yes and so what? How does that help us?"

Sara sighed as she thought how great her brother was in a fight, but not always so brilliant in figuring out ideas before the fight. "It's easy brother, we find this person, Regni, I think his name is, and we get him to kill all but the little child and then we take her home with us."

Michael stood quietly for a second and then smiled at his sister's plan. As usual, she was as efficient as she was lethal. "Yes sister, you're right. Let's go find this Regni and help him find his prey."

Once more Sara stopped her brother and shook her head.

"No Michael, you follow the vehicles and find out where they are going. I will find the ones we seek and enlist their help."

Michael frowned and thought about the idea of being separated from Sara, but knew that she was better in dealing with people and probably would have better luck without him getting in the way. "Alright sister, but where do we meet?"

"Remember where the portal is?"

"Yes."

"Then once you find where they are staying, that's where I will be with the ones we need."

"Okay," Michael said as he headed out to follow the cars, but stopped at Sara's next words.

"Oh and Michael?" Sara growled, her voice a low deep sound.

"Yes?"

"Don't go it alone, Michael dear. I would hate to lose you to the demon, and so would mother."

Michael stared at Sara and then shuddered at the thought of his mother. "You aren't going to tell mother are you?"

Sara grinned and looked at her brother. "Of course not brother, just stick to the plan alright?"

"Yes Sara," Michael said as he headed off to follow the demons and their helpers; the smell of the demons wafting in the air making it easier to follow where they may have gone.

Sara watched her brother head off into the dark, cold night and thought that it was such a good thing that she loved her brother so because there were times where it would be easier to get rid of him than to put up with him.

Well, who knew maybe when they got home mother would tire of him and give Michael to her to play with. Then Sara shuddered as Michael had earlier when she thought of her mother. If they didn't return home soon, her mother may be mad enough to have some fun with both of them and that was never an idea to contemplate, especially when she had seen what was left of her mother's playthings after she was done with them.

෩෨෩෨෩෨

As we drove away from our home, I thought I caught sight of two black shadows standing near the garages but didn't mention anything as everyone seemed so on edge and in a rush to get to this new place that Roc had in mind.

It was probably only my imagination anyways from everything that had happened this winter's night. My thoughts drifted back to all that had happened and then the quick packing that had followed.

"Come on girls, we don't have all night," Mom said as she

zipped back down the hall toward her bedroom, then suddenly she was back in the doorway of my room with that look that I knew so well. The one that said I wasn't going to like the wisdom she was going to pass on to me, but I was going to follow it, "Ceri when Dad said the necessities he did not mean your gaming stuff."

I looked at the gaming system and the few disks I was packing in my duffle bag and then back at my mom. "Uhm this are my necessities in my life, Mom," I answered looking over at Jamie for some help and moral support.

"Don't look at me; I don't even know what any of that stuff is," she said looking a little put out at being dragged into our conversation.

Mom smiled at Jamie and then turned back to me. "See Ceri there are kids out there that can live without gaming. Now dump that stuff and pack some clothes, and only the necessities that you need to function with, young lady," Mom said as she popped out of the room once more.

"Suck up," I said turning to Jaime as Mom popped her head back into the room again.

Jamie stuck her tongue out at me with a smile as Mom gave me a frown. "And Ceri don't forget your laptop." Then she was gone again.

I dumped my duffle out on my bed and had started emptying out my drawers when my Dad popped his head into my room and looked at my bed where all my gaming stuff now lay. "Ceri, you can't take all that gaming stuff with us," he said.

Jamie gave out a small laugh at the look on my face. "Yeah I know, Dad, Mom told me," I said with some frustration inflecting my voice.

"Oh well okay then, but let's get a move on in case we have any more visitors," he said as he too disappeared toward the living room like my mom had done only minutes earlier.

I looked at Jamie who was now rolling on my bed, laughing at me and threw some of my clothes at her. "Here as soon as you're done having a fit, how about you help me pack."

It took the two of us no time at all until we had the things we needed all packed and ready to rock and roll. Pulling my duffle off the bed and throwing it over my shoulder, Jamie grabbed up the two small suitcases that were lying on the floor and we followed my parents out to the living room.

Roc looked at what we were carrying and a look of determination crossed his face. "Princess, I think you need to leave some of that stuff behind. Where we are going we won't really have the place or time for you to do this gaming stuff you do so much."

I stopped and looked Roc up and down and threw my bag down at his feet as Mom and Dad came out of the kitchen with a small box of food. "Okay to let everyone know, there are no games in my stuff, and this is the necessities that two girls need, okay?"

The three adults looked at Jamie and I then down at the bags. I could see that Dad was opening his mouth to say something when Mom poked him from behind. "It's alright, Ceri, I understand, just grab up your stuff," Mom said with a small smile playing across her lips.

"Yeah okay," I said still not mollified that everyone thought that I would sneak my game stuff in my bags. Yeah well, okay maybe the thought did cross my mind, but with Jamie in my room, I thought it would be prudent to follow orders this one time.

"Okay, here is how we should do this," Roc said as he looked us all over. "I'll take point with the trolls, Jenna and Dede behind me then the girls and Bill will bring up the rear. Also, I think that Jenna should carry Dede in case we need to move fast. Any questions?"

No one answered so Roc turned toward the door when I picked up my bag and threw it once more over my shoulders. Mom was loaded down with Dede and her backpack. While Dad had two duffle bags like mine and the box of food in his hands.

"Uhm, hey dragon," I asked as I looked at all the stuff that everyone was loaded down with, "a little help here?"

Roc stopped and Dad smiled and shook his head. "It's alright Ceri. Roc needs his hands empty in case there is someone waiting out there for us. Now let's not waste any more time and get this show on the road, okay everyone?"

I shrugged my shoulders and followed my Mom out the door with Jamie right behind me. I looked back as Dad shut the door, but I didn't see him lock it as we started down the steps. "Uhm Dad what if someone gets in," I asked.

"Ceri, whatever is in there doesn't matter anymore, for we probably won't be back after this."

I stopped and then started down again as I thought over what I had heard. "Oh I see, I guess," I said as we hit the cars and started to load our stuff into the trunk.

We split up and then all headed to this new place that was Roc's hidey hole. Driving through town, watching all the other people walking and driving getting ready for the holidays I felt a little resentful that my life seemed to be such a mess. Here I was some normal girl leaving everything behind that I knew because some creatures of myth and fairy tales were after me. My life was so weird right now.

❦❦❦❦❦❦

When we finally arrived at Roc's place we followed the reverse of how we came out of our apartment, with Roc and the trolls leading and the rest of us following with Dad bringing up the rear guard.

I don't know what I was expecting, but you think with a

dragon hoard that he kept bragging about Roc could have afforded a bigger place than the little two bedroom, one bath condo we entered.

"This is your hidey hole?" I asked my voice filled with doubt and a little bit of scorn.

"It's supposed to be a place to hide Princess, not a place to vacation," Roc said looking around him with some pride and love.

"It will do Roc, thanks for letting us use it," Mom said as she moved into the small living room with a sleeping Dede lying in her arms. "Where can I put her?" Mom asked.

"Use the bedroom on the left," Roc answered, pointing down the short hall. "You and Bill can bunk there with the little one. There is a small cot in the closet that will fit her."

"And what of Jamie and me, where do we sleep?" I asked as I headed down toward the other room with Jamie following close behind me.

Roc stepped in front of us and pointed at the two large couches in the living room. "Really, are you serious?" I asked as I spied the couches one of which Tessa had hopped up on and the other that Scom was trying to get on with little success.

"There are blankets and pillows in this hall closet," Roc answered my inquiry while opening a folding door to his right with a smile.

I was opening my mouth to let him know in no uncertain terms that we would not be sleeping on those couches when my dad stepped in front of me and laid his arms on my shoulders. "Listen, Ceri, we all need to live in this small area without causing trouble," he said as he looked around the small condo.

"Yeah, sure Dad no problem," I said now feeling guilty at my attitude.

"Good. Roc and I are going to get the rest of the stuff in from the car and then we are going to ditch them, so we will be back in a little while. Let your mom know where we are."

I stared at the two men as they walked out of the condo and shut the door. Damn, we must really be in trouble if the two of them thought that we needed to get rid of our vehicles to throw off whoever they thought was after us. Turning to Jamie, I looked over at our new beds and asked her, "So flip you for the one without the cat on it?"

Jamie smiled and walked over to where Tessa was lying and picked up the mangy looking cat and hugged her to her chest. "It's okay, I'll take this one." Tessa purred loudly in the witch's arms and twitched her nose at me. This cat was almost as annoying as a certain dragon I knew.

Michael looked up at the building from across the train tracks deep within the shadows of the park trees. He saw which apartment that his prey was in because they never took the precaution of closing the drapes that could have hidden the room. Seeing the mother and little one in a small back room, he thought maybe he could steal his prize for him and his sister thereby precluding the need of getting outside help from some lowly creatures in this world. All he needed to do was be patient and watch for his chance.

❧❧❧❧❧❧

About fifteen minutes after Dad and Roc dropped off the last of our bags and then left on their car dumping mission, Mom came back into the living room shutting the door to the back room that Dede was in.

"How are you girls doing?" Mom asked as she flopped down in a small armchair near the edge of the living room. "Damn and where did your dad and Roc get to?" she then asked looking around the room and seeing neither of them.

"They left to hide the vehicles," Jamie said as she fluffed out the blankets she had found in the closet.

Mom frowned then looked at me standing at the large glass doors that overlooked the park below and the ocean beyond that. "Ceri, are you alright?" she asked.

"Yeah, no prob, Mom," I said as I stared at the blackness outside the window. When Jamie had turned out the living room lights I could see easier out the windows and watched the dark trees below us and the few lights of the ships that were out plying the ocean on this cold winter night.

I turned to look at my mom and saw by the dim light coming from the kitchen that she looked haggard with worry and tired to boot. "Who are we running from Mom?" I asked.

Mom looked at me and then over at Jamie. "Your dad thought that Jamie's teacher had a slight smell of angels about him. If that is true then we may all be in real trouble," she said with a large sigh.

"Oh, okay," I said as I looked out the glass doors once more. A dark shift in the shadows at the base of the building caught my eyes for a second, and then all was still once again. I turned and looked at my mom and the worry on her face. "Are these angels really as bad as you and Dad think?"

"Yeah honey, they are worse than even your mother. They have no compunction in killing a living being. Believe me; do not be fooled by the name."

"But what do they want with you and Dad?"

"They want us because your Dad is the last in line of those that rule the demons on our world. They think that if they bring us back to our world they can make the rest of the demons do whatever they want."

Both Jamie and I looked at each other at this turn of events and our "OH" echoed each other.

Mom looked at us amused by the expressions on our face and laughed. "Don't worry girls; if there were angels out there I'm sure that we lost them when we came across town."

❧❧❧❧❧❧

Michael quietly moved up the side of the building, climbing to the window of the back room where he had seen the mother demon put down the child he wanted. Slowly he crawled up, stopping only when he thought the one girl looking out the glass doors had seen him.

Getting up the building was not hard for an angel, but it was still work that he was not used to. Getting next to the now dark window, he quickly looked in and saw the small bundle he was looking for laying on a cot at the end of a bigger bed in the room.

Reaching up, he moved his hand over the window and slid it to the side after he heard the lock open. Now all he needed to do was get in without those in the other room hearing him and steal his prize and then he could be his mother's favorite, even if he was a boy.

Climbing through the window like a common thief, he looked down at the bundle sleeping on the cot and thought how jealous Sara was going to be when he showed up at the portal with this child.

As he reached down to lift the child up into his arms with a smile playing over his face at the thought of all the glory he would reap, the door opened and into the room walked the two girls that should have been in the living room. Michael froze for a second then threw a freeze spell at the first girl through the door.

❧❧❧❧❧❧

I was twitchy standing in the room thinking that something was wrong, but not being able to put my finger exactly on what. I started toward the back room, stopping and looking at Mom as she dozed off in the chair she had flopped down in.

Jamie sat up and looked at me. "Where you going Ceri?" she asked with some concern in her voice.

I walked back to the couch she had claimed for her bed and then knelt down next to her. "I don't know, just want to go and check on Dede, I guess. I have this feeling that something is wrong or we are missing something and I want to check on her."

"Oh good, I thought it was just me then. I'll go with you." And with that Jamie rolled out of bed and started toward the back room before I could even stand up again.

We tiptoed down the hall, Jamie opening the door and stepping in the room. As she looked over her shoulder to say something to me, I saw a dark shadow within the room standing over Dede's cot. There was a flash and then Jamie was silently dropping to the floor.

I gave a yell and flung a fireball that connected with the shadow, throwing it against the wall. I dived into the room and grabbed the bundle that was Dede and then jumped out the room's door once again. As I hit the floor, I saw a flame hit the door and char the wood on its edge above my head.

I rolled into Mom's legs and we all went down in a tangle of legs, arms and one small eight-year-old crying in my arms. I threw Dede into Mom's arms and told her to head back down the hallway as I moved back to the bedroom to check on the shadow and the friend I had left in the room.

I peeked around the doorframe and then ducked back, leaning up against the wall. Since no more flashes of flame came at me I lowered myself to the ground to change my position and took a longer look into the dark room.

I stood up and slowly walked into the room, my head swiveling from side to side looking for danger as I flipped on the overhead light, but the room was devoid of any dark flame throwing shadows, or for that matter young witches.

I looked around the room one more time as I slowly walked up to the open window and took a quick peek outside when a noise behind me made me jump and spin around. There was Mom with Dede in her arms, both stifling a gasp and looking at the hand I had cocked back ready to throw a fireball I didn't even remember conjuring up.

"Uhm Ceri you going to throw that at us or put it out?"

Mom asked as Dede buried her head in Mom's shoulder.

"Oh sorry," I said as I snuffed the flame out and then reached up and closed the window. "You guys just startled me."

"Yeah, no worries. Uhm where is Jamie?" Mom asked as she spied the empty room.

"I think whoever was in here grabbed her when I ran out of the room with Dede."

"Oh," was all Mom could muster as she stood in the doorway and looked at me then at the small child lying in her arms.

"Let's wait in the living room until Dad and Roc get back. I don't think it would be a good idea to be in separate rooms right now."

Mom nodded and then stopped dead in her tracks with this peculiar expression on her face. She sniffed the air and then frowning, glanced at Dede and saw she was asleep again and then looked at me. "Oh damn – angels, I smell angels."

I slid the lock on the window and herded the two of them back into the living room. As we entered the room, I could see Tessa standing before the front door and Scom standing at the big glass doors in the living room.

I glanced at them and then at Mom whereas she answered my unasked question. "I told them to keep watch on the other two main entrances, in case there was more than one intruder."

"Yeah good idea, I guess, but a little late for Jamie," I said with a depressed sigh. "Now what do we do?"

Mom laid Dede down on my makeshift bed and covered her up before turning to me and giving me a hug. "As hard as it is going to be, we need to wait until your dad and Roc get back. That's all we can do, because if we rush off after an angel by ourselves we won't be helping Jamie."

I flopped down on the floor and let the misery flow over me as I thought of my friend in the hands of some creatures. Yeah wait, that seems like all I was good at, was waiting.

CHAPTER 16

Michael carried the unconscious girl over his shoulder, walking down the dark wooded gravel path. His chest heavy with pain where the other girl had hit him with the ball of magic she had thrown at him before she grabbed up his prize. His prize, he thought, well that was fine because he now had something of hers.

He stopped on the path, where it dipped deep down into the darkest part of the park and laid his burden down. Two scruffy figures approached him from the other end of the path, both moving in an erratic fashion.

"Hey there fellow, what's you got there?" the smaller of the two asked.

Michael stood there and watched as the two men walked within five feet of him and his burden and stopped, casting glances between Michael and the girl on the ground.

"My friend Jasper here asked you a question boy, what's you got there?" the bigger of the two men asked.

Michael once again remained quiet just taking in the appearance of the two men, the mismatched clothes that reeked of dirt, sweat, and lots of alcohol.

The smaller man glanced at his companion and smiled, taking in the small kid in front of him and the girl that lay on the ground at his feet. "I don't know Oscar, I think maybe he means to hurt that little thing, don't you?"

The bigger man smiled and took a few steps forward, saying with a nasty laugh, "Yeah maybe you're right Jasper; maybe we should rescue her. Who knows how grateful she may be later."

The two of them now looked at each other and nodded and as one started to jump forward at the young kid before them.

Michael waved his hand in front of Jasper who froze in his tracks as he lunged at Oscar and met him in mid-air, the both of them rolling off the path into the dark.

From his vantage point, Jasper could see the bushes moving in the dark, but could hear no sounds from his partner, until he heard what sounded like a fire hose let go and then the gurgle of someone trying to take a breath.

It was quiet then in the dark that is until the sound of something munching down food sounded from the bushes. Jasper could feel the sweat start to build and run down his face as he could not move from the spot that he was frozen to.

After a couple of minutes, the young boy moved out of the dark and walked over to where Jasper stood still as a statue. Seeing the blood and gore that now covered the boy, Jasper tried with all the willpower he could muster to get his feet moving in the right direction away from this walking nightmare, but no matter how hard he tried he couldn't move.

Michael walked up to the smaller man before him, his pain from the earlier wound now diminished since he had fed. The taste of the bigger man was pretty rancid, but food is food he thought as he smiled at his next meal.

Jasper closed his eyes, not wanted the sight of those teeth, the ones with pieces of Oscar smeared all over them to be the last thing he saw in this world as a sharpness closed around his throat and bit down.

⌘❧⌘❧⌘❧

Jamie slowly rose out of the fog that she was in and opened her eyes slightly to take in the horror before her, but her mind closed up at the sight and she slowly slipped back halfway down into the quiet of darkness once again.

Soon through the fog of the darkness, she could feel herself lifted up and thrown over something hard and unyielding. With the movement of whatever she was lying over again, the darkness reached out and enveloped her totally, this time, taking the pain within her body away in her deep oblivion.

❧❧❧❧❧❧

Sara moved around the group gathered around, her impatience showing as Regni came up and once again demanded to know where her brother was. "You know we don't have all night here angel, we need to find the Princess and get her head back to the Queen," the large man said.

"Just take it easy, dragon. I told you my brother will be here and he will be as soon as he knows where our prey has nested."

Regni looked at the young girl before him and wondered for the fifth time in the last fifteen minutes if it had been such a good idea to put in with these creatures. Sure she said that they would hand over the Princess and they would take the ones they were after, but something about this little girl spooked him, and dragons never liked that feeling.

Regni looked around at the creatures that had met up at the back of the mall and, counting heads, he noticed quite a few missing Others that should have responded to his summons.

"What's bothering you, dragon? Soon you will have your precious Princess and I'll have what I want," the little girl before him said with a smile now lighting her face.

"Yeah, I don't trust you, angel, you are no better than witches. You treat my kind as trash and kill us for fun," Regni looked around once more at his diminished forces and then back at the girl. "In fact, you are probably the reason why so many of us are missing tonight, aren't you?"

The girl looked around her and laughed. "Now dragon how could you think a thing like that about me. Didn't I tell you it was that witch that was killing your people off and didn't my brother and I take care of him for you?"

"So you say, angel," Regni replied in a sulky voice.

"You and your people need to chill, dragon, for once my brother and I have our prize we will reward all those that help us."

One of the ogres stood close to the angel and dragon quietly listening to them talk and processed all that was being said. As he was an ogre, the process of thought was slow, but still he formed his own opinion and remembered what the dragon that beat him earlier in the fight outside the princess's house had said. As he moved into a dark corner to think some more without any interference, he heard the guards that were out keeping an eye on things give a shout.

❧☙❧☙❧☙

Michael moved through the cold night with the witch over his shoulder, making for the place where he knew that his sister waited for him. He felt better now that he had fed, even though the two creatures that he had fed on did leave a nasty taste in his mouth; still the pain from the magic was now pretty much gone. Damn, he thought, who would have thought that such a small thing as her could inflict pain on one such as him.

Soon he was standing under an overpass near the mall, late night traffic zipping above him. All those worthless creatures living lives that were no more important than bugs, he thought with a smile.

Then the smile slowly slipped from his face as he thought about how mad his sister would be at his little try at taking their prize by himself. Well, he thought, she needed him so that whatever she would do to him would be mild; unless that is, she told mother what he had done.

With that thought, his whole body chilled and broke out in sweat as he thought of the consequences of that reaction from his sister. Maybe it was time that Sara was sort of lost, never to return to home, and then he would be mother's favorite. Yes, that thought had been recurring more and more in his head lately.

Michael stopped looking around the dark area he was resting in and sniffed the wind as it flowed under the overpass. Yes, his sister had come through; he could smell her and some Other creatures up by the large building where they had first come into this world. Smiling at the thought of once more being with Sara, all previous dark thoughts vanished from his mind and Michael once again threw the girl over his shoulder and headed toward where his sister waited for him.

Sara moved over to the see what the commotion was all about when she saw her brother walk into the light thrown off the building behind her. Her smile faltered as she noticed that Michael was carrying something over his shoulder.

"Michael! What did you do?" Sara asked as she walked up to her brother.

Seeing what the bundle was as he laid it down, Sara stepped up to her brother and slashed him across the face, her hands turning to claws as they raked his face from his left eye to his chin.

Michael stood silently, the blood dripping down his face, the crowd around him hushed by the sudden attack from one angel on another. "I asked you, Michael, what did you do?" Sara whispered into the dark.

Michael stared at his sister then looked around at the crowd of creatures around them with a grimace. "I had our prize in my hands, but some girl interrupted me so I took one of theirs, a witch by the smell of her," Michael whispered back.

Sara sighed and stepped up to her brother and laid a hand over his damaged cheek. He flinched ever so slightly as if expecting another blow, but relaxed when the bleeding stopped with the pain. As Sara removed her hand from the wound, all the creatures closest to the pair could see that there were no marks on the angel's face anymore.

Sara looked down at the unconscious girl on the ground and then at Michael. "Just get rid of it, brother, and then tell us where the demons and the Princess are, okay?"

As Michael bent down to do his sister's bidding, Regni stepped up between them and made his presence known. "Wait you two, we can use her."

"Dragon, have you lost your mind? This witch is of no use to us. Do as I told you, Michael," Sara said with a tinge of anger and annoyance in her voice.

"STOP!" Regni yelled. "Her friends will come to us and we can meet them on our turf and not in a place of their own choosing."

Sara looked at Regni with a little respect in her eyes as she thought over the dragon's statement. "Okay, go on dragon, tell me more."

Regni took a deep breath in and then let it out figuring he had dodged a bullet in that the female angel was listening to him instead of flaying him alive right now. "Easy, we move this party to the park down the block and then send the demons a message letting them know where they can find their friend."

Sara thought this idea over for a couple of minutes and then slowly nodded her head. "Alright dragon, we will give your idea a try." Then she grabbed Regni's arm, digging in claws that once more drew blood from the flesh they were wrapped around, "But if this idea does not work you will be my next meal, understand dragon?"

Regni shook his head and then gulped at the hungry look in the angel's eyes. "Yeah, sure I got it, angel."

"Good then let's get to this park," Sara barked at the creatures all around her. "Michael, pick up that trash and bring her along."

Michael bent over and obeyed his sister as the others headed into the night toward the park. All but one that is; one giant shadow that had been hanging back in the dark. This shadow headed off on his own mission.

৵৵৵৵৵৵

Just waiting can suck! It seemed like every noise we heard was some creature trying to get into the condo, ready to finish the job it had started. Even Tessa and Scom were starting to get pretty jumpy, startling at any noise in the night.

Suddenly a thought flashed across my mind and I jumped up from the floor and headed toward the end of the couch that had been my bed muttering to myself. "Oh man, why didn't I remember him before."

'What is it Ceri?" Mom asked.

"What Princess?" both Scom and Tessa hissed at me.

I dug into my new backpack without saying a word and pulled Mr. Blue from its depths. I looked around at the other three a little embarrassed that I had forgotten all about my big friend in all the excitement around here.

"Maybe a little or should I say a big demon protector could help us right now," I said as I tossed Mr. Blue into the air toward the middle of the room and snapped my fingers.

Yeah, I forgot that the condo had regular ceilings and not the tall ones at our apartment. Mr. Blue rolled across the floor as a teddy bear and then stood up in his demon form. Unfortunately, when he came up his horns were stuck into the ceiling of Roc's condo.

Oh yeah, forgot that the big fuzzy was that large, especially with those two big horns sticking out the side of his head. Mr. Blue sneezed from the plaster that covered his head and face, unfortunately, for him, this only brought down more of the ceiling plaster on him.

Dede, who by this time had awakened from her sleep, and Mom were looking at the demon protector and giggled at the sight while Scom and Tessa sniffed and went back to their places to watch for any bad guys. Mr. Blue glanced at me with an embarrassed look on his face. "Sit down big guy and I'll clean you up," I said as I went to look for a rag in the kitchen.

I heard a thump and a fresh load of giggles from the living room as I wet down a large dish towel in the kitchen sink. Walking back into the living room, I couldn't help but smile at the big fuzzy demon as he wagged his tail at me, but the smile disappeared as I looked up at the ceiling and the two holes that were now gouged into Roc's condo. Well, I thought, he did say he had a dragon hoard, so I guess he could afford a hole or two in his ceiling.

Walking over to Mr. Blue and starting to wipe his face off, I heard the front door handle rattle and start to open when several things happened at once. Tessa and Scom both jumped in front of the three of us; while Mom, Dede, and I all faced the door with various balls of magic erupting in our hands. Of course, Mr. Blue jumped up in reaction to the rest of us thus once again sticking his horns into the ceiling of the living room.

So there the six of us were standing when my dad and Roc walked into the condo. Both men stopped as if they weren't sure if they should keep coming in the door or to retreat back outside.

"Uhm hi everyone," Dad said with some hesitation. Then looking around asked, "Where is Jamie?"

That's when everyone seemed to relax and Mom, I and the trolls all tried to tell the two men what had happened in their absence. Dad held up his hand and looked at all of us as we quieted down, then smiling he pointed at Mr. Blue standing behind me and said, "Sit!"

Once again I heard a thump behind me and turning I saw that the big fuzz ball was covered in even more ceiling plaster than before. As Roc and Dad closed the front door and came further into the living room, I turned to finish the clean up job I had started figuring Mom could let the two men know what had been going on.

"Oh man, what did that big dog do to my home," Roc asked as he looked at four sets of holes in his condo ceiling.

"Oh chill out, Roc it's only a couple of holes. Anyways we probably will need to leave after all this is done," Mom said with a smile chasing across her face as she swatted Roc on his arm. Roc did quiet down, but he didn't look too happy as he kept glancing up at the holes.

❧❧❧❧❧❧

After cleaning up one demon protector and Mom and I telling the two men what had happened while they were gone, an hour had passed and I was getting a little impatient with the lack of action in finding my friend and rescuing her.

After a little break in which everyone sat quietly with their own thoughts, I couldn't help but blurt out my ideas for what we should do. "Uhm so what are we going to do now, guys? We have to save Jamie; I mean she would do the same for me."

Everyone looked at me as if I had grown another head then looked at each other before Roc spoke up. "Sorry Princess, but we don't even know where they took her."

"Well yeah, but then we go out and look for her, guys," I said now my frustration really showing especially since both Mom and Dad weren't saying a word to help me.

"Princess, Bellingham is a small town, but it isn't that small of a town. Where do you wish for us to start looking for your friend?"

I finally had it with this dragon's attitude and I stomped over to him and stood on my tiptoes to get in his face as much as I could, me being as small as I was and him being, well a mountain. "Listen, I don't care how we do it let's get out there and get my friend back, understand that dragon?' I said as I flicked a small fireball that singed his eyebrows and made him step back from me.

Mom and Dad jumped up from where they were sitting and grabbed my arms and pulled me from Roc as Dede let out a little laugh and muttered something about finally me causing some trouble in this family.

I pulled out of my parent's arms and glared over at my little sister. She glared back and laughed as she stuck out her tongue at me, but the smile disappeared as Mom gave her one of her famous 'not now' looks.

We all stopped and turned to look at Roc as he was leaning against the wall holding his side and laughing his head off. Now Dad must have been getting a little frustrated too because he glared at Roc and snarled, "I'm glad you can find something amusing in all this dragon, but I find none of it funny at all."

Roc stopped laughing and a serious look crossed his face as he took us all in. "You are right, demon, there is nothing funny at all in this situation, but the fight in this little one," he said as he pointed to me, "reminds me so much of her father."

Dad and Mom looked at the dragon and shook their head almost in unison. That's when I stepped up and tried to make my point once again.

"Well this is fine and all, but what are we going to do about Jamie?" I whined.

"Princess, I didn't say we wouldn't find her. I said it would be very hard to find her."

"Okay, so where do we start then?" I asked as I glanced at all three adults.

Before anyone could say anything there was a loud pounding knock at the door. All of us froze in place and then Roc walked over to the door and looked out the peephole. He waved us down as he opened the door and then let in a big man that made Roc look tiny.

"How did you find us, ogre?" Roc asked as he shut the door behind the large man.

"I told you before, dragon, we ogres are trackers."

"Okay, and why did you find us, my big friend?" Roc asked.

The ogre looked at all of us and then zeroed in on me. "Princess," he said kneeling on the floor and looking up at me with awe. "I know where they take the witch girl."

"Oh okay then, and why are you helping us?" I asked looking down at the large mountain of a man kneeling before us.

The ogre looked up at me, smiled and pointed at Roc. "Because this dragon told me that you would come and save our world from your mother."

I looked around, not knowing what to say to the ogre or anyone else that seemed to be staring at me. How does this always seem to come around once again to me going back to some world and getting rid of some obscure family member to save their world?

I let out a sigh, of course, there was only one thing I could do and that was to play along so that we could save Jamie. "Alright ogre so where is Jamie, and please get up off the floor, won't you?"

The ogre stood with a puzzled look on his face. "What is a Jamie?"

"The witch girl," Roc said as he chuckled.

"Oh yes, they take her to a woods by the place they call mall."

"You mean Cornwall Park?" I asked.

"Uhm sure, I guess," the ogre said as he scratched his head with his big hands, looking over at Roc as for help.

"Makes sense that they would set up there. Plenty of space

and this late at night no one around to cause them any trouble," Dad said with a thoughtful look.

"Well, we know where they are so let's go," I said as I marched toward the door.

CHAPTER 17

The large group of creatures moved down the street unimpeded and arrived at the dark park with no trouble at all, even with an unconscious girl hanging over Michael's shoulders. Walking past the parking lot and the large playground set, the group came across a wooden structure with picnic tables lined up inside it.

Michael and Sara looked around the area and sniffed the air taking in all the different scents left by the people that used this area. "What is this building for?" Sara asked looking out the open sided park building, taking in the various playground and water fountain areas.

Regni smiled and pointed out the different areas. "This is one of the places that the people of this world bring their children to play."

The two angels looked around at all the different areas and laughed. "No wonder this world is so backward, to waste all this space on letting a child play."

Regni's smile disappeared off his face as he looked at the two angels standing before him. "Yeah, well, don't forget this world has the witches to protect it, along with technology."

"Oh please, spare me. Others of our kind been to this world before; their technology does not scare us," Michael said as he puffed his chest out walking over to a table where he had dropped the girl. He looked down at her unconscious figure, "And I'm certainly not afraid of something like this witch."

"You angels have not been to this world in awhile, have you?" Regni asked.

Michael and Sara looked at each other then back at the dragon with smirks lighting their faces. "No, we have not visited this world for a long time, not since the first of our kind came here," Sara said. "But it matters not, for they have no real magic, so they are worthless."

One of the other older dragons who had survived in this world the longest chuckled at the two angel's arrogance. "These creatures in this world have technology that can destroy a whole city in a blink of the eye. What can you two do again?"

"Hush Adler," Regni said as he glanced at the dragon sitting on one of the other picnic tables in the open building. Then he turned to look at the two surprised angels before him.

"What is he talking about?" Michael whispered.

Regni sighed and looked between the two angels before him thinking that for such advanced creatures as they thought they were these two could be pretty stupid. "The people of this world have taken their technology and can make it do terrible things, whether to the individual or to a group; they have learned whole new ways of destruction."

"Oh, well fine then we finish what we came here to do and leave. Alright with you, dragon?" Sara asked Regni, but taking in all the Others that were crowded around them.

"Fine," Regni answered, "just don't underestimate the creatures here is all we are saying."

"Yeah, yeah, got that," Sara said impatiently waving her hands in the air as if to wipe out all the doubt around her. "Now that we are here in this park, is it? What are your plans to get the demons and your princess here?"

Regni smiled and pointed out three of the creatures that stood together. "These three will follow your brother's scent back to where the demons are and tell them where they can find their friend."

"I can go back and get them," Michael said with a pout.

"NO! You have caused enough trouble, brother. You will stay here where I can watch you."

Michael ducked his head whether from the harshness in his sister's voice or the quiet laughter from the other creatures around him Regni wasn't sure, but what he did know, looking at the hatred in the angel's eyes, was that this one would need to have a close eye kept on him.

He tore his eyes off of Michael to pay attention to what Sara was saying and had to ask her to repeat herself.

"I said, dragon, why will these three, uhm creatures be able to backtrack my brother and find the ones we want."

Regni smiled and looked at the three men that were now seemingly dancing in place, their movements showing their eagerness in tracking down their unsuspecting prey. "These three are part of a wolf shifter pack that is in this world. Ogres are great trackers, but give me a shifter any day for tracking down prey and running them to ground."

"Okay then, well what are you waiting for?" Sara asked as she stared at the three men. "Go deliver this message: Tell the demons that if they want to see their little witch alive again, they will all come down here to the park."

The three shifters stood there looking at the angel waiting to see if there was more to the message when Sara stomped her foot and clapped her hands sharply together. "Let's go now gentlemen, now."

With that all three shifters jumped up and turned in mid-air and were soon lost in the darkness, two seconds later all the creatures around the open building heard a wolf howl echoed by two others.

Regni looked at the angels and smiled. "Now that the

messengers are away, how do you want to do this?"

The two looked around at the rest of the creatures around them. It wasn't a big crowd, but Sara and Michael figured it would have to do to capture two demons and this princess of the Others. "What are our forces here, dragon?" Sara asked.

Regni looked about at the creatures and smiled. "I think we have what we need to take care of anything that comes into the park. We have three dragons, including me, ten more wolf shifters and eight ogres."

"Uhm Regni," a rough voice interrupted from the dark. "We are missing one of our own," one of the ogres said as he walked nervously into the light.

"And where did this one ogre go and why are you just telling us now?" Sara whispered in a quiet, deadly voice.

The ogre stood there and looked at the angel with a dull look and then shrugged his shoulders.

"It doesn't matter, angel. We have what we need here. One more ogre more or less will not make a difference to us or them," Regni said as he looked down at the angels.

"Yes, you are probably right, but did it cross your mind that the ogre could have gone and warned the demons where we were headed too," Sara asked.

"Okay, so what does it matter if they know from some ogre or from the shifters we sent, just so that we get them to the park, right?"

Sara looked at Regni for several minutes then glanced over at her brother. She saw though that Michael was not paying any attention to the conversation as he was sulking from her previous rebuke. "Yes, you are right this one time, dragon. So how about we send the shifters to the other end of the park to watch for our guests and the rest of you spread out in the dark? As they come in here to collect the witch, we all close in on them and then we all get what we want, okay?"

"Yeah that sounds good, angel," said Regni as he started to move off with the other creatures around them.

Sara grabbed the dragon's arm and laughed. "Oh not you, dragon; I think I want you here with us."

Regni stared down at the hand on his arm and then shrugged his shoulders. "Whatever, angel, just so in the end I get the Princess's head to bring back to my Queen."

Sara smiled again at the dragon. "Oh you will get what's coming to you, dragon," she said as she let go of Regni's arm and turned to her brother.

"Michael," she hissed as she walked up to him and grabbed his face in her two hands. "You need to snap out of this mood you are in."

"They laughed at me, Sara," he whispered so low that Sara wasn't sure at first if her brother had even spoken. "You made them laugh at me."

Once more Sara stared into her brother's eyes, thinking that she really didn't need this kind of problem happening right now with Michael, and cursed the day that her mother sent her brother with her. "Alright, I'm sorry, okay? But you need to pull it together now. I certainly can't trust these other creatures around here, so you are all I have right now, brother dear," she whispered clamping both her hands tighter on her brother's cheeks to get his attention.

Michael looked into the eyes of his sister and nodded his head at her. "I will be here for you sister, as always," he whispered back and then straightened his back and turned to walk away from his sister.

As her hands slowly fell from her brother's face Sara worried as she watched her brother walk over to a bench at the far side of the building and sit down and stare off into space. The thought flashed through her mind that maybe her brother had been away too long from her mother's influence and that after this little adventure was done she needed to take him home, no matter the outcome.

❧❧❧

With one look between them, Roc and the ogre stepped in front of me blocking the door and my way out of this place. Just as I reached down inside of me to pull up a ball of fire in my hand I could feel my dad put his two hands on my shoulders and turn me around to face him.

"Ceri, you need to chill out for a second and let us think

this through," Dad said.

"What's to think about? We know where Jamie is, we go there, we kick butt and we bring her back home with us, no thinking needed, Dad."

"Listen, it's just not that simple. Besides, you are not going with."

"Oh so you want to leave Dede and me here, is that it? You know in the place where they already know where we are and have broken into so easily before, is that it?" I asked.

Dad looked at Mom then over at Roc. Roc looked at all of us, not liking that he was the center of everyone's attention. "Don't everyone look at me; this is the only other place I had in this town."

"But you do have another place, right?" Mom asked with some hopefulness coloring her voice.

Roc now really looked uncertain before he answered. "Well, yeah, but it's down in Seattle. I mean that's two hours down there, maybe less at this time of night. Then a half hour or so to get the girl's settled and two hours back. I just don't think we have that kind of time."

The ogre stepped forward and looked at all of us. "You do know too that there are Others that have moved down to this Seattle place, right?"

I smiled and looked at my dad. "See you can't leave us down there. Jamie probably doesn't have that much time to be rescued and Dede and I would still be in trouble with creatures down there looking for us, so we have to go with you guys."

"Fine you can stay here and we will leave the trolls here with you," Dad growled.

"Right, so you, Mom, and Roc are going to take on two angels and who knows how many Others all by your lonesome. Now there is a winning plan, and what are Dede and I to do if you guys don't come back, then what?"

"Okay let's all settle down now and think this through calmly," Mom said.

Everyone agreed Mom was right as we all moved into the living room to figure out what we were going to do to get Jamie back from the creatures that had her. Of course, what I didn't tell any of them was that if we didn't come up with something quick I was going all by myself to get her if I had to.

"Alright Roc and Ceri have a point," Dad said. "We don't have time to take the girls down to Seattle and we probably will need the help of the trolls to get Jamie back."

"Yes, you're right dear but I don't like the idea of the girls staying here with no one else to watch them," Mom said.

"We can leave Mr. Blue here with them, Jenna."

"What so if we really need you, you guys are still gonna be across town," I said butting into my parent's conversation.

Mom and Dad looked at me and then over at Dede still sitting on the couch in her P.J.s then glanced at each other like they do when they have these silent conversations.

After a couple of minutes, Dad sighed and shook his head. "Alright you girls can come to the park with us, but . . ." he said as both Dede and I cheered, "you will stay by the car with Mr. Blue while the rest of us get Jamie. At least this way you will be close to us in case we need to help you."

"Yeah and we can be your back up," Dede said as she jumped off the couch and fluttered a small fireball in the air.

"NO, no back up, you guys stay by the car with Mr. Blue and that is final, understand me, girls?" Dad said his voice rumbling into that deep down 'dad voice' he has when he expects no back talk on a subject.

Dede froze in her tracks and meekly nodded her head 'yes' at his command and the stern look he threw her way. Then he turned to me with the same look, and I knew what to say, "Oh, yeah, sure Dad, I understand." (Even if I wasn't going to necessarily follow what he said.)

Dad stared at me for a minute as if he knew what was flowing through my thoughts then slowly turned to Mom. "Alright I guess if we are going to bring the girls, why don't you get Dede dressed warmly while Roc and I go get a vehicle for all of us."

Mom nodded and took Dede by the hand and led her into

the back bedroom. As Dad moved to head to the front door, Roc put his arm out and blocked his way. "You stay here Bill, with your family; me and my big friend here will go get us a set of wheels."

"You sure?" Dad asked even though I could tell that the idea of staying here with us sounded pretty good to him.

"Yeah, the two of us can handle it," Roc said as he looked over at the large ogre. "Come on my big friend; let's go find a big car."

The ogre smiled and walked out the door with Roc. Dad stood there for a moment looking at the door then without looking at me, walked into the back bedroom where Mom and Dede were getting ready for our rescue mission.

Well okay then, I thought, I guess I'll go and get some warm stuff on for our little trip.

❧❦❧❦❧❦

The three shifters easily found the place where the angel had been. Now they were hanging low watching the building in which the demons were now hiding. "I say we go in and deliver the message like the angel wanted us to," the smallest of the shifters said.

The largest shifter, the Beta of the pack in this world, growled in reply. "We wait for a few minutes and scope out the place first."

All three shifters settled down in the cold night air, watching the building. Each thinking of the tender flesh that they would be able to dine on if all went well with tonight's plan. Who knew? If they got the Princess's head they could go back to their own world and take retribution on the shifters that had spurned them.

After half an hour, the largest of the shifters made to move toward the building to deliver the message given him when the lights of a large truck washed over their hiding place. Since the truck turned into the parking lot of the building they were watching, he slunk back into the shadows to wait once more.

੭੶੭੶੭੶

Roc got out of the truck's cab and watched as the ogre hopped out of the back of the large truck they had borrowed. As the two of them walked toward the front door of his hidey hole, he stopped and looked across the street at some bushes.

"What is wrong, dragon?"

"What? Uhm I don't know; thought I saw a flash of something across the way there."

The ogre walked over to where Roc stood and stared at the bushes and then sniffed the air, but the wind was going in the wrong direction so that he couldn't smell anything. "Do you want to go look there, dragon?"

Roc stood there looking at the area for a few minutes more, shook his head and started back up the path toward his condo. "No, I must be getting old and seeing things. Let's go get the others and get to the park so we can rescue the little witch."

"Yes, that is very strange that the Princess and her family would help one such as her," the ogre said as he followed Roc to the front door.

"Yeah, well what can I say, my big friend? I guess that is what makes her a Princess and me just a dragon and you an ogre."

The ogre stopped at the door and scratched his head in thought, then laughed. "You know for a dragon, you are half-smart."

Roc looked at the ogre and laughed right back at this remark. "Yeah well, if I was so smart I think I would be headed down to Seattle to hide and not going to some park to save a witch," he said as he unlocked the front door and walked into the condo.

❧❧❧❧❧❧

All three shifters stepped out of the shadows and watched with fiery red eyes as the door of the condo shut.

"That ogre was with us at the mall, I know he was," the smallest of the shifters whined.

"Quiet, I know where he was. Let me think for a second," the Beta said as he looked over at the two other shifters. He knew that the smallest of them would be useless in a fight and made up his mind what he would do.

"You," he said pointing at the whining shifter. "Head back to the park and let them know about the ogre. We'll stay here a little bit and if they don't move in a half hour then we will give them the message."

"Well what about the ogre, though?" the smallest whined again.

The leader spun around and grabbed his pack member up by the scruff of the neck and lifted him off the ground as he pushed him up against the side of a small building. "I said, head back to the park and let them know what we saw here. We will take care of the ogre if needed."

He took the smaller shifter and threw him to the ground and growled, "Now get out of here."

The small shifter scrambled to his feet and tore down the street, headed back toward the park as if a nest of hornets was on his tail.

"He does have a small point you know. The ogre could be a problem," the third shifter whispered.

The leader turned and growled a warning but then stopped as he thought over what his companion had said. "Yeah you could be right, but what the hell you can't live forever can you?"

This seemed funny to both shifters and they each quietly chuckled as they thought that as wolf shifters their life span was never very long anyways, especially in this world.

⚜⚜⚜

Now that Roc and the ogre were back, everyone seemed to be almost ready to go and finally rescue Jamie. It was about time, I thought, as we once again gathered in the living room of Roc's condo, waiting for my mom and Dede.

"Princess, you need to as you say, chill, we will have your friend back soon," Roc said as he watched me fidget back and forth.

"I don't want them hurting Jamie; I mean it's my entire fault that they took her."

Roc walked over and looked at me and smiled. "Princess you saved your sister; there was no time in this battle to do more. Your friend will be safe as long as she is of some use to the angels, do not worry."

"Yeah, easy for you to say dragon she is not your friend and you didn't lose her, I did."

"You are right Princess, she is not my friend, but she is yours and therefore just as important as you are to me."

"Oh," was all I could get out of my mouth as my mom came out of the back of the condo with my little sister in hand. "Okay we are ready to go after having our second pit stop," Mom said with some exasperation in her voice.

Dad looked at all of us and with a big sigh started for the door. "I still don't like this, but I guess we have no choice in this matter," he mumbled as he opened the front door. We all followed him and Roc down to the truck, me with Scom tucked in my backpack with Mr. Blue once again and Tessa wrapped around Roc's neck.

Dad looked at the large four-door truck that Roc had borrowed from some unsuspecting owner and laughed. "Well, I guess we will have enough room for everyone in that . . ."

He stopped talking as two figures that had been crossing the street caught his eyes. All of us looked at the two men and knew from how they were walking toward us that whoever they were, they were not here to help us in our rescue of Jamie.

The ogre stepped in front of us and sniffed the wind that was now blowing toward us and growled. "Shifters. Get in truck, I will take care of them," he said as he marched toward the two men.

Roc started to go after the ogre, but Dad grabbed him by the arm and pushed him to the driver's side of the truck. We all piled in and the last we saw as we headed out of the parking lot was the two shifters changing forms and one very peeved ogre growling a challenge.

CHAPTER 18

The shifter, named Jonna, stopped running as he hit the edge of the park. He bent over to catch his breath, wondering if it was such a good idea to finish his mission like his Beta had told him or just disappear in the night.

"What are you are you doing here Jonna? Where are the other two?" the voice of his Alpha growled from the dark woods on the edge of the park.

Jonna startled and jumped and then looked at the big shifter and three others that were now bearing down on him. "I asked you a question Jonna? Where are the others?"

"Hold on sir, let me catch my breath . . ." Jonna started to say, but his voice was cut off from the big meaty hand that wrapped around his throat and lifted him off the ground so that his toes barely were grazing the sidewalk where he had stood.

The big man brought Jonna's face inches from his, his breath smelling of decay washing over the frightened shifter's face. "I'm sorry, Jonna, I don't remember giving you permission to breathe. Now where's the rest of my pack?"

With that last word, the large Alpha dropped Jonna to the ground and as Jonna looked up, he saw he was surrounded by some very unhappy pack members. Yeah, should have run when I had the chance, he thought, as he once more focused on the Alpha's face.

"I was sent back here to tell you that there was an ogre at the demon's house, one of the beasts that were at the mall."

"And the others? Where are they?" the Alpha growled.

"They are back at the demon house, they decided to wait and see if the ogre told them where the witch was or see if they still needed to deliver the message the angel sent."

The Alpha stood and thought, his small mean eyes glowing in the dark. Jonna knew that this was a sign that his leader wasn't far from going on a killing spree, and he also knew who the target of that spree would be.

After a minute or so, Jonna saw those murderous eyes lose the glow and relaxed somewhat with a sigh of relief. Of course, his relief didn't last long as the alpha picked him up off the ground and threw him into the arms of two other shifters. "Take him to the angel; she will see if he is telling the truth."

"NO, wait, really I'm tell . . ." Jonna tried to tell his leader he was telling the truth, but his voice was cut off by the hand that had half shifted into a large wolf paw, the claws of which dug into his cheek and kept him from uttering any more sounds as he was led away toward the other end of the park.

The Alpha looked at the other shifters around him and ignored the muffled screams coming from the receding men as they moved toward where the others were. "Alright, I want you all to spread out and find a good place upwind. If they come here first, I want no one attacking until I give the order, everyone understand?"

The small group of shifters all nodded and headed into the dark. The alpha shifter looked down the street and then glanced back at where he knew the angel was probably having fun with the coward of his pack. Well, no big loss that one, he thought, as he moved off into the dark with the rest of his pack. He hoped that his beta and companion made it back in time for all the fun this night seemed to promise.

❧❦❧❦❧❦

The two shifters were now in their half wolf form, a form in size and viciousness that would scare most any normal person, but the ogre smiled and laughed as the thought crossed his mind that it had been awhile since he had had shifter steaks.

The shifter's form was not only scary to look at, but ugly as well. Each shifter's face was elongated in the jaw area so that the shifters looked like they carried a muzzle full of razor sharp teeth. Along with the mouth full of teeth, each shifter sported long pointed claws on the end of their hands and feet that now popped on overextended muscled legs and arms.

As they hit the sidewalk, the smaller of the shifters jumped at the ogre's head as the larger one veered off to follow the truck that was speeding down the road. "Oh no you don't," the ogre growled as he ducked under the first shifter's jump and reached up into the air grabbing him around the center of his body and threw him into the other shifter.

The flying body connected with the running shifter and sent both of them slamming into a low brick wall that was near the condo's parking lot. As they both lay there dazed for a second, the ogre stomped over to continue the fight he had started.

The ogre reached down and pulled the smaller shifter off of the pile of claws and teeth by the scruff of the neck. As he stood up, the larger of the shifters reached out and clamped his teeth around the ogre's arm, slashing his head side to side trying to tear the arm off of the ogre's body.

"UGH! BAD DOGGIE!" the ogre screamed as he slammed the smaller shifter into his companion. Then turning he threw the shifter in his hand back behind him and heard a crunch as that shifter hit the side of a car.

Now breathing hard from the exertion and pain, the ogre

reached down and grabbed the shifter that was still latched onto his arm behind the head and squeezed. "Let go, bad boy," the ogre grunted as he put as much pressure as he could on the head of the shifter.

Soon there was a whimper from the shifter, but he refused to let go of the ogre's arm and seemed to be jerking his head back and forth harder than before. The ogre grunted and squeezed harder and soon in the quiet night air there was heard a loud creak and then a snap as the shifter suddenly went limp and the fire died in his eyes.

The ogre pried the dead jaws of the large shifter off of his arm and, picking up the carcass, walked over to a large green garbage can by the wall of the parking lot and threw the body inside of it. "I told you, bad doggie, to let go," the ogre said as he slammed the lid down on the garbage can.

As he turned to go collect the other shifter to put him with his companion, a large ball of teeth and claws erupted from the ground in front of him. Oops, guess he not dead thought the ogre as he tried to keep the other shifter from ripping his throat out.

The weight of the shifter slammed both of them back against the garbage can behind the ogre. His big hands wrapped around the neck of the fierce set of teeth that were trying to connect with his throat.

Trying to get some purchase, the shifter kept clawing into the ogre's chest and belly until the ogre finally threw him away where once again the shifter slammed into the side of a car in the parking lot.

The ogre slowly slid down the side of the garbage can, both of the combatants looking at the other. As the shifter catches his breath, he looks at the ogre and sees that he probably isn't going anywhere soon and slowly moves around him, staying out of his reach, so that he can head back toward the park where the real fun is going to be.

He growls at the ogre to let him know that he will be back and with friends but the ogre looks at the shifter and smiles. With that the shifter takes off at a slow trot, all he can muster after the fight he has been in with this creature, never once looking back at the ogre and that is his last mistake.

The ogre slowly stands up holding himself against the garbage can and the low wall. He reaches down with his big hand and grabs a long metal piece of ornamental fence off the top of the wall. The piece he grabs is about four feet long, black, and has a sharp point on its end. With a smile, the ogre puts the last of his strength into throwing his makeshift spear.

The black death flies through the air and hits the moving shifter in the back of the head, exiting out his mouth where the force causes the shifter to roll head over tail down the road fifteen feet. The ogre looks at the shifter's body and then slowly sinks back down on the ground, smiling. "Damn must be getting old, I was aiming for doggie's back," he said with a groan.

Nearly panting in pain, the ogre takes in all his injuries and slowly rips up his shirt, or what's left of it for some band aids. As he slowly tries to cover his wounds; his head, little by little, lowers to his chest and his eyes close.

⇛❧⇛❧⇛❧

As I looked out the back window of the truck, I could see the two men crossing the street and changing into the hideous forms of a half wolf, half man heading for the lone large figure of the ogre that was helping us. "I don't think that was such a good idea to leave him there you guys," I said turning back to the front of the truck.

Mom and Dad turned and glanced back out the window, but by this time we had moved out of sight from Roc's condo. "I know Ceri, but if we want to save your friend then we need to go now."

"I don't like running either Princess, but we have no time to fight every Other that wants to take us on right now. Besides, ogres are one of the hardest creatures to kill in our world," Roc mumbled.

As we drove through town, Dede slowly laid her head down on my lap and was asleep once again. Must be nice to be young and sleep whenever you like, I thought, as I looked out at the deserted streets of the town, wide awake even at this late hour of the night.

The truck stopping made me start and I realized that despite my last thought I had fallen asleep. I looked around trying to figure out why we had stopped in an all night store's parking lot that was a few blocks away from the park, then noticed that Dad and Roc were now climbing out of the truck.

"Uhm, where are you guys going?" I asked trying to disentangle myself from my sleeping sister.

Dad smiled and looked over at us in the back seat as Dede slowly woke up from her nap and was sitting up now looking around at where we were. "Roc and I are going to do a quick scout. We will be back in about a half hour or so, sit tight with your mother until we get back," Dad said as he slammed the door of the truck and headed down the street with Roc leading the way.

No one said anything for a few minutes until Dede's small voice popped up in the dark. "Uhm Mommy, I need the bathroom."

My mom looked at me and I laughed. "Don't look at me, I don't have to go."

Mom sighed and opened the front door of the truck as Dede crawled over the front seat and Tessa and Scom hopped out of the truck with them. Looking at me, she waited for a second before saying anything. "Uhm, don't you think you should come with us Ceri?"

"Really, Mom, all the bad guys are in the park not wandering the streets looking for me, I'll be fine."

Mom stood there, undecided until Dede started to whine

that she really, really needed to go now. "Well alright, but dig out Mr. Blue from your backpack just in case, okay?"

"Really Mom?"

"Just humor me Ceri, okay?"

I smiled and pointed at my dancing sister with the grimace of pain painting her face. "Sure I'll dig him out, but you had better hurry with her if you don't want her to explode."

Mom laughed as she grabbed Dede up and hurried toward the lights of the store with the two trolls following behind them. I sat in the dark for a few minutes with the thought of following my mom into the store after all when I remembered to dig Mr. Blue out of my pack.

"Well, Mr. Blue should we stay here where it's quiet or go in and listen to the little troublemaker inside whine?" I asked my stuffed teddy bear.

I looked at him and wondered if the big fuzz ball could hear and see me while he was in this shape. It would be nice to know that all those late night conversations I had had growing up hadn't been wasted on a stuffed teddy bear after all.

After about ten minutes of sitting around in the dark cold night, I decided that maybe I should go in and see if I couldn't wheedle a late night snack out of Mom for Dede and me. After all, a girl needs to keep her energy up while waiting to go rescue her friend, I thought.

I looked in the front and saw that the keys had been left in the ignition and climbed in the front seat with the idea of warming up the truck when my stomach growled and won out in the competition on whether to stay out here or go into the store and get some food.

"Well let's go get some eats, Mr. Blue," I said as I hopped out of the truck and locked the door, but turned slowly as I heard a voice out of the dark with the quiet snickering of three others at my back.

"Well, well, what do we have here boys? Looks like a little lost girl, don't you think?" the voice growled.

Turning, I could see that I was right from the sound that there were four of them standing about five feet from the truck and me. Teach me for woolgathering and not paying any attention to my surroundings. "What do you guys want?"

"Why we want a little fun," the leader of the small bunch said.

I looked at all four guys closer and knew they were going to be trouble for me. All four were as short as I was, but each of them looked like they had spent considerable time in their local gym. They all sported shirts that showed off that even their muscles had muscles on them. Yeah, I definitely was in trouble.

"Uhm listen, guys, my mom ran into the store and will be back out any second so how about you go find your fun somewhere else?"

"Oh, I don't think so, little honey. I think you should be nice to us, who knows after tonight you may need friends like us," the leader said as he took a few steps nearer to me with his three friends snickering in the background.

Suddenly out of nowhere, I got a flash and standing before me were four goblins and then they were four large guys again. "Oh, I see," I said as I looked at the four of them. "And what is happening tonight?"

All four laughed and flexed their muscles as they looked at each other and admiring themselves. Oh lord, save me from boneheads like these, I thought as I watched them posture and strut their stuff.

"We have some friends that are taking care of business in the park, and once they are gone me and my friends are going to take over this little town and run it the way it should be run," the leader said.

"Pretty confident aren't you that your friends will take care of this business of theirs."

The leader smiled and stepped a little closer to me. "Oh they are very bad people, but like I said, they are leaving soon so then we get to show how bad we are."

"You know as the Princess I don't think I can let you do that," I said with an evil smile of my own.

The leader of the group looked at me for a second then

glanced back at his companions and whispered, "The Princess?"

As he turned back to me, I tossed Mr. Blue into his hands. "Here's a present for you," I laughed as the look on his face was great. The poor guy looked down at the teddy bear and then back at me with puzzlement written all over his face, that is until I snapped my fingers.

Mr. Blue grew into his demon form, squishing the goblin that held him under his heavy bulk. The other three goblins stood there looking at the spot, where seconds ago, their leader had met his demise.

Mr. Blue reached down and grabbed the two closest goblins, smashed their bodies together and stuffed them into his mouth before they could move. This sight seemed to spur the fourth goblin into action and he turned and started to run.

I stepped around Mr. Blue as he crunched down on his snack and threw an earth ball of magic, hitting the goblin in the middle of the back and stopping him in his tracks. Mr. Blur stood up and smiled down at me and walked over to the goblin statue that was now adorning the store parking lot.

Before I could stop Mr. Blue his large furry fist came down on the rock goblin pulverizing it to dust. I glanced down at where the goblin leader had stood and then looked away from the mess on the parking lot.

Hearing some voices in the dark from the store, I walked around the truck and saw that Dede, Mom, and the two trolls were now coming out of the store carrying some shopping bags. I looked around the parking lot and the surrounding areas and saw that no one had seen our little actions here.

As the four of them came up to the truck, Mom looked over my shoulder to the other side of the truck. "Uhm Ceri? What is Mr. Blue eating?"

I glanced over where the demon was picking something off of the ground and stuffing it into his mouth. "Uhm nothing, don't worry about it, Mom. What did you get in the bags?"

Mom glanced at Mr. Blue again and then again toward me and shrugged her shoulders. "Just some snacks to get up our energy, because magic can use it up fast."

"Oh look there's Dad and Roc," Dede said as we all looked down the block where we could see the two of them walking back to the store.

"That was quick," Mom said as she took the keys out of my hand and unlocked the door of the truck. "Come on Dede, hop in and I'll start the truck so that we can warm up."

I looked at Mr. Blue, who by this time, had wandered over to me with a big satisfied look on his face. "Hope that your snack was good, big guy," I whispered.

It must have been pretty good in his opinion as his tail was wagging away as I snapped my fingers once again and turned him into a little teddy bear. Now hopefully, I thought, Mom brought some good stuff for our snacks. Of course, anything would be better than goblin right now for a snack.

CHAPTER 19

The Alpha spied the two men that were scouting the park and watched them closely with grudging respect as they moved through the area. These two were warriors, he thought, as they slowly looked over each area before they moved on to the next. Taking his eyes off of them for a second, he checked his own forces. Making sure that none of his men gave away their position, as the two scouts moved along the path that leads back to where the angel and the Others were stationed.

He was pleased to see that his pack was disciplined enough not to attack this first thrust into their territory, knowing that the demons would be scouting out the park for the enemy's positions as he would in their situation. The Alpha wanted to catch all their prey in one swoop, the demons, the Princess, and whoever else was with them – this ended tonight, he thought.

As he ghosted the two scouts through the woods of the park, the Alpha made a small wager with himself on where the two men would stop their scouting mission. A few minutes later, he won that bet as they stopped almost five feet from where the Alpha himself would have stopped.

The bigger of the two men slowly crept forward then stopped suddenly as he stared off to his left into another small grove of trees. The Alpha couldn't see any of his men and he watched alertly as the big man took small sniffs of the air. After a few seconds, the big man moved closer to his goal, the small bridge that crossed the creek dividing the two sides of the park.

Then a small sound to the left of him caught his ear as the man disappeared into the darkness of the bridge. The Alpha cursed whichever one of his pack had made this slip and vowed he would not live to see the morning.

As this thought crossed his mind, he observed the big man once again materialize from the dark bridge and join up with his companion and head off toward where they had both entered the park.

Minutes later, a whisper of sound behind him alerted the Alpha and he turned in a flash seeing two of his shifters dragging a dead ogre between them. "He made some sounds when the two men were near, so we quieted him, sir."

The Alpha looked at the ogre and smiled as he saw the way the head hung on the body at an odd angle. He knew exactly how his men had quieted the annoying creature and approved. "Get rid of the body quietly so the others don't see him."

Both shifters started to move when the Alpha stopped them. "Someone is following the two back through the park, right?"

"Yes sir, four scouts are still with them and will report back when they leave the park," the second shifter reported.

"Good, I'm going to check in with Regni and the angels. Now get rid of that trash."

The two shifters moved off through the trees with their burden between them as the Alpha trotted across the bridge and up over to where the two angels and Regni waited. As he got closer, he could see that Regni sat at the far end of the open building and that the male angel seemed to be in a better mood than he had before.

He stopped as he came up to the building as something hanging from one of the open spaces caught his eye. It was his man, Jonna, or at least what was left of him spread out in an X across the open space, each arm and leg tied to a separate post. The Alpha looked on his carcass and once again wondered if it was such a good idea to hook up with the likes of the two angels.

"Well, why are you here?" The sweet female voice sounded to his left causing his eyes to tear away from the sight before them.

It was the female angel and she wore a scowl on her face that made the Alpha wary of her, especially when he once more glanced at what was left of his man. "I came to tell you that two of them scouted out this position and they should be coming back in force soon."

"Yes, I know. So?" Sara said.

"Do you want us to take them as they enter the park?"

"No we stick to the plan, let them come here and we will all be in on the kill. Remember that the youngest demon is not to be hurt."

"Yeah, yeah I know and I have told all my men the same."

"Yes well, remind them again, for if the little one is hurt by anyone here then what I do to them will make what I did to your man there seem like a walk in the park," Sara said as she patted what was left of Jonna with a shrill laugh incredibly a low moan issued from the shifter.

"And what about the witch there, what are you going to do with her?" the Alpha asked pointing at the still prone form lying on one of the wooden tables.

"You and your men can have her as an added bonus as long as I get the little demon child unharmed."

The Alpha smiled at the angel and took a quick look at the girl and then back at the hanging figure before him. "Yeah that sounds like a deal," he said as he trotted off into the night to remind his men of their mission.

"Pretty sure of yourself aren't you, angel, that all will go your way?" Regni asked.

"Don't worry dragon, when the time comes we will take down the adults and you will have your Princess and my brother and I will have our prize. We can't lose."

Regni looked at the two angels and felt a shiver run down his spine, remembering how quick the Princess had taken out one of his own back in his world. He didn't think it would be as easy as these angels thought it would be. Echoing the thought of the Alpha Regni began to regret ever throwing in with these two, no matter what promises they had made.

Mom had warmed up the truck and handed out some late night food to us by the time Roc and Dad had gotten back. Mom must have had plenty on her mind because I could see that the snacks had Dede's influence written all over them. Not one healthy food group in either bag. Well, I guess fighting angels and Others does have some advantages after all.

When Roc and Dad finally got settled and warmed up enough, I couldn't hold in my curiosity anymore and asked the question most on my mind. "Well did you see Jamie, and is she alright?"

Dad looked at Roc who swallowed a big bite of food and then answered. "Yeah I saw her Princess and they are keeping her safe for the time being."

"Where are they at?" Mom asked before I could blurt out my other questions.

"They are over by the playground inside some open-ended building," Roc said, again between bites.

"Okay, so let's go then," I said finishing up my food and throwing the wrappers down on the floor of the truck.

"Ceri, pick that up please," Mom said as she looked over the seat at the trash on the floor.

"Really Mom? This isn't even our truck," I whined.

Mom looked at me and then shrugged her shoulders. Dad smiled and then looked over at us all. "Okay, guys enough; we are going over to the park and get your friend while your sister and you stay here."

"And just who is this 'we' that is going with you, Dad?"

"Roc, Mom, the trolls and I will hit the park while you and Dede wait here with Mr. Blue. That way with you guys here we don't have to worry about you while we take your friend from the angels."

"Uhm yeah, that may not work as well as you think Dad," I whispered.

Mom looked at me with narrowed eyes as I told them about the encounter that Mr. Blue and I had had with the four goblins while everyone was out doing their own thing.

"I knew there was something up when we came out of the

store," Mom said looking at me then down at Mr. Blue sitting next to me in his teddy bear form.

Dad looked between Mom and me and wisely kept his mouth shut as Mom lit into me about how this wasn't a game and I needed to grow up and realize that right now. As her lecture lost steam, I gave the same look that I had seen Dede do numerous times before that usually got her out of Mom's dog house.

"Sorry Mom, won't happen again, okay?" I said trying to pacify her.

"I worry about you girls," Mom answered as she turned in her seat and leaned against the passenger door of the truck.

Roc who was also quiet throughout Mom's tirade cleared his throat as he tossed his trash over the seat which landed next to mine on the floor of the truck. Mom gave him a dirty look but kept silent.

"I think we need to bring the girls along with us. We can leave the truck at the end of the park where we entered Bill, that way the girls will be near us in case there is trouble, and the truck will also be near for a quick getaway once we get the witch back."

I could see Dad was thinking over what Roc had said so I kept quiet, hoping that he would bring us along for the fight. After a couple of what I thought was wasted minutes, Dad sighed as though he had made up his mind, but wasn't happy with the decision he came to.

"Alright the girls will come with us, but they stay by the truck with Mr. Blue and we leave Scom and Tessa about half way between them and where Jamie is."

"WHAT, but why?" I asked

"Because that way if we need help the trolls can come help us and if you guys need help they can come to you quicker that way."

"But . . ." I started to say.

"That's the way it will be, no back talk young lady," Dad said with some anger tinting his voice now. I could see Roc shake his head at me and I quickly shut my mouth.

With that seemingly settled we all got ready to go as Roc pulled out of the parking lot of the store and headed down the street toward the park.

It was a quick ride as Roc pulled into the parking lot of some church or daycare that was next to the park. The woods came right to the edge of the parking lot and the darkness and late night and lack of lights in the park made the night look ominous.

"Hold on," Roc said before anyone could open their door. Reaching back in the truck, he grabbed the cover of the small light in the middle of the roof and pulled it off, then popped the bulbs out of the fixture.

"Okay, now we're ready," Roc growled.

We all climbed out of the truck except Dede who climbed over to the front seat and settled down in the middle. Dad looked around at the cloudy, quiet night and then down at the trolls.

"How about you guys head out and find a good place to settle?"

"Alright," both trolls answered as they disappeared into the night.

Then Dad looked at me and then down at Mr. Blue who was resting in the crook of my arm. "Oh yeah," I said as I set him on the ground and snapped my fingers.

Mr. Blue was once again his big fuzzy demon self and he seemed pretty happy about that if the motion of his tail was any indication.

"Hey big guy," I whispered with a smile.

Mr. Blue's tail seemed to move with even more wild abandonment than before if that was possible as he walked back over to me.

"Mr. Blue," Dad whispered.

Mr. Blue stopped dead in his tracks and turned to face Dad all indications of the happiness he showed just seconds ago were gone.

"I need you to stay here and watch the girls, Mr. Blue, and oh yeah make sure that Ceri stays with the truck and doesn't follow us into the park," Dad whispered again.

"Really," I mumbled under my breath as Mr. Blue glanced at me and then looked back to my dad.

"Okay," Mr. Blue growled.

I looked at the big fuzz ball and then at my parents standing there with these grins all plastered across their faces. "He can talk?" I asked them then turned to Mr. Blue. "You can talk?"

Mr. Blue shrugged his shoulders and smiled once again at me, wagging his tail. "You big idiot," I said as I smacked him on the arm affectionately.

Everyone gave a quiet chuckle as I danced around with my sore hand. I forgot that when the big guy was in this form he wasn't the soft teddy bear anymore. Mom came up to me and hugged me and then went over and did the same with Dede.

"Don't be mad at him," Dad said. "He can talk, but he has very limited words, after all, he is for protection, not conversation." Then he gave me a hug as Mom had and moved off to give my sister hers.

I looked over at Mr. Blue who was standing there tail and ears drooping and rubbed his arm where I had smacked him, not that it hurt of course. "Alright big guy, quit the act you're forgiven."

Mr. Blue's tail once again gained a life of its own as the

happy look returned to his face.

Roc came up to me and looked around the dark area of the park and leaned in close to me. "Listen, Princess, be ready for anything. We could be coming back here in a hurry so be ready to move and don't let your guard down for a second, understand?"

"Yeah, I got it Roc. Take care of my parents for me, okay?"

"Yeah no problem, Princess."

With one last look around at us and then the surroundings, the adults disappeared into the cold dark. "Will Mom and Dad be alright, Ceri?" Dede's voice floated out of the truck.

"Yeah kiddo, they will be fine and they will be back in no time with Jamie and all the bad guys gone. Now, why don't you lie down and cover up with that jacket on the seat and try to sleep some."

Dede looked at me for a second and then snuggled down under the jacket and soon was fast asleep as only a little kid could do. Sometimes I envied her in that I don't think she fully understood all that was happening with us this night.

CHAPTER 20

Roc moved slowly through the park with the two demons behind him. He stopped every few feet looking and listening to the dark night for any sign of unwanted company. He tried to pick out where the two trolls were hiding when he got to the spot they should be, but was glad that he couldn't detect any sign of either of them. Just before he came to the narrow bridge before him, he stopped and let the two demons catch up.

"What's up, dragon?" Bill whispered as both he and Jenna crouched next to Roc.

"Well, we have two choices here. We can go over this narrow bridge or we can follow this path around and come out behind the building the angels are in," Roc said as he pointed out a small path that split into two in front of them.

"Does it really matter? I'm sure they have eyes out here in the woods and know we are coming."

"Yeah I know, thought we might take them by surprise."

"How about you two pick a way and let's get Jamie and get this done," Mom said with a hushed hiss in her voice.

Both men looked at her and then at each other before Jenna stood up and headed for the bridge, saying, "Oh for heaven sakes, and they say women can't make up their minds."

Both men grinned at Jenna's back and hopped up off the ground and followed her down to the bridge. They slowly crossed the bridge looking all around them for any surprises.

Once they reached the other side of the bridge, they stopped while still under cover of the surrounding foliage and took a breath. Roc looked behind them and then peeked around the end of some bushes before looking at the two demons.

"I don't like this you guys, this seems too easy," Roc whispered.

"Yeah I know, we should have met some of the Others by now you would think," Bill whispered back.

Roc nodded in agreement then looked at Jenna with a wicked smile on his face. "Well like the lady said, no sense in waiting let's go get the little witch."

With that, all three stepped out from behind the foliage and started to walk across the open ground toward the building, where they saw Regni and the two angels were waiting. As they passed some playground equipment, Bill lit up a fireball in each of his hands as Jenna, walking beside him, reached behind her for a hidden sheath and pulled out a small curved knife that glowed silver in the moonlight.

Roc looked down at the knife in the demon's hand and saw that the silver light glowed with runes that were written up and down the foot long sharp blade. "Uhm nice butter knife you got there," Roc said with a laugh.

"My mother's," Jenna said with a smile. "She always said I might need it someday."

The three of them kept walking until they were about ten feet from the building and then spread out to give each other room enough to move in a fight.

"Well, well brother what do we have here? Two demons and, what, a dragon?" Sara sang out with laughter in her voice.

"Hello, Regni. See you are still keeping bad company," Roc said as he spotted the other dragon.

"Yeah well, I think you should have brought more friends with you, Roc," Regni said as he raised his arm then dropped it.

Out of the dark, from the sides and behind them ogres and shifters moved into the light so that the trio was now surrounded by Others. The three of them looked around slowly at the numbers they were facing and then at each other.

"Yeah looks like I bought enough friends for this if these are all the scum you have," Roc said turning to face Regni again with an evil smile lighting his face.

"Dragon, you are going to die," Michael said as he lurched forward toward the opening of the building, but was stopped in his tracks by the look of disdain on Roc's face. Michael was shocked as he had never in his life seen that look thrown at him from any lowly creature.

Roc looked at Michael for a few more seconds and then looked back at the other dragon. "Where is the witch, Regni?"

"Don't worry she is fine now . . ."

"We want to see her now before you say anything else," Roc said his voice rising in anger.

Regni smiled and raised both hands in the air as in surrender. "Chill brother, you will see her."

"I'm not your brother, Regni. Bring out the witch now!"

Regni looked to his left and growled something that the trio couldn't make out. A door on the inside of the building marked women's opened and Jamie walked out with a shifter right behind her. The shifter was large and had both of Jamie's arms pinned down to the side of her body in a tight grip.

As they moved up next to Regni, he glanced over at the witch and then back at the trio before him. "See one witch, unharmed for the most part," Regni laughed.

"Okay Regni, what do you want for her?"

"We want the demon child," Sara said stepping up next to Regni.

Roc gave Sara the same look as he had Michael as he heard two muttered curses come from Bill and Jenna. Then he looked over at Regni once again who shrugged his shoulders.

"You know what I want Roc, the Princess."

"Yeah neither of those things are going to happen Regni, so how about you and your friends leave and go back home."

Regni stood there, head bowed as if he was giving it serious consideration then looked up at Roc shaking his head. "Well you see, Roc, you and I both know that if I go back home without the Princess's head, I won't see the next sunset."

"Not my problem, dragon," Roc growled.

Jamie watched this interplay between the adults, wondering, not for the first time how all of them were going to get out of this mess without getting hurt or killed in the process.

All she knew for sure was that she had been awakened by the angel called Michael about half an hour ago and thrust into the smelly bathroom to wait for this moment.

While in the bathroom, she had slowly been gathering what power she had left in her body concentrating on being able to hit the claws of the shifter that held her in such a tight grip at the right second. The angel Michael let out a scream of frustration at the conversation and she saw Sara light up a red ball of magic and throw it in the direction of the three adults.

That's when Jamie shoved all the power she had left into the hands and arms of the shifter holding her. She could feel the shifter dance around as the power surged throughout his body like an electric charge.

As the power finally drained, Jamie moved forward a step then turned bringing her knee up between the legs of the shifter driving all her power into that soft spot that she knew all men had. As the shifter grunted and started to bend over, his hands automatically going to his crotch, Jamie brought her left hand, palm up, into the nose of the shifter breaking the bone and putting it through his brain. The light went out of the shifter's eyes before he even hit the ground.

Without looking around, Jamie ran to the other side of the building ducking a ball of magic thrown her way. The blast splattered against a wall, dripping dark green magic all over. It hissed and sizzled as it dripped to the ground. Reaching the low wall at the other side of the building, Jamie hopped over it and soon disappeared into the night with the sounds of battle echoing behind her.

∽⋍∽⋍∽⋍∽⋍

The trio saw Michael scream in frustration and they all crouched down as a ball of magic thrown by Sara sailed over their heads and impacted on the playground equipment behind them. The plastic slide the magic hit lit up a bright red then melted and fell into a twisted mess on the sand below.

"I think she is serious about this," Roc said with a grin as he stood to fight the various ogres and shifters that were rushing out from the dark night.

As Roc grabbed two shifters that jumped at him by the throat and smashed their heads together, he saw what Jamie did to her opponent and her escape into the night. Throwing the two bodies that he held at the chest of a charging dragon he nodded in satisfaction as all three went down in a tangle of limbs and bodies.

Hearing grunting behind him, he turned and saw that Bill and Jenna each were fighting one of the angels. Bill stood off with Michael each of them throwing small balls of magic that deflected off into the air by the demon and angel before they could score a hit. While Jenna and Sara were locked hand to hand in their own struggle; Jenna with the wicked knife she carried and Sara with teeth and claws that deformed the once beautiful face into a grotesque mask.

As Roc stepped forward to help Jenna, he felt a hand on his shoulder and a voice growl behind him. "Where do you think you're going, dragon?"

Roc turned to the ogre behind him and felt the punch thrown at him all the way down to his toes. His body hit the ground as the ogre stepped up to bring his large foot down onto the dragon when a hefty ball of magic hit the ogre in the middle of the chest. The ogre looked down at the big smoking hole in his chest for a second and then his eyes rolled back into his head and he toppled like a tree. Roc rolled out from under the falling ogre, noticing that he could see all the way through the ogre and see the stars above in the night sky. As he stood he made a quick mental note that getting hit with those balls of magic that were flying through the air would not be a good idea right now.

As he looked around for more creatures to fight, he heard a scream behind him and turning saw that Jenna had buried her knife into the middle of Sara's chest. He watched as Sara stood there for a second with surprise written all over her face.

Then slowly her body disintegrated into dust before everyone's eyes. Rushing over to Jenna, Roc caught her just as she collapsed to the ground. Looking down at her wounds, the dragon could see that Jenna's face and arms were covered with deep scratches and cuts from the now deceased angel, but that she was still breathing.

Roc looked up as he saw three more ogres growl their battle cry and stood to meet their charge. Unfortunately, for the front two ogres, they never made it to Roc as they were attacked from the side, by two dark, red-eyed creatures trailing flame and smoke. Each creature hit one ogre taking them to the ground amid snarls and spits of fury. The third ogre stopped, looked at his two companions that were receiving the worst of the fight and turned and ran off into the night.

Roc turned back to check on Jenna when he heard a loud pop and saw Bill fly through the air and land close to where Jenna lay. Looking up he saw Michael step toward the two demons when Regni grabbed him by the arm and pulled him toward the entrance of the park.

Roc ran over to the two demons as the trolls joined him leaving their deceased enemies behind. "Keep an eye out for any more Others," Roc told the two trolls still in their own hellhound form as he bent down to check on Bill and Jenna.

He saw that both demons, though unconscious and covered with cuts and bruises, were breathing without any problems. Looking around once more, Roc gathered both of the demons close together and with some difficulty managed to get each one over a shoulder. Standing up with his heavy burden, he looked at both trolls.

"Tessa, you take the lead back to the truck and Scom you

watch our backs." And then all three headed back toward the truck.

❧❦❧❦❧❦

Jamie ran into the woods then headed back around the large open building for the one place that she knew she could power up with magic again. The ley line was not far away and all she needed to do was power up and she could head back to help the adults fighting in the park.

Jamie heard a noise behind her as she reached the baseball field that was her marker for the ley line. As she looked behind her she saw a large ugly ogre burst out of the bushes and make a grab for her. She managed to slip out of his grasp and run down the hill toward where the ley line was, but she tripped before she reached it and rolled past the magic line and into a tree on the edge of the woods.

"Got you now, little witch," the ogre growled as he reached down and picked up the small girl by the front of her outfit, lifting her in the air right over the ley line.

Jamie could feel the power seeping into her body and smiled at the ogre, causing a look of confusion to cross his face. Never before had a meal he had been about to eat looked as happy as this one did.

"Here's a little trick, I learned all on my own, big guy," Jamie said as she grabbed tightly to the ogre's arms with her own and opened herself up to the power flowing through the ley line.

The power swarmed up through Jamie and into the ogre, freezing him in place. As the power filled him up, Jamie opened up more and let the flow fill him up until she screamed, "EAT THIS!" and as she did the ogre's head popped off his shoulders like a cork out of a champagne bottle, flying back and over the body that was now falling.

The lifeless hands let go of Jamie and she jumped to the side, away from the body hitting the ground, running back to where she could hear a large popping noise. Jamie made it to the edge of the clearing where the playground equipment was when she saw Roc and the two trolls head off into the dark of the woods.

❧❦❧❦❧❦

I could barely hear the fighting that was going on, but I heard enough that I knew I needed to be there to help. Taking a few steps away from the truck toward the sound from the other end of the park, I heard a low growl behind me.

I turned and there stood Mr. Blue with a scowl written all across his face looking at me as his huge head shook from side to side. "I wasn't going anywhere, big guy," I said as I once more looked at where a fight was going on.

After a while it got quiet and then off to the side, I heard a rough voice. "Well men, look what we have here."

I turned and looked at five large men that had come running silently out of the dark from the woods in the park.

Looking them over I got that flash again that told me these guys were shifters and from the way they looked and smelled, they were not the shifters that I knew from the Other's world.

Mr. Blue came around the other side of the truck growling when the biggest of the men pointed at him. "You three take him," he said to the shifters closest to Mr. Blue. "You come with me and get the girl," he then said to the man standing next to him.

As the three men jumped Mr. Blue and buried him in a pile of shifters, I dropped the magic that hid my true appearance and grabbed both swords from behind me. The sudden change stopped the biggest shifter for a heartbeat, leaving only one of them moving forward at me.

As I pulled out the swords, I swung both in a backhanded motion so that both blades swept across the path of the shifter in front of me. Running right into the arc of the blades, first, the fire blade sliced into the upper part of the shifter and the ice blade sliced across the lower half of him.

He let out one quick scream before his upper body burst into flames and the lower part turned to ice and then shattered. I turned to the large shifter and took two steps toward him and smiled.

⚜⚜⚜

Dede watched Mr. Blue go down under the three men that tackled him and then watched her big sister dispatch one of the ones in front of her. Watching, she saw one of the men was thrown by Mr. Blue over the truck and heard a thump as his body hit the ground. She knew she should stay in the truck, but the one man that Ceri faced looked so much bigger than her and she did so want to help. She quietly slid out of the truck and peeked around the door, when she heard a noise behind her. Dede started to turn when the world went black.

❧◞❧◞❧◞

I watched as the shifter's face and hands started to change into some hideous form. The face looked like he had the muzzle of a wolf and the claws that grew from his fingertips looked as sharp as daggers.

With a snarl and growl, the large shifter charged me his maw gaping and his claws extended to rip me apart. The only problem for the shifter was that he never reached me as a huge, dark blur hit him from the side, lifted him in the air and tore him in two.

I looked over at my rescuer and saw that it was the ogre that we had left at the condo. His chest and arms were covered with makeshift bandages. He smiled at me and then looked down at the two pieces of shifter at his feet. "Bad doggie," he said

"Yeah, really bad doggie," I said then ran around the truck to help Mr. Blue in his fight.

Mr. Blue had one of the shifters down on the ground and

was finishing off the second when I came up to him. He picked this last shifter off his back and threw him into the nearest tree. From the large splat, I figured that that was one less shifter we had to worry about.

Mr. Blue grinned at me as he started to reach down to pick up the nearest shifter when we heard sounds like someone coming down the sidewalk to our left. Both Mr. Blue and I turned to face this new danger before I saw that it was Roc and the two trolls hurrying toward us.

I couldn't make out what Roc was carrying until he almost got right up next to the truck. "Mom, Dad, what happened to them."

"They will be fine Ceri. Here help me get them into the back of the truck."

Oh dang this was so not good, I thought, as we put them side by side on the back seat of the truck. "How about Jamie, where is she?"

Roc looked at me and was about to answer when we heard feet running up to the truck and then out of the night, there she was.

"Hey guys, miss me?" Jamie said.

"There is the witch. Now we need to get your parents to my place so that I can better check their wounds. They still may not be out of danger yet," Roc said as he climbed into the driver's side of the truck.

As Mr. Blue and the ogre hopped into the back of the truck and I threw Scom and Tessa in with them, I looked around for a second and then noticed what was missing from our little group. "Uhm where's Dede guys?"

Everything stopped in mid motion as we all looked around us for the little troublemaker.

CHAPTER 21

Hessa jumped with the other two shifters on the large fuzzy demon by the truck as the Alpha and his companion attacked the girl. In the fight with the demon, he felt himself flying through the air and landing on the other side of the truck. Rolling to the side of the vehicle to catch his breath, Hessa watched a young girl slide out of the front seat and peek around the door at the fight.

Moving without thought, Hessa launched himself up off the ground delivering a blow to the back of her head that knocked her out cold. He kneeled there for a second, listening to the fight that did not sound like it was going the shifter's way.

Ripping off his jacket, he wrapped the girl and then threw the bundle over his shoulder and headed toward the back of the truck to make an escape. Bending down and using the truck as cover from those still fighting at the front of it, he ran across the street and headed back toward the mall where the angels and the Others had first met.

Jogging along, Hessa wasn't sure why he had grabbed the child from the truck, but what the hell if she turned out worthless then, at least, he would have a tasty little meal to chow down on, he thought.

After about fifteen minutes, Hessa and his package had made it back to the mall and he had dumped his small bundle on the ground when he heard two quiet voices behind him. Turning, he saw that it was the male angel and the dragon, Regni.

They both stopped talking as they came up to the shifter and eyed the bundle on the ground that his jacket hid.

"What's you got there, shifter?" Regni asked.

"It's mine, I got it from the truck."

Michael smiled as he walked up to the shifter and then waved his hand at him, freezing the shifter in his tracks. "Yes well, dog, it may have been yours, but now it's mine," Michael purred.

Regni bent over the bundle and opened the jacket and saw a small child wrapped within its folds while Michael slowly circled the frozen shifter looking at him as if he was his next meal.

"It's a child, a girl," Regni said looking up at Michael with a smile.

Michael bent over and glanced at the unconscious child and smiled right back at Regni. "Well, well, the little demon child," Michael said.

He turned toward the shifter and smiled once again, this time, the smile was so wide that it showed a mouth full of teeth that frightened the shifter. "I want to thank you for bringing me my prize, dog, I'm ever so grateful."

Hessa let out a small breath he didn't even know he had been holding until Michael's next words slammed into his ears. "I also want to thank you for providing me with the meal I need to gain back my power," Michael said as he launched himself at the shifter. As he hit the immobile shifter, the force knocked both of them into the dark where Regni was spared the sight of the angel feeding on his snack.

After a few minutes, the grotesque sounds coming from the dark ended and Michael walked out of the dark wiping his face on some rags – all that was left of Hessa. "Now I will take my prize, dragon, if you don't mind. That is unless you want to end up like your, uhm, friend back there."

"Listen, angel, how about we make a deal."

Michael stopped and stared at the dragon." You have nothing I want, dragon. All I need is what is on the ground by your feet."

"What? You don't want the ones that killed your sister, angel?"

This caused Michael to stop and think for a few seconds, staring off into the night sky, and then he looked back down at Regni. "Alright dragon, you have my attention."

"We bring the girl back to my world, to my Queen and then the Princess and her parents will follow and I can get her head there."

"I thought your Queen wanted the Princess killed here, not in your world."

Regni thought the same thing about his Queen and shivered at the idea of what would be in store for him if his Queen didn't like this small change in plans. "I know, but with you beside me maybe we can get her to see how this plan would be better?" Regni asked with some hope filtering through his voice.

Michael stood there looking down at Regni and then laughed. "Alright dragon, we will try it your way. If it doesn't work then I still have my prize and I get to see what your little Queen will do to you. If it works, I still get my prize and the killer of my sister."

With a deep sigh of relief, Regni picked up the bundle and threw it over his shoulder and the dragon and angel walked over to where the portal was and disappeared from this world.

We all looked around the truck for Dede until I could hear Mom groaning in the back seat. Roc grabbed my arm and pulled me to the back door and pointed at my parents.

"Listen Princess we need to take them back to my place to check them out now."

"I'm not leaving my sister out here," I said as I tore my arm out of his hand and started to head out into the woods to find Dede.

Roc grabbed me again in a tighter grip and spun me around to face him. "She is not out there Princess, they have her and you won't do her any favors by maybe letting your parents die while you search for her."

"Fine Roc, you take my parents and I'll stay here and look for my sister."

"Yeah, that's not happening Princess."

I looked around at the little band of people and creatures gathered around the truck and knew deep down that Roc had a point. I couldn't hope to get my sister back by myself and my parents did need help.

Then I looked down at the two trolls and smiled for the first time in the last couple of minutes. Crouching down, calling over the two trolls they came up to me and watched me with their full attention. "Listen you two, I need you to follow my sister wherever they take her, do you two understand?"

Both trolls glanced at each other and then back at me with a nod of each of their heads, then sniffing the ground they ran into the dark toward the mall. I took a step toward them but stopped as I heard another groan come from the back of the truck.

I turned to Roc and then pointed to Mr. Blue and the ogre. "Come on guys, get in the back and let's get going."

Everyone jumped into the truck and Roc started back down the road toward the condo. About a block down the road, Roc looked at me as I sat staring out the front window. Leaning around Jamie, Roc asked, "What are you thinking about now, Princess?"

"I'm thinking Roc, that this is war. This is war with any angel or Other that has my sister in this world or any other world. I'm also thinking we can't go back to your condo as the Others know where it is. So we need to find a new place to take my parents."

ABOUT THE AUTHOR

Robert is the author of the Witch Way Book series. Robert lives in Bellingham, Washington with his wife and youngest child (along with his imaginary friend Percy, the dragon). Look for Robert's next book, Walk the Stars, slated for publication October 2016. For more information you can visit witchwaybooks.com or visit him on Facebook.

Made in the USA
Columbia, SC
03 December 2021

50132571R00193